SEE NO EVIL

Seeing Double

Tom Crewe and Amber Wells

First published in 1998
by HEADLINE BOOK PUBLISHING

A HEADLINE LIAISON paperback

10 9 8 7 6 5 4 3 2 1

ISBN 0 7472 5857 0

Typeset by CBS, Felixstowe, Suffolk

Printed and bound in Great Britain by
Mackays of Chatham plc, Chatham, Kent

HEADLINE BOOK PUBLISHING
A division of Hodder Headline PLC
338 Euston Road
London NW1 3BH

Seeing Double

Chapter One

Waiting for her lover was almost the most difficult part for Charmayne – and also, perhaps, the most exciting.

For the third or fourth time she checked that all was well with the soufflé in the automatic oven, that the bottles of Pouilly Fumé were chilling nicely – better get another one down from the rack, just in case – and that the flowers on the garden table hadn't started to wilt.

Everything was perfect. She looked at her watch, an expensive lover's gift for her birthday, two months ago, her twenty-fifth. Twelve forty-five. Given a clear run most of the way but allowing for the odd road works or build-up of traffic, how long would it take to drive back from a nine o'clock meeting in Birmingham? Sometimes, she felt those long journeys – though necessary – were getting in the way of her life. Business, business, always business. They might be sitting down somewhere, a nice meal in a country restaurant, perhaps, a hand lingering suggestively on a black-stockinged thigh, and then the bloody phone would go, its insistent beep-beep-beep making her jump. Sometimes she wished she could have taken that mobile phone and thrown it out of the window but business was business and an appointment was an appointment. And it wasn't always Birmingham, either. Three weeks ago they'd had an idyllic couple of days in Bern on the old expenses and there'd been a couple of expensive trips to South Africa back in the winter.

Still, it wasn't all bad and besides, it was her lover's business acumen that had brought her to this garden, and this house, and the black BMW convertible on the drive, and the bank accounts , and the foreign holidays they occasionally managed to steal together, without mobile phones and a Filofax full of meetings.

The phone rang. Excited, she all but dropped the salad servers as she rushed indoors. But it was only some stupid kitchen supplier, cold-calling. Charmayne's kitchen was new only last year, had cost upwards of thirty grand, and she sure as hell didn't think she needed a new one. A new car maybe – the BMW was eighteen months old and there was still the slight stain on the back seat when they'd got a little silly in the car park at the Wembley Conference Centre after that big presentation that had gone so well. But she didn't need a kitchen and besides, Compact Kitchens who just happened to be in her area didn't sound like the kind of outfit she'd be interested in. No genuine Carrara marble there, it would be jumped-up Formica and horrid little doors that worked loose in a matter of months. Hers closed with a satisfying thunk, just like the doors on the BMW. She liked things that worked nicely. She liked things, period.

She washed some salad and then went upstairs to change.

Charmayne showered and picked up a long, loose, flowered dress from her walk-in wardrobe. It was the one she'd been asked to wear, but it was the one she would have chosen anyway. She laid it carefully on the bed. Her fingers trailed an invisible line along the pillows. Was that a hair she saw? No, it was some of her own, so much finer. But that unmistakable smell of Calvin Klein hung in the air still, even after forty-eight hours.

She stepped out of her robe, studied herself in the mirror. She liked what she saw, a tall slim woman in her mid-twenties, long legs, sizeable and quite exquisite breasts, a flat stomach. She turned round and considered her backside. Was that a hint of cellulite? She pinched the flesh between her fingers, but it was just a trick of the light, thank goodness.

She felt good. She was looking forward to lunch together and then a long, slow afternoon of love-making. Half-formed images of tongues and lips passed through her mind, meeting in passion. For some reason she thought of a finger in her vagina, then two, then three. Mmmmm – she was looking forward to it all. She had learned to value the moments they could snatch together. Three or four hours was a rare luxury, especially here. There would always be a meeting, or a fax, or something that needed attending to. She knew how necessary it all was but it was difficult, all the same.

She considered drinking a glass of Pouilly Fumé but it was too early. There might be a hold-up on the motorway, the unwelcome phone call, the apologies, an hour's delay or longer. By the time they were together she would have half-finished the bottle and the soufflé would have been ruined. Stay cool, she told herself. Enjoy yourself. Just relax. Everything will be fine.

She opened her lingerie drawer. She knew what she wanted to wear, knew the reaction it would have. It worked every time.

She took out a crisp new packet of stockings, very pale, lace top. She often wore stockings to please her lover, and other things besides. They each knew what the other liked.

Then a suspender belt, Janet Reger of course, in cream satin, trimmed with the most beautiful lace she had ever run her fingers over. It had been an early Christmas present, last year. The two of them had gone to the familiar, discreet shop in Beauchamp Place and gone wild on the company's credit card. She wondered what the assistants had thought but they were very tactful and in any case most of the other customers in the shop seemed to be businessmen and their mistresses.

She put on the filigree garment, sat on the bed and rolled the stockings one by one over her smooth, freshly waxed thighs. My, she loved that feeling of the cool, soft nylon against her skin. Silk stockings were even nicer. She clipped the suspenders in place and made sure they were straight, standing in front of the mirror.

She loved the way her suspenders framed her dark bush. She had trimmed it herself only last night as a surprise, a delicate heart shape. Was it the same both sides? She came closer to the mirror, to reassure herself. She had long legs and found it difficult to get stockings that were the right length, but these were just right. They ought to be, at more than twelve pounds a pair. Silk was a lot dearer and they laddered too soon when worn for sex.

3

She looked again – one way and another, Charmayne spent a lot of tine in front of mirrors. The effect wasn't quite right in her stockinged feet so she put on a pair of high-heeled gold sandals and that was much better.

She spent quite a while looking at herself like that. God, she said to herself, you look a real wet dream. She tried to imagine what some of the guys from the office would think if they could see her now.

She liked that feeling, of wondering what other people thought of her, whether she was turning them on, whether she was making the juices flow and the heart beat a little faster. She was aware of organs moistening, filling with blood. She turned round, bent over and presented her backside to their imaginary gaze.

Like what you see, do you? she breathed and then she bent a little further and spread her legs slightly. She could just see her pink pouting pussy lips amid their nest of curls. She found pussies exciting. She liked to look at pictures of other women, naked, even the hardcore ones.

She seemed to be getting hornier with every minute. Then, suddenly, the sound of a vehicle on the drive. Bare-breasted, she rushed to the bedroom window, but it was only the wine-merchant's delivery van. She'd forgotten he was due but she didn't need to answer the bell. He knew to leave the boxes in the garage and to push the delivery note through the door.

He was a good-looking boy, could only have been twenty or so, if that. He wore tight blue jeans and she liked his neat ass. She wondered what he would have thought if he had known a beautiful woman dressed only in stockings, high-heeled sandals and a Janet Reger suspender belt was looking at him, wondering what it would be like to suck his cock. She was sure he would be full of spunk. He looked the type. Young, dumb and full of come.

But it didn't do to think thoughts like that. She had a lover coming to her arms inside an hour at the most and she would have to be patient. It was difficult though – it was a warm noon and she was feeling so very sexy about herself and what was to follow.

It was no good. She moved away from the curtains and

4

took a sleek ivory instrument from a drawer by the bed. This wasn't your typical twenty-quid sex-store vibro. This was the real thing, a proper late-Victorian godemiche, the kind of thing they used in those funny old books, *The Pearl* and that diary by that dirty old perve, what was his name? Albert or Walter or somebody. They had bought it in an antique shop in Vienna and everyone knew what it was, even if they pretended otherwise. It cost a lot of money and not just on account of the delicate filigree silverwork at the handle end. In the antique trade there was a premium on nine-inch ivory dildoes. They had a history, naturally enough. This one was supposed to have belonged to Bismarck's mistress.

As she lay on the bed and ran its cool rounded tip over her labia, Charmayne wondered at the women that it had pleasured in its time. The surface was barely marked but she knew that it must have brought rapture to many, in beds and hotel rooms, on rugs before an open fire, sitting on laps in armchairs, wherever and whenever the opportunity and the desire arose.

Very quickly she found her clitoris and began gently to massage it. She didn't want to become orgasmic, not yet anyway, but she just wanted to feel something down there, something more than her own fingers could achieve. As the van drove off she thought again of the delivery boy, his blond hair and his tight butt. She had another dildo in her drawer, the strap-on kind, and she could have used it to fuck him in the butt with, if he had been so minded. She'd done that kind of thing before. She liked it, pretending to be a man and wondering what it felt like to have a dick.

She lay back on the bed, careful of her stockings, the cool ivory nestling amid her heated lips. At this moment she had no images or fantasies that she would masturbate over, just a general feeling of desire and wantonness and pleasurability. She was, in short, on heat, lying there on the bed – their bed – in her stockings and high-heeled shoes, perfumed and made-up to perfection, her legs spread wide, waiting.

She was penetrating herself but her thoughts were of tongues. She imagined lips brushing against her nipples, teeth expertly nipping her clitty in the way she knew would drive her wild, clean over the edge. She thought of her lover's tongue probing her labia, that amazing feeling when it went right into her. She squeezed her pelvic floor muscles and clenched the beautiful dildo in her vagina. Soon, soon, she wanted it to be soon. She couldn't wait and yet she knew she had to.

'*Oh God*,' she cried, heedless of anybody who might at that moment be below on the drive. '*I want you to do my cunt right now.*'

And then the moment seemed to pass. She rose to her feet, left the godemiche by the side of the bed – for later, maybe? – and completed her dressing. She had a cream silk teddy decorated with mother of pearl and she loved the way the lace brushed her still-damp crotch as she pulled the thin straps over her shoulders. The back was deeply scooped, the front heavily infilled with lace that revealed almost every succulent inch of her breasts. This was another of the spoils from their great pre-Christmas shopping bonanza.

Checking over and remaking-up her face didn't take long. Charmayne had the kind of complexion that didn't need much cosmeticising, though she always bought the best of what she did use – a little powder, a little blusher, rather more of eye-shadow and mascara. She liked the heavy-eyed look in the middle of the day. There was something appealingly wanton about it, like wearing a corset and black seamed stockings. It gave out messages.

Oh Christ, she thought – the soufflé! She pulled on her dress and rushed downstairs but it was fine. She turned the oven off and at that moment the kitchen phone beeped.

'Hi, sugar,' said the familiar deep voice.

'Hi,' said Charmayne. 'Where are you?'

'Just turning off the motorway. I'll be with you in ten minutes.'

'Oh, great. I thought you were going to be late or something. How did it go?'

'Fine. I think we'll clinch it. But I'll tell you more in a minute. Pour me a glass of wine, will you? I hope it's nice and cool – I'm parched.'

'Of course it is. I put three bottles in.'

'Good, I think we're going to need them. I'm dying for a fuck.'

Earlier that morning, an excited hubbub of people had gathered in a large exhibition hall. Some were suited businessmen, others were ordinary members of the public, keen to sneak a glance when they heard the rumours about who was coming.

But it hadn't been an easy morning for Tina Scully. First, the agency had rung her at seven-thirty to say Mulder had a temperature of a hundred and one and felt like he'd been hit by a runaway train, and she'd have to do this one on her own. Then the mini-cab taking her to her secret destination had been late and there had been an almighty and unseemly dash through the rush-hour traffic to get her there on time. The guy driving it smoked cheap cigars, too – she was already feeling a bit sick with her usual nerves and this made it ten times worse. Once she almost had to ask him to pull over so she could throw up – what the world at large would have made of that she didn't dare think, an anonymous-looking Toyota suddenly veering over to the side of the road and the door flies open and there's a red-headed girl looking like Agent Scully from *The X Files* puking her guts up in the gutter.

Then, earlier on that morning, she realised her period was starting a couple of days early – a relief in some ways but a great big pain in the butt in others. She could handle that with the aid of the usual painkillers but then she always got a bit irritable at these times and to cap it all a ball-point pen had leaked in her handbag and she'd got a slight stain on her shirt. It wasn't one of her own, either, she had borrowed it for the occasion and she felt anxious about it. She buttoned her familiar black jacket around it and hoped no one would notice.

That was before she'd even got there. Once in the place, things went from bad to worse. She got a message on her mobile that Kenny, her usual minder from the agency, had been involved in a rear-end shunt somewhere on the orbital ring-road so she was even more on her own, even without Mulder. Mulder drank too much and got on her nerves but

Kenny was a good man, she relied on him.

In the sanctity of the ladies' washroom she gave her red hair a final brushing, checked her lipstick and took a series of deep breaths the way she had been taught. Never let them sense your anxiety, they had told her. If they sense your fear, they'll rip you apart like a pack of wolves.

Once outside, she strode confidently down the aisle and up to the podium. Familiar music played over the PA, too loud as always. She gave them Agent Scully's famous pout and then the same speech she'd given two dozen times before. It was ten minutes long, timed to the second. It was aspirational and inspirational all at the same time, designed to inculcate a sense of undying loyalty to The Cause in all who heard it. It worked every time, even if she didn't understand the half of it. The audience, though, seemed to lap it up, clapping like crazy when it was all over.

Afterwards, the marketing people were fine but there were some sales guys there as well and they were acting well to type. Some of them came over all greasy and fawning and one of them kept trying to peek up her skirt whenever she sat down and crossed her legs. It looked good on her but it was kind of short. She kept her jacket wrapped around her as she mingled and chatted.

There was some big-cheese company director-type topping up her drink – just a white wine with soda, if you please – and he was just boring her into the ground with all this shit about the secret services and the paranormal and stuff, about the weird and wonderful things that went on and people didn't realise the half of it, the authenticated UFO sightings and the crop circles and the strange marking that they'd found on the top of Nelson's Column. He'd seen the photos, he knew it was true even though they'd tried to hush it up like they always did. She wanted to say to him, look, sonny, I don't give a toss for any of it. You shouldn't believe that bullshit. But she didn't. She nodded and pouted and brushed her hair back the way Ronnie had suggested, and wished it was time to go. I have a banging headache, she screamed inwardly at him, I've got period cramps and I'll need to change my tampon soon.

There were a couple of *X-Files* junkies who were easier to handle. She didn't need to do much, just to be there and make polite conversation and let them imagine. And then there was the roller-bearing man, this pillock barely five-feet-five so she just towered over him, and he got her over to one side when they broke for coffee – which tasted like instant, and supermarket own-brand at that – and let fly with absolutely everything there was to know about the manufacture of high-adhesion lubricants and their industrial applications and the challenge of the new markets, especially in Eastern Europe and the Pacific Rim countries, and after a while she just wanted to handbag him. She gave even less of a toss for high-adhesion lubricants than she did for creatures from beyond the stars, all she wanted was to get her fee in cash from Ronnie and then she could get home in the minicab and get the shopping done. They usually sold off the beef and lamb cheap on a Tuesday afternoon at Asda and if she didn't get there by two-thirty, all that would be left would be a few scraggy chops and a bit of topside.

She stood it for the best part of an hour, chatting with every semblance of gaiety in the familiar fashion, the hurt look in the eyes, the faraway glance, the toss of the famous red hair, but inwardly seething and wishing they would all go away. Then they dimmed the lights so they could watch this big video presentation of their new hydrocarbonates and she managed to slip out to the lav for a fag.

God, that felt good. She sat on the lid and hauled the smoke down into her lungs, feeling her head beginning to spin slightly as it always did when she'd not had a smoke for a few hours. It could be pretty difficult sometimes. The Cigarette Man was one thing but as Agent Scully she was not expected to light up in public, even at the launch of a new range of PVC industrial piping or the opening of a factory extension in Walsall. It was one of those things, she'd learned, that just wasn't done, even if you smoked Bensons rather than Lambert & Butler. There was always gallons of free booze swimming round at these dos and could she get her hands on any of it? She had to make do with a glass or two of dry white, if she was lucky. Mulder, however, drank like a fish.

She reckoned that was why he wasn't there this morning – and not for the first time either. She didn't believe a word about the flu symptoms – in January maybe but certainly not at this time of year.

She smoked in silence. She'd just had the electricity bill that morning and it wasn't an estimated bill this time. The kids needed new school clothes too and now that she and her husband were living apart, that was something else to worry about. She couldn't just ask him for the money like she used to and he was absolutely fucking useless about the maintenance. People assumed that she lived in some plush mansion in Hollywood or Washington DC because of who she was supposed to be and what she did but the reality was different, a council maisonette in Balsall Heath.

She chucked the fag end down the bog and flushed. She was just standing in front of the mirror, doing her hair, when a woman came out of one of the other cubicles. She did a double-take and then laughed.

'Oh, I'm sorry,' she said as she washed her hands at the basin. 'For a moment I thought you were, you know—'

She was smartly dressed in a business suit but she had a nice face, really pretty but friendly too. Tina put her down as mid-twenties but she could have been a year or two older. Her eyes lingered over her clothes, the hair, the make-up.

'It's just me job. I do Scully, you know, from the telly. I'm a lookalike.'

'I know. I can see. What's it like being Agent Scully?'

'Sometimes I'd rather be meself, to be honest.' Now that her guard was down, traces of Black Country came through in her California-tinged voice. Actually she'd always felt she did Scully's accent rather well, she'd always been a good mimic at school. But it was an effort to keep it going even for the minimum two hours for which she was usually booked. This was a three-hour gig, with lunch, which wasn't always a whole bunch of fun.

'Things not too good?'

'It gets a bit wearing sometimes. I think they ask me to do too much.'

She wondered why she was saying all this to a complete

stranger but there was something in the woman's manner that she felt she could trust.

'Who is "they"?'

'The agency I work for.'

'Not *the* agency? The Department?'

They both laughed.

'No, not that one. Hey, you're not with Silurian Carbons, are you?'

'I don't think so. Who are they?'

'The people giving the presentation. They make industrial lubricants or something. They hired me to help launch their new product range. Polyhydrocarbonates or something.'

'They're in Hall D I think. We're next door. British Federation of Model Agencies.'

'Oh, right. Actually, I work for the Ideal Model Agency, do you know them? They're in Edgbaston.' Though she nodded, she felt the other woman didn't really know. The Ideal Model Agency was pretty small beer. This woman, she guessed, would do ads, commercials, maybe a bit of TV cast work.

'Tell me about them,' she said, applying lipstick.

'What?'

'The agency. The one you're with.'

It had been building up inside her for ages, the series of cock-ups this morning, the way they were always late paying her, all the frustrations that had built up inside her. She tried to be tactful but she didn't really realise how much anger had built up inside her.

While she summed it all up in one sentence, the woman was looking in her bag. She produced a card, gave it to her. It looked very posh.

'If you really are dissatisfied with your agency, give me a call,' she said. 'My name's on the card. What's yours?'

'Tina. Tina Richardson.'

'You're the best Scully I've ever seen, Tina.'

'Thanks very much.'

'No, I mean it. I'm sure you can do much better than Silurian Carbons and supermarket openings, you know.'

'I go where the work is, I guess. Or where they put me.'

11

'How much are you paid, if you don't mind my asking?'

Tina named a figure. It was actually about half as much again as her usual hourly rate, but the woman in the suit winced.

'I'm sure we could do a lot better than that,' she said. She sprayed a little perfume behind her ears and then she was gone.

Tina sniffed. She knew her perfumes. This was the new Calvin Klein. She'd had a whiff of it in Debenhams on Saturday. It was way outside her price range, she knew that.

Charmayne was sitting in the garden with a glass of Pouilly Fumé when she heard the car on the drive. She felt confidant, beautiful, desired. She didn't get up, but waited there where she was.

She could hear doors opening and closing. A female blackbird landed on the lawn and began looking for grubs. It came to within only two or three feet away from her and chirruped.

'Hello,' she said, momentarily distracted. The next thing she knew, someone had bent down behind her and kissed her ear.

'Where's that glass you had ready for me?' said the familiar deep voice.

'Hi, darling,' said Charmayne. She stood up, and they embraced each other, kissed one another on the lips.

'You look beautiful, Charmayne. I really love that dress.'

'Thanks. You don't look too bad yourself.' They kissed again.

'Hey, mind my lipstick. I've just put fresh on.'

The other woman sat down as Charmayne poured her a glass of cold wine.

'How was work, honey?'

'Not so much fun without you. I'll fill you in later. I'll just have a drink and get changed. I met this amazing Scully lookalike. You know – from *The X Files*.'

'Where? At the conference?'

'No. In the ladies'. She was doing some PR for this awful lubricants firm. But I'll tell you later. The garden's looking lovely.'

They sat sipping their wine for a couple of minutes. Charmayne's hand rested on her lover's knee – she could feel it through the severe woollen business suit. It was good that Lesley was back. She'd only been gone a couple of days and she'd missed her like hell.

While Lesley was getting changed, Charmayne brought the lunch things out. The blackbird was still busy, a beakful of worms and other unmentionable things. It seemed to be a time of plenty and abundance for all.

Lesley reappeared, simply dressed in tight black cut-off jeans and a white shirt, open at the neck. Her thick black hair, which she'd worn up, was now loose around her shoulders. She'd put fresh lipstick on, the colour of strawberries.

It tasted like strawberries too, as Charmayne kissed her. For a second or two their tongues met, playfully, and then Lesley patter her lover on the hip.

'You know what I'd like now, don't you?' she said, her eyes twinkling.

Charmayne smiled back. Of course she knew. It was all a part of the deal, like the dress and the lace-top stockings, the cut-off shorts so tight she could see the outline of Lesley's labia through them.

She knelt down until her eyes were level with Lesley's hips, put her arms around her, drew her lover to her. She pressed the side of her face against her flat belly, felt the soft stone-washed denim against her skin. Lesley ran her fingers through her hair.

Then she kissed her thighs, aware of the soft golden downy hairs. She ran her tongue up and down the muscles, the flesh taut and already browned by the summer sun.

'Mmmmmm,' breathed Lesley. 'That feels good. Do it again.'

Once more she ran her tongue up and down Lesley's thighs and then, when she felt the moment was right, she reached out her hands and unbuttoned her shorts.

She pressed her face against the bare flesh of her belly, feeling a pulse against the warm skin. Her's, Lesley's, what did it matter? Then another finger on the zipper and she was pulling Lesley's shorts down over her thighs, exposing brief panties of intricate black lace. She pressed her nose right up against them and inhaled deeply and appreciatively, the musky perfume of a woman undeniably on heat. The soufflé, once again, was forgotten, cooling on the table beside them.

She pulled shorts and pants down until they were around Lesley's knees and then she inserted her tongue between her thighs. She was surprised at how wet she was already. She licked and lapped for long enough to set her juices flowing even more and then, in a swift movement, Lesley kicked off her clothes and spread her legs invitingly.

Charmayne buried her face deep in her lover's dark muff. She kissed and licked and then, with infinite subtlety, began to draw little patterns of desire along those dark-rimmed labia.

'Oh God,' breathed Lesley, 'I can't tell you how long I've been waiting for this.'

Charmayne smiled secretly to herself, burying her tongue deeper into Lesley's salty recesses. She loved to go down on her, to have Lesley go down on her in turn, for them both to do it together. It took her a long time but Lesley came off very quickly.

She had her hands on Lesley's buttocks and she drew her body even closer to her, practically pressing herself into her, her tongue busy with its butterfly flutterings and lascivious licks, as promiscuity and lasciviousness mingled wildly in her heated imagination. Here, in the garden, in the middle of the day, with her tongue up another woman's pussy and her own seeping its juices all over her expensive tart's lingerie. Could this really be Charmayne Kirtley, once derided by her schoolmates as fat and unfanciable, denied a place in sixth-form college, now within ten years rich and successful and a senior partner in a model agency, sexually experienced, beautifully bi?

It was, of course. She felt happy and fulfilled, even as Lesley clasped her shoulders and thrust her pussy against her probing mouth, and she could even feel the tremulous shudder of her orgasm through the infinitely delicate nerve-endings of her tongue.

'C'mon,' said Lesley, pulling her pants back on. 'I'm hungry.'

Lunch was long, slow and delicious. So, thought Charmayne, would be their love-making afterwards. A whole lascivious afternoon of it.

Tina Richardson didn't make Asda after all. Actually there was quite a nice guy at the presentation that she got talking to. She was booked from eleven until two but it was getting on for half-past before she realised that the guy hopping up and down on the edge of the group was the mini-cab driver, a different one this time who hopefully didn't smoke cut-price cigars. Griff from the agency wouldn't be happy about this, an extra half-hour at no extra charge. Well, it was his bloody fault if he didn't send anyone with her, not counting Denise from the office who showed up just before lunch with her money, gave her a couple of faxes from Griff and then said she had to go off and take her mam down the clinic, and would Tina mind not telling because Griff said she was to stay with her until it was over but her mam had been six weeks getting an appointment and she wanted Denise to drive her there, not her dad who was nervous about clinics and places which only made things worse.

So Tina said yes to this and yes to that, and then Denise clattered off and for the next hour or so she did the Scully bit for all she was worth – about two hundred and thirty pounds overdrawn at the last count, and after tomorrow's shout up in Manchester it would be next week before she got another gig – but the reps and people were mostly too pissed to notice by then.

And then this nice guy came up, Christopher he said his name was, and he treated her just like she was a real person, not like she was royalty. She could have been dark, or red-headed, or quite short – actually she was a whisper under five-six, a little shorter than the real Scully but that was good because it didn't intimidate the men so much, Griff used to say. He got her a couple of paracetamols when she said she had a headache and he was funny without being one of those endless-fund-of-anecdotes raconteurs, and he didn't once talk about his job, which made a welcome change. He didn't say a word about the programme, which he didn't seem to have ever seen, or about the Department. He just talked to her as a person whom he seemed to find interesting.

It was such a relief. She assumed he was with Silurian Carbons but he didn't seem their type at all. When he discreetly asked her for her phone number, very quietly while the chairman made a couple of announcements, she gave it to him without a second thought.

He gave her his business card. She didn't look at it until she got home after picking up the kids from school – the other mums had got used to Agent Scully turning up at the school gates, but she still had to affect the dark glasses and a baseball cap worn low over her face.

'Christopher Francombe,' the card read. 'Creative Director.'

The company had one of those meaningless names like Protech or Infonet, but it had the word communications in there somewhere so she assumed he was something to do with advertising or PR or whatever. God knows what he was doing at the presentation, unless Silurian Carbons were one of his clients.

Still, he was a nice guy. She wondered if he would ring her, after all. At that moment she was, as they say, unattached, and if he asked her out she knew she would say yes. She and Ray hadn't made any kind of formal arrangements but she knew he was seeing other women and she'd been out with other guys too. The divorce wouldn't be long anyway so the whole awful bloody thing was as good as over.

It would be something nice, she knew that – a country restaurant or something, not a quick tandoori and then trying to get his hand up her skirt in the front of the car, and the endless 'go on do the voice, luv' requests that they came out with while the fantasies ran riot around their tiny brains. She knew Ray, her soon-to-be ex, was a bag of shit but some of the guys she'd been out with since were a whole effing sewage farm.

And there was the other card she'd got, from the nice woman in the ladies' lavvy. She took that out of her bag too and put it on her dressing table. She'd liked her as well. If things didn't shape up with Griff in the next little while, she might give her a ring. Lesley Carmody, it said in tiny little serif letters, above the name Carmody Kirtley Agency. And the amazing thing was, she was a Creative Director too.

Lesley Carmody was indeed a highly creative lady. At that very moment, lunch being over, she was dextrously undoing all the tiny buttons on Charmayne's summer dress. Charmayne was sitting on her lap at the table in the garden. She'd already helped Lesley out of her crisp white blouse and decorously licked her nipples which – being unusually large – now stood up, pert and alert.

'Mmmmm,' murmured Charmayne as the last button was undone and Lesley slid the dress off her shoulders. Her lover's fingers ran over her own breasts in turn, scooping them up, straying longingly over the expensive whispers of lace that enshrouded them.

Charmayne threw her arms around Lesley's waist and their lips met in a long, drawn-out kiss. She could feel Lesley's breasts against her own naked flesh, felt wantonness stir deliciously inside her. She began to move her hand around the waistband of Lesley's tight black cut-off jeans, a gesture always calculated to increase their mutual arousal. The flesh was firm, like marble, and warm in the afternoon sun.

Now Lesley was cupping her breasts, gently squeezing them, rubbing the erect nipples against the open palm of her hand. Charmayne leaned forward slightly so she could take their full weight. Charmayne had full, luscious breasts. They were a source of enormous pleasure to her, and to her lovers.

'Let's go upstairs now, shall we?'

Lesley was the one who usually took the initiative in these matters. They disentangled, instinctively smoothed out creases in their clothing – real or imaginary – and together left the table. Charmayne held Lesley's hand while, with her other hand, modestly pulled her gaping dress together.

They climbed the stairs to their room. The windows were open and a soft breeze played over their skin. The room was light and spacious, quietly luxurious. Charmayne let her dress fall to the floor and stood there in her ivory satin lingerie, the suspenders tight against her long thighs.

17

'I do love it when you wear stockings for me,' breathed Lesley. She knelt down, bare-breasted, and placed her tongue between her lover's legs. Charmayne gasped with pleasure as Lesley traced little wet trails around the firm flesh of her thighs. Her teddy was loose at the crotch and, with very little difficulty, Lesley soon inserted her tongue inside and found the warm, wet places that were barely concealed by those wispy scraps of satin and lace.

Charmayne was very damp – she always was when she felt aroused. She could feel Lesley's tongue darting around outside the entrance to her womb, playing with the folded labia, exploring her hidden, musky recesses. No one – man or woman – had ever been able to pleasure her with their tongue quite as well as Lesley could.

She paused for breath, and then renewed her delicious game. Charmayne ran her hands through the thick, dark-brown hair that spilled on to her shoulders, excited by the glimpses of her lover's darting tongue. She wanted her to find her clitoris and yet at the same time she did not – she wanted to save that moment of release for later.

She could see herself in the mirrors opposite the bed, a tall woman in her early to mid-twenties, dressed to thrill in Janet Reger lingerie and gold Bally sandals. Men liked her like this – and so did Lesley.

The phone rang suddenly on the bedside table. It only rang a couple of times, softly, until the answerphone cut in, but it seemed to break the reverie, at least for the moment. Lesley paused, her nose against Charmayne's luxuriant pubic bush, and then kissed those deeper, pinker lips a final time.

She stood up. Soundlessly, the two women undressed each other. Lesley's creamy teddy and Lesley's black lace panties lay side by side like friends on the thick carpet. They climbed on the bed together, Lesley naked, Charmayne still in her stockings and suspender belt. Charmayne lay back and Lesley climbed on top of her, pushing her legs open with her knees until their naked pussies were together, blonde muff and dark muff rubbing gently, tongue seeking tongue, breast crushed against breast.

They lay like this for some little while, gently moving against one another, until Charmayne sighed softly and tried to turn away.

'Guess I ate more than I should,' she murmured. 'I feel stuffed.'

'Am I too heavy for you, darling?'

'In a word, yes. It makes me feel uncomfortable, lying on top.'

Lesley kissed her on the tip of her nose and rolled to one side. They cuddled up close together, their legs interlocked, face to face.

'You miss me last night?'

'Sure I did. Did you?'

'Mmmmm. Press me again, there, like that.'

'Did you, you know, play with yourself?'

Charmayne could detect a little frisson running through her lover's body. A hand slid down over her stockinged thigh and cupped her pubic mound.

'Sure I did.'

'Did you think of me?'

'Maybe.'

'Who else, then?'

'That would be telling.'

'Go on.'

Lesley insinuated just the tip of her index finger into Charmayne's pussy, but her inquisitor wouldn't be distracted quite so easily.

'Go on, tell me who?'

'Have a guess?'

'I don't know. That woman from *Neighbours*? Uma Thurman?'

'No.' Another finger.

'The Spice Girls.'

'Which one?'

'The one you fancy.'

'Mmmmm – imagine licking her out. I've heard things about her.'

'I know you have.'

'Who told you?'

'Never you mind. Can't you guess?' Another finger.

Charmayne put her hand on Lesley's pussy and was amazed how wet it was.

'No, I give up.'

'Rudolph Valentino.'

'Are you kidding?'

'I'm not. Haven't you ever seen *The Sheik*? God, I nearly wet myself every time I see it.'

'I thought you went for the pale and interesting type.'

'A girl can change her mind.'

'What was he doing to you?'

'He was kissing me, and things.'

'Where?'

'In a garden somewhere. A big, ornamental garden. At night. There were people somewhere near. I think they could see us.'

'I like the idea of people watching. Did you fuck him?'

'Of course. He was huge! And I sucked him off.'

'Did you swallow it?'

'Of course.'

'You ever done that with a guy?'

'Sure. Have you?'

'Just once. I didn't like it. But I like it when you come in my mouth.'

'It's different for girls.'

'I think I've realised that by now. Not quite so messy.'

They fell silent. Swiftly and expertly now their fingers probed each other's hidden recesses, as delicate as bees' wings brushing a flower. Charmayne's touch on Lesley's clitoris was as infinitesimal as the movement of a second hand on a watch, but it brought her to orgasm all the same. Gently, always so very gently, she caressed that tiny bud, a rhythm that it seemed she had known all her life, so slow and sure. Others may have quickened the pace but Charmayne actually slowed down as she heard Lesley's breathing change and knew she was close.

They turned their heads on the pillow to face each other, opened their eyes. Lesley's tongue flickered out from between her lips and Charmayne felt a fresh wave of desire surge through her. She licked the tip of Lesley's tongue with her own, all the while her fingers moving so slowly and gently, and then she felt Lesley stiffen and the first waves of her orgasm hit her.

She quickly followed when Lesley went down on her. No sooner had she got her breath back than her dark-haired lover was down there between her legs, the sheets thrown heedlessly back. Charmayne looked up at the ceiling, helpless and wide-eyed, as she felt herself being explored by that questing, restless tongue. There was no doubt about it, no one knew better how to bring a woman off than another woman.

She could feel herself slipping closer to the edge. It felt like some slow, deliciously soothing anaesthetic was taking over her body. Her body seemed to be becoming number and yet more alive at the same time – or was it just that her sensations were totally focused in that divine triangle? And then, when the first little pulses began to spread outwards and through her whole body, she held her breath and let herself go, fell over the edge of the world as easily as a drunk slipping off a bar stool, and lay still while Lesley lay there, still licking her gently, her dark hair spread out on her thighs.

Tina realised with a start that she was fresh out of hair colour. She was naturally red herself but she had to keep it up, that little extra orangey-coppery tint that made all the difference. She had a very good stylist, Emily, who used to work in make-up at Central Television and knew more about Tina's hair than she did herself, but once the two of them had figured out what to do it was just a matter of letting rip with the bottles once a week.

There were all kinds of things in the bathroom cabinet but not the one she wanted. She'd have to make do with something else, she decided. She had a gig tomorrow – some show-business charity lunch up in Manchester, an evening do this time so it wasn't such an early start – but she reckoned her hair would pass muster as it was, just. After that it was the weekend and she could relax. She didn't have to work again till Wednesday but it worried her in a way, she could certainly use the money.

She checked the kids were asleep, thought about the half-full bottle of Frascati in the fridge and then the doorbell went. It was a little after eight which meant it had to be Daisy from the flat across the way, who had people coming for dinner and always managed to run out of herbs or stock cubes at the crucial moment. It was a day for running out of things, one way and another.

It wasn't Daisy, though. It was Ray, her soon-to-be ex. She'd changed the locks the day he finally left but it didn't always deter him.

'Don't wait to be asked in, will you?' she said to him as he brushed past. She could smell whisky on his breath. He sure as hell wasn't having any of her half-bottle of wine. It was all she had in the house and after her day with the manufacturers of high-quality lubricants for the automotive industry, she reckoned she deserved it.

He went into the living room, looked around.

'Got a new stereo, then?' he said, pointing at the smart black midi system on its little table by the window. 'You must be raking it in.'

He was always difficult about money. He had been a welder at Babcock Valves when they first met but they'd shut down three years ago and anyway she had really carried the weight for most of their married life, which mercifully had been pretty short. She knew he did a bit here, a bit there and had driven a lorry for some mate of his who must have had more money than sense – because Ray was a nutter behind a wheel – but he was still signing on. A couple of times he'd bummed money off her, a hundred and fifty, twice. He'd promised he'd pay her back but she knew he never would. She wasn't going to fall for that one again in a hurry.

'I got it in part payment for a job, actually. A company in Cambridge makes them. I did their sales conference a couple of months back and they let me have it cheap when I said I was looking for a new one. And no, I'm not raking it in at the moment. The bank stopped two cheques last week and you've not paid us any maintenance since Easter.'

He affected not to hear her, just went over and looked at the little black boxes.

'They must have liked you, to let you have something like

this. Top of the range stuff, this. What did you do, give the sales director a blow-job?'

'Ray!'

'Not that it bothers me what you do. How's that lawyer of yours getting on?'

'Not fast enough for you, that's for sure. I just want the settlement to be fair.'

'She'll get nothing out of me, I can tell you. I'm fucking skint.'

'They're your kids, Ray. As far as I'm concerned you can just piss off for good but you do owe it to them, you know.'

'Don't give me that sanctimonious crap. You sound like me dad.'

'I'm not. I'm just reminding you of your rights and duties as their father.'

He looked at her. He didn't look drunk but she could tell he'd had a glass or two, or maybe three. Ray always drank doubles.

'What is it you want? Why are you here, Ray?'

'I happened to be in the area so I thought I'd call in. Any post for me?'

'No. I always forward it. You know that.'

'I just thought there might be something, that was all.'

There wasn't any post for him, she knew it was just an excuse. He just wanted to niggle her, like the kids did with each other sometimes.

She heard the timer going on the oven. She made to go and switch it off but he suddenly grabbed her by the wrist and pulled her close to him. She could tell he had an erection. The whisky smell was equally overpowering.

She didn't do anything, waiting for him to relax his grip.

'Ray,' she said when he didn't move. 'Let me go, will you? I've got a quiche in the oven.'

'Fuck the quiche,' he said and pushed her over backwards on to the sofa. 'Fucking artsy-fartsy food.'

Her housecoat fell open revealing bare, newly shaved legs. She tried to cover herself but he was too quick for her, and too strong. In a second he had his hand between her legs and she was trying to push him off.

'Stop it, will you? I don't want this.'

He tried to kiss her. She turned her head away in disgust, but she could feel his tongue trailing wetly over her chin.

She struggled hard in an attempt to push him off but he had his weight on her upper body and her left arm was trapped underneath her.

She wanted to scream but she was afraid for the kids and besides old Mrs Hetherington next door was as deaf as a post and had the telly way up.

'Look, Ray, I don't want this,' she hissed.

He looked at her and sneered.

'You really are a fucked-up bastard, aren't you?' she yelled at him.

He paused for a moment.

'Don't sound like Scully now, do you, bitch?'

'Oh let me go, Ray. Why are you doing this? Can't you see it's over between us?'

Then he let go of her. He stepped back, his shoulders slumping, as if all the bravado had gone out of him.

He turned suddenly and walked out of the door, leaving it wide open in the clear suburban dusk. She could hear the music for the next programme on Mrs Hetherington's telly. She didn't know what it was. It sounded like it was being played backwards or something.

Chapter Two

In the early 1990s, things had been looking pretty rough on board that ship of fortune that was known as the advertising industry. Danny Kirkpatrick had kept his head above water, but he still found the seas choppier than some. He began to wonder whether the time might have come to jump ship.

He'd left art college in the North of England with a stack of commendations and diplomas. Some of the major agencies and studios had seen his degree show and liked what they saw. They suggested he come down south to see how the land lay. Creative Directors left their cards, he had a couple of good lunches and he quickly picked up plenty of work as an illustrator. It was good quality stuff, too – car manufacturers and TV companies, supermarket chains, that kind of thing. He'd hit the big league straight away. He worked in a couple of studios and after going on for three years he took the plunge and plucked up courage to go freelance. He was just twenty-five.

At first, it had been brilliant. Money, job satisfaction, seeing his work – and his name – in the right magazines, not just in Britain and Europe but in the States, Japan too. That brought in even more jobs. But then, after a couple of years, things started to get tighter, and tighter, and tighter. The budgets just weren't there any more – or was it that the agencies were getting greedier? A job that could easily have pulled in a couple of K was now going for seven-fifty, tops. Guys who had been around in the eighties, when you could come up with the most ludicrous fee you could imagine, double it, and still get the money, were aghast.

The faxes didn't come in quite so often, either. Instead of firm commissions, Danny found himself doing more and more work on spec, pitching for jobs that never came. Seven-fifty came down to six-fifty and there were quite a few that didn't even crawl past the five hundred mark. He could spend anything up to a fortnight on any one particular piece of work and this was bad news with a capital B and a big fat N. He was feeling pretty down about it all.

One night, in the pub, he met a mate who still worked full-time for one of the big studios. They were shooting a promo video for some new synthetic girlie band that had been invented by a guy in Wardour Street with a thousand-a-week habit and no imagination. They needed extras, didn't want to go through the usual agencies, it would be cash up front, a hundred and fifty a day. Danny knew Tot was doing him a favour, but he bit the bullet all the same. The phone hadn't rung in two weeks.

After the promo video there was some stuff for a theme park and then a catalogue of upmarket country clothes – Danny had that dark, relaxed style that looked good in a waxed jacket, though he was strictly leather and T-shirts himself – and after that a whole string of modelling and film extra jobs. He was happy to accept as many of them as he could, in between the diminishing number of 'proper' jobs.

It didn't satisfy him very much, sitting on his butt all day waiting for 'the right kind of light', but it paid the rent and it sure as hell beat waiting around wishing the phone would ring. He did the modelling work for eighteen months or so in the increasingly long gaps between commissions for his day job, but then things picked up and he was able to get hold of a pretty good computer graphics system by way of another friend and generally get himself back on the straight and narrow again.

Before long he was busier than ever, working freelance, doing design work as well as illustration – and still a couple of years short of his thirtieth birthday. He had an offer to go back to working for the same studios but he relished his freedom too much. He even took on an assistant, George, fresh out of college and keen to learn. He still kept up with the modelling assignments if they were interesting or lucrative enough – they provided him, among other things, with a steady stream of one-night stands and other optional extras. In the end, it became almost a hobby with him, an occasional indulgence to keep his eye in – it didn't harm his prospects to have two strings to his bow. So he didn't bother over-much if modelling power tools in Wolverhampton for a hundred and fifty pounds didn't come off but he screwed a five-day soft-drinks shoot in Nassau out of Gresley Thompson Peppercorn and screwed the director's assistant into the bargain. She was a twenty-two-year-old honey called Chantal who subsequently became his girlfriend. After a month or so, they moved in together.

He got a few more jobs by way of Chantal but then he took on another big identity scheme for a major Japanese-based car manufacturer and lost sight of his bit-part career for a while. Things came back with a vengeance, though, when he took on the hair-care job.

This came through an agency called Kirtley Carmody and basically it entailed little more than sitting on a horse for three highly paid days in Leicestershire. Danny's last contact with a saddle had been via a donkey named Rosie on the beach at Dawlish but he didn't need to ride, just to sit there, which was just as well because it was all he could do not to fall off. He'd been squeezed into trousers so tight that you could count the change in his pocket and this became even more excruciatingly uncomfortable every time Amelia rode into view.

Amelia was the real star of the ad. Her job was to come galloping through the covers, ride up to Danny, take off her riding helmet and shake loose her flowing blonde hair, freshly washed in Deneuve 103 with vitamin B and miracle secret formula Clearophen for added bounce. Then he took off his hat and shook his long hair free too. Actually, the pretty blonde woman from Kirtley Carmody told him, it was exactly the same stuff that Tesco sold at half the price, but who cared about things like that in this make-believe world? It took three full days to film the sequence and the director reckoned this was good going – they'd budgeted for six.

Amelia was a professional model and also an accomplished horsewoman – you could tell that by the effortless way she handled the chestnut mare. She was drop-dead gorgeous, had an ass that would have looked sensational in army fatigues, let alone jodhpurs, tits to match and enough sex appeal to burn a hole through armour plate. Danny went weak at the knees every time he thought of her.

And the extraordinary thing was, she was giving him the big come-on right from the off. Maybe it was his pony-tail that did it – it certainly couldn't have been as a result of her admiration of his riding skills. His Manchester accent was still quite strong and that probably didn't do him any favours either.

On day one there had been some guy in a Range Rover hanging around her but he'd quickly pissed off back to London and she was on her own, with only a mobile phone for company, which seemed to be glued permanently to her ear. They were staying in a three-star hotel with windows festooned with *Good Food Guide* stickers and over the lobster gallant Danny made his move. It was about as difficult as getting your spoon into a scoop of melting ice-cream.

Of course there was Chantal back in town but she and Danny had an understanding about these things and besides, she was many, many miles away. The girl from Kirtley Carmody didn't seem to mind. Amelia didn't appear to have an awful lot between the ears but that wasn't the point. She looked the business and Danny was in the mood to make a few stains on the three-star bedsheets.

Neither of them did anything overt, just the odd glance at the right moment, the usual stuff to let each other know how many beans made five. There were the others around, of course, the director who was half-pissed most of the time, various crew and assorted handlers. Conversation was anecdotal, the usual film crew/advertising business trade talk. Remember that time in Wolverhampton? The man with the three-legged dog on the beach at Biarritz? The time Lofty Smallweed got his leg over that MP's daughter? I'll never forget old Whatshisname . . .

There might have been a dozen of them around the big table by the open hearth, racking up the expenses like there was no tomorrow and very little left of today. They only had a little bit of second-unit stuff to do and everyone was feeling pretty mellow. Danny, however, went very easy on the Australian red and the fine old brandy that followed, on the director's insistence, as a matter of course.

It seemed the most natural thing in the world, when the party broke up, to slip back to his room, brush his teeth, fix his hair, check he had a clean shirt and a clean willy, give her another ten minutes and then tap on Amelia's door.

She opened it almost immediately. He knew she had been waiting for him. She was still fully dressed, in jeans and a loose silk shirt, which surprised him – he was sure she'd be the negligée type. Perhaps she hadn't packed one.

Danny had a bottle of champagne with him, and two glasses. She closed the door quickly behind him. They managed a glass and a half each and some faltering and inconsequential conversation before he was on the bed with her, busy with the buttons on that mauve silk blouse.

Her tits, scooped up in a white half-cup bra, were sensational. Without the bra they looked even better. She was practically thrusting them into his face, urging him to kiss them and lick them, encouraging him to nuzzle on her nipples as if he was a baby animal. He was absolutely crazy for her, so turned on that he was hoping he wouldn't cream himself.

All the while, her hand was rubbing against his cock from the outside. He was aware of how monstrously stiff he was, so stiff that it was becoming quite uncomfortable. He wished he could will his clothing to auto-destruct, so they could be naked together as God and Danny intended.

Next to go were her jeans and then he finally had his hands on that divine ass. Two lovely moons winked at him, dimpling prettily. They were made to look even more lusciously biteable by the frail lacy wisp of a G-string. Danny's heart felt as if it was about to explode. His chest was too small for it. Something had to give pretty soon.

He squeezed her cheeks and snogged her hugely, two wet tongues slobbering against one another in a wanton orgy of desire. He got his shirt off and she ran her hands over his pectoral muscles, with their covering of dark fine hair. Somehow Danny was able to kick his shoes off and struggle out of his jeans. She turned round with her face in the pillow and stuck her ass out at him, pulling down her panties at the same time so he could see the wet coral crack of her pussy, inviting him in.

And then he was up behind her, his cock purple and hugely distended, bobbing about in a frenzy of lust and male pride, already starting to leak spunk. She was so wet that he went straight in almost at the first push and then he was fucking her for all he was worth, reaching round to cup those suckably huge melon breasts while she murmured sweet pornography into the pillow with her eyes closed and her tongue lolling in the corner of her mouth.

He could get a long way into her like that and he gave her everything he had, which was far from inconsequential as various discerning ladies had pointed out to him in the past. They fucked each other with such abandon that their pubic hair was quickly matted with each other's secretions in this wild exchange of bodily fluids. She seemed able to open her legs impossibly wide – maybe it was all those years of sitting on horseback – and it got so that she was just like one enormous cunt and he was just one enormous dick, blurring together in naked lust, soaking wet, crazed into delicious obscenity.

He was hardly aware of the moment of spunking into her for it had all seemed like one gigantic orgasm from the instant he first entered her. One moment he was slewing in an out of her, leaning back and arching his back until it seemed that his cock would snap off right at the root, and the next he had thrust forward again, big and bursting and then, finally, came the big fat pulses. He shouted out something and she was gasping words too, grinding her arse at him while those gorgeous melon tits swung provocatively and heavily over the tangled sheets, and then he was suddenly empty, draped over her back with his nose against her ear, smelling her expensive and pervasive perfume, trying to get his breath back and feeling that he was losing the battle and would die of asphyxia and sexual rapture in equal measure.

They had more champagne and she invited him to stay the night, which was something of a foregone conclusion in

Danny's mind. Conversation was fairly restricted in its scope, which didn't greatly distress him. She showed no interest in anything other than her own social life. Did he know Simon this and Sacha that? Did he go to this or that party? Had he been to Johnny Depp's club in New York? She was like a page from *The Tatler* come to life.

In the end, he thrust his big thick dick into her mouth just to shut her up. She sucked him up to a nice fat cockstand and then climbed on top of him, so that her luscious breasts were hanging there right before his eyes, those highly edible nipples brushing against his chest. This time, it seemed, she was going to fuck him.

She bobbed up and down for a while and then gave him the big squeeze with her pussy muscles. It was extraordinary, the power and finesse she seemed to have there between her legs. Even though he'd come hugely not twenty minutes before, it was all Danny could do not to shoot off there and then, but he was anxious to sample everything that was on the menu that night.

So he lay back, with his cock sticking up like some primitive tribal totem, and she spitted herself on him and rode him up and down, up and down, like it was some new dance craze she'd learned at Johnny Depp's place. Every now and then she'd stop and he'd have a suck on those gorgeous nipples or else she'd work her magic with her vaginal muscles. She had so much control, it was like she was giving him a blow-job with her cunt – and the real thing, done with her mouth, had been pretty good too.

He looked down between her big melon breasts at the blonde thatch of pussy fur, matted now with their bodily juices. Her lips were slick and engorged, unusually prominent so they looked like a mouth. It was fascinating to see his cock disappear far inside her with every movement, only to come sliding back down again, almost to the tip of the glans.

She wasn't the tightest woman he had ever screwed but she sure as hell knew how to use what she'd got. She treated his cock like it was her own private dildo, fucking herself with it, riding him like the stallions she was evidently so adept at handling. At that moment it was the only part of his body that she seemed interested in – she didn't seem to give a flying fuck for his mind – and pretty soon she brought herself off again, a long, slow, shuddering climax that just seemed to go on and on. He felt the ripples and waves surging around her body and then, slowly, start to ebb away.

She sank down beside him and his cock, still erect and as yet unspunked, flopped over on to his belly.

Amelia lay still for some while, running her fingers through his pony tail. Then she opened her eyes and looked at him intently, as if studying every detail of his face.

'Hey,' she said, 'you really do look like Tom Cruise.'

Danny laughed. He was six feet two, spoke with the mild trace of a Manchester accent and had never heard that in his life before.

'No, I mean it. With your hair back from your face like that, it's uncanny. Hasn't anyone said that to you?'

'No – I don't believe anyone has.'

'You're kidding me. Your eyes are even the same colour.'

'You big on Tom Cruise, then?'

'Sure, I've seen all his pictures. I saw him once at a party in New York but there were people all around him, you couldn't get near him. I saw his wife in the powder room, though, what's her name?'

'Nicole Kidman.'

'That's right. I said Hi and she smiled, didn't say anything. I didn't see them again until they were leaving. He's a little guy—'

'So what? Lots of big name actors are. Dustin Hoffman, even Paul Newman.'

'Paul Newman? Are you kidding?'

'Johnny Depp.'

'Yeah, I know. I met him once. I went to his club, did I tell you? Sean Penn was going to come but he didn't show. He's no taller than I am, I'm sure. How tall are you?'

'Six-two.'

'That's big.'

'For an Englishman, maybe.'

'I like big guys.'

'You just said you like little guys.'

'I like little guys too. Best of all is a big guy who looks like Tom Cruise. Paul Newman's old. Even Sean Penn's a bit old for me now, you know what I mean?'

'Ever imagine doing it with someone like that?'

It was like an electric shock had gone through her.

'What do you mean?'

'Oh, come on, you know what I mean. Going to bed with them, having sex, all that kind of thing. Ever wonder what it's like?'

'Maybe. What kind of things?'

'You know. Kissing him. Screwing him. All those things. All those sexy scenes you see in movies. Ever imagine you were there?'

'Mmmmm. Sure I do. Doesn't everyone?'

'I screw actresses, given the choice. In my head, natch.'

'Who do you fancy, then?'

'Greta Scacchi, for one. Isabel Huppert.'

She didn't seem to have heard of either of them. She soon lost interest in this side of the conversation, and went off into a world of her own. Danny saw her hand stray down to her groin.

'I bet his cock's really nice to suck,' she said at length. Her voice was distant, dreamy. She had her hand between her thighs. It was obvious she wanted to play games, use her imagination.

'Sure. Why don't you pretend you're doing just that?' said Danny, quietly suggestive. 'I bet you do it just beautifully.'

Amelia needed no second bidding. She slid down the bed, her tongue tracing a wet trail down Danny's lean and muscular body. She spent an age teasing him, running her fingers and her lips over his thighs, across his belly, anywhere except where he wanted her to put them. She reached up and tweaked his nipples between her thumb and forefinger, something guaranteed to drive him to the peak of desire.

'Suck me, for God's sake,' he said with urgency in his voice.

'Say please,' she replied but she didn't wait for him. Instead she opened those rich, full lips and swallowed him right up, taking the whole of his cock in at once, right up to the root. God, it was an extraordinary feeling, like screwing a vacuum

33

cleaner that was running in reverse.

And then she started to move her head up and down, up and down, always with his cock half-way down her throat like few women could ever really do to a guy. The wet, velvety suction was so great that he almost came off there and then, even though he'd already come twice.

To calm himself down he opened his eyes. Amelia was lying on her side, frigging herself while she sucked his cock. She seemed to be in a world of her own but then she sensed his eyes on her, looked up at him and smiled dreamily. She took it out of her mouth and it surprised him just how much came out, like his cock was twice its normal size.

She winked at him, and then her tongue flickered out wickedly and she licked just the very tip of his cock. For a while she played with him like this, running her tongue down the dark eye which seemed to open up and welcome the probing of her tongue, exploring the mysterious ridges of his glans.

And then she opened her lips again and took all of him in once more, cupping his balls in her hand. As she did so, he could feel the spunk beginning to rise inside him. His mind aflame with pleasure and lust, he did nothing to resist the feeling but instead pushed his hips towards her, so that he too was lying half on his side, half on top of her, fucking her in her welcoming mouth. He came in an almighty torrent and he knew that she was expecting him to, because she didn't gag or cough, just sucked him dry and swallowed everything, and then when the pulsing had ceased and he lay back on the tangled sheet, she licked him all over like a cat that had got the cream.

She was far away in a world of her own imagining. He turned off the bedside light and went to sleep.

He woke up with a start, scarcely aware of where he was, and who was sucking his cock. Then he remembered. He was at home with Chantal. He was lying on the bed, naked, his legs apart. He couldn't remember the last time he had had his cock sucked with such finesse, such obvious relish. She was the best he had ever known. He lay back with his eyes closed,

34

savouring the moment. He wanted to banish all sensation other than that of her tongue, lips and hands.

She was using just the tip of her tongue to coax little jagged shards of electricity from him. That was what had woken him up. A clock by the bedside told him it was twelve minutes past four.

The physical pleasure made him melt, made his mind go shooting off somewhere into the ether. She licked the tip of his penis as though it were a species of exotic fruit, reassuringly expensive, whose juice was to be savoured slowly, one sip at a time.

He couldn't see her face in the darkness. Somehow he preferred it that way. That made things too specific being able to see who he was with. He recalled what she'd said about her fantasies and he wondered, just who she thought she was in bed with.

They lay thus for many long minutes, her tongue washing over him. At times she seemed to be trying to probe down into the little oval-shaped hole with its supremely sensitive skin. She didn't seem to want him to do anything, just to lie there and let him roam free through the realm of his senses.

Gradually she drew all of him into her mouth. He was conscious only of his stiffness and of how her ministrations seemed to soothe and seduce him. He was alive purely for the moment, and felt no need to push her on to her back, force her legs apart, take her in haste and excitement. Only what was now was of any importance and what was now was all-absorbing.

Her lips closed over the ridge of his glans as if she were sucking a plum. Her teeth nipped him lightly and deliberately, but it served only to enhance rather than interrupt his consciousness of the moment. He moaned gently. He didn't want her to stop. He wanted this moment to go on forever.

Then she was moving down the thick stalk of his penis, pursing her lips to take him all in. He could feel her tongue swirling against him and the soft pressure of her lips. He seemed to penetrate deeper and deeper inside her, until he could feel her nose against his thick pubic bush. He wondered she didn't choke herself.

She was gently bobbing her head up and down now and involuntarily he found himself responding to her rhythm. He made to move his hips up to meet her thrusts but she seemed to try to stop him, to make some cautionary noise from the back of her cock-filled throat. He settled back on the soft bed and touched her lightly on the shoulders in acknowledgement of her wishes.

The bobbing became as regular and hypnotic as the surging of waves, one following another as surely as the motion of the moon. He found himself breathing in and breathing out with infinite slowness, trying to match to perfection the movements of her mouth. Soon he could no longer tell when one breath ended and the new one began. It was like an anaesthetic drug.

He opened his eyes and he realised she wasn't there any more. Had he fallen asleep? No, he was far too conscious of his bodily sensations for that to have happened. He had, he realised, simply floated away into an ecstasy where the barriers between what was her body and what was his had simply ceased to be relevant any longer.

Time went by. An hour. A minute. An atomic fraction of a second. His tongue sought hers. She sucked in his lower lip and nibbled it, nipping it gently with her teeth.

He was feeling more aroused than he had ever done in his life before. She pushed her hips up against him, meeting him thrust for thrust, willing him to move deeper inside her. He arched his back, pushed into her, and almost immediately he came inside her in short, rhythmic pulses.

He lay his head down on her shoulders and she ran her fingers through his thick, tangled hair. He could feel his penis trail across her thighs, damp and sticky with their mingled juices. She pressed her leg against him, took his hand and squeezed it gently.

Then she led it towards the warm moist place between her thighs.

He rolled over once more until he was face to face with her. The bedding rustled. Everything was tangled. He kissed her on the tip of her nose and his hands flickered up and down her body, stroking the sensitive flesh of her upper arms and the delicate nape of her neck. It felt good. The palms of his hands were strong and confident but in his fingertips he had magic. She seemed to like just to lie there and let the subtle little waves of pleasure wash over her.

They were in no hurry, they had no end-point to reach. His penis lay snugly against her leg, warm and limp, detumescent. Gradually, consciousness of the room and the cold night air began to slip away from her. His fingers began to draw little patterns around her breasts, hardly touching them, but just getting near enough to make her nipples pucker up in anticipation. She sighed and moved closer to him, feeling his breath against her neck. The sensation of being held back became almost maddening after a while. She started to want him to take her.

Now he was pushing his palms against her breasts and she felt almost embarrassed by how erect her nipples had become. Her vagina, too, seemed exceptionally moist and succulent, the lips engorged with the blood that hammered through her from her pounding heart.

'Suck my tits,' she breathed, urging him into action. She liked him to do that.

And he needed no second bidding. His tongue flickered down around her bosom, across each soft white breast in turn, lingering tenderly at her nipples. She pushed herself against him, holding her breasts up for him, offering them. Her nipples were as hard and swollen as rosehips.

He sucked almost all of her right breast into his mouth – it was an extraordinary feeling, the sensation of his tongue crammed against her wet nipple, the level of suction he was able to exert. Then he turned his attention to the other breast, drawing that in almost whole, his hand between her thighs now, seeking her wet places as she gladly parted her legs.

He slid down her body, his tongue tracing a line down across her firm, flat belly. She pushed him away. It was too soon, there were other things she wanted him to do first. He understood the meaning of her movements and instead planted soft, butterfly kisses against her pudenda, stroking her thighs, reaching out for her own hand to take in his.

Minutes went by, which seemed like hours. She seemed to swirl away into another level of consciousness and then came back, refreshed and eager, as though she had been away for light years instead of seconds.

He focused all his attention on his lover and the waves of pleasure that were coming through her. She came as he tongued the slick, widening gap between her legs, the pulsing eddies of pleasure becoming almost unbearable at the end, as if she were being tormented rather than pleasured by him. She had to make him stop, or he would have carried on all morning, making love to her in that fashion.

'I always knew you'd be good,' she breathed. 'Even when I first met you.'

It took a while for him to understand what she'd said. Aware once again of her role, she took hold of his penis and guided it to her mouth. She seemed possessed of an irresistible energy and so was he. There was a levity now in their love-making, a joy that had not been there before, until their bodily lusts had hurled themselves against each other and exhausted themselves. Rawness and fire were being replaced by tenderness and warmth. It wasn't fucking any more, it was more like making love. He thought guiltily of Amelia, back at the hotel.

Chantal was sitting half-upright on the bed and he was kneeling up to let her suck him. She frigged his shaft a few times and then her tongue flickered out and she teased the tender nerve endings of his glans, gliding over its spongy surface, nibbling with practised teeth.

'Do you think I look like Tom Cruise?'

'Hmmmmmmm?'

'I said, do you think I look like Tom Cruise?'

'Never thought about it. Will you lick me again, please?'

He pushed her on to her back and spread her legs. Before he began he asked her again.

'Look like who?' she asked.

'Tom Cruise.'

'Don't talk with your mouth full. Didn't your mummy tell you?'

He would get no sense out of her until he'd brought her off. He pushed his tongue back in between her labia and did her for all he was worth.

'What was that you were asking me?' Chantal said when the earthquake had finally subsided.

'I said, do you think I look like Tom Cruise?'

'Who?'

'Me, obviously. Tom Cruise looks like Tom Cruise.'

'Do I think you look like Tom Cruise?'

'That's right. Now do you understand?'

'I wouldn't have said so – except maybe around the eyes.'

'Is that all?'

'I don't know. Your hair's the wrong colour, for a start. And it's too long.'

'What if I had it falling forward, like he does?'

'Maybe. I don't know.'

She began fellating him again. He was surprised by how much she liked to suck his dick. She took it deep into her mouth, tasting his saltiness and the mixture of their juices, her own tang as well as the ammoniac flavour of his come. She bobbed her head up and down with practised ease, swirling her tongue around the sensitive tip, nipping him playfully with her teeth so that he winced and laughed and protested. She knew he liked it the way she did it. She would have been happy to suck him all night if he wanted her to.

With his glans just inside her mouth, she formed her lips into a tight ring and managed to insinuate the tip of her tongue into the little dark slit at the end of his cock. As her lips massaged the ridge around his penis she stroked his shaft with a firm, regular rhythm. He moved backwards a little, perhaps rocking back and forth slightly on his heels, gently fucking her in her mouth in the darkness, inserting and withdrawing his cock no more than an inch or two at a time.

She could hear him moan but she didn't look up, concentrating instead on what she was doing. When he came she would have almost choked had she not taken a deep breath when she felt his balls contracting, so great was the rush of semen into her mouth.

She wanted him to fuck her when he was ready again and he wished he could but he was tired, so very tired. On top of his guilt about Amelia, it made him feel even worse.

He held her close, stroked her hair. 'Look,' he said as softly as he could. 'I just want to get to sleep now. I was up at six this morning.'

'Yesterday morning.'

'Exactly. That's why I want to sleep now.'

'Okay.'

'So you don't think I look like Tom Cruise?'

'Yes. No. Oh, I don't know. Why all this Tom Cruise all of a sudden?'

'Oh, somebody said there was a resemblance.'

'Who?'

'Oh, just somebody I met.'

'When?'

'When I was away.'

'A woman?'

'Maybe.'

'You sleep with her?'

'What?'

'You sleep with her?'

'Why d'you ask that?'

'What kind of woman says to a guy, "Hey, you look just like Tom Cruise," if she doesn't fancy him?'

'She didn't say "just like", just "a bit like".'

'Don't get technical. So it was a woman then?'

'Sure, it was a woman.'

'And you did sleep with her.'

Silence.

'I don't mind. You know that. Just don't lie to me, that's all.'

Another silence, longer this time.

'So I do look like Tom Cruise.'

'Maybe a little. Your eyes are the same colour, anyway.'

'How do you know what colour eyes he's got? You never said you fancied him.'

'I don't. He's not my type at all. Besides, I'd tower over him. I can't get on with little guys.'

'Paul Newman's not that tall, you know. And you go ape over him. Remember that time we went to see that double bill, *The Hustler* and the sequel to it, you know, what do they call it. The one with Johnny Depp or whoever—'

But Chantal was asleep. He, funnily enough, now felt wide awake and, moreover, he had a woolly-bully on him like a copper's night-stick.

Next morning, when a client unexpectedly rang up and cancelled their meeting, Danny booked an appointment at a hair salon. He told himself he'd had his hair long and tied back in a pony tail for long enough now and it was time for a change. Actually, it was because he wanted to see what he looked like.

He had his hair coloured too, several shades lighter than his own. It felt weird. He took a lot of care of his appearance but he'd never done anything quite like this before.

'Hey,' said the girl when she'd almost finished drying his hair. 'You look just like Tom Cruise, you know.'

Danny tried to laugh it off. Inwardly he was quite pleased. That was what he'd been rather hoping to hear.

'He one of your favourites, then?'

'You bet. I see all his films.'

Danny stood up, all six-feet-two of him, and scooped little strands of hair from inside his collar.

'He's only a little guy, though,' he said, casually.

'Is he? I didn't know that. I thought he'd be quite tall.'

'Oh no, not at all.'

'Still, it wouldn't matter that much, would it? I'm only five-feet-one myself.'

He peered down at the top of her head. What was it with all these small people?

On the way to where he'd parked the car, he kept checking his appearance in shop windows. One or two people looked at him, too, as if they'd clocked him, a mystified expression on their faces. Unfortunately no women bared their breasts for him to autograph, or offered to blow him there and then on the pavement, or even offered him their phone numbers.

He had one last look at himself in the rear-view mirror and then drove round to the agency.

'Bloody hell,' said Charmayne.
'Bloody hell,' said Lesley.

They looked at Danny, standing in front of them in their office. He'd turned up suddenly in reception and asked to see them. He hadn't been one of their major assets until then but when he swept into the office and took off his baseball cap, he'd instantly become a star.

'I thought there was a resemblance,' said Charmayne after a long pause. 'I wish I'd said so earlier.'

'It's incredible,' said Lesley. 'Can you do an American accent?'

Danny tried but he wasn't very good. He was an illustrator and a part-time male model and now they seemed to want him to be an actor as well.

They were pretty pushy, these two women. He was sure they were lesbians. The blonde one, Charmayne, he could sense there was something there, that she fancied blokes as well, but not the other one, as far as he could tell. They were both pretty glam but that was the fashion these days, wasn't it?

'Danny?' said the dark one, Lesley. 'Would you just go and wait in the outer office for a minute. There's something I want to discuss with Charmayne.'

He hung around the photocopier for a while. He knew they were setting something up. He could hear low voices, like they were on the phone. Then Lesley stuck her head round the door.

'We want to make a deal with you,' she said when he was seated again. 'Forget the modelling for the time being. How much do you make as an illustrator?'

'Three-fifty a day. Twelve a week. It depends on the client and the job. Obviously I don't make that kind of money every day.'

'What would you say if we offered you two grand a week to be Tom Cruise?'

'For how long?'

'As long as it lasts.'

'Doing what?'

'The things that lookalikes do. Gala openings, private parties, promotion work, that kind of thing.'

'Where's the work going to come from?'

'Oh, we'll find it, don't you worry about that. We've got contacts, we know the networks.'

'What about the day job? I mean, I've got clients, I've got commissions. I don't want to let them go.'

'Provided nothing clashes, there's no reason why you shouldn't carry on. But for the time being, you should regard Kirtley Carmody as your main client. We'd want an exclusive, of course, but as far as your design work's concerned, you're your own boss. All we ask is that it doesn't get in the way.'

Danny thought quickly. He had a couple of identities to develop, they'd bring in six or seven grand each over the next three months, he couldn't let them go, they might lead on to bigger things. Other than that, though, things were getting a bit quieter than they had been, but then they usually were at this time of year. There was a few little things on top of that but he could get George, his assistant, to handle them.

'Okay,' he said at length.

'Oh good,' said Lesley, looking relieved. 'We'll fax you when we know more. It might take a couple of days.'

'That's fine,' said Danny. 'I've got plenty to go on with.'

'Just one thing, though. With the baseball cap on, you look more like yourself again. Could you be a bit, you know, circumspect from now on?'

'Dark glasses?'

'That kind of thing, yeah. We don't want people to see too much of you, not in public anyway. You know what I mean.'

'I see what you mean, now,' said Chantal. Danny'd rung her at the ad agency where she worked, said he had something important to tell her and it couldn't wait. It was gone seven-thirty but she'd worked really late the last three days on the trot and her boss ruefully conceded that maybe she ought to see daylight once in a while. 'But be back tomorrow at eight,' he called after her. 'We've got those chewing gum people coming in to discuss concepts.'

They'd driven out west, over the river away from the bustle, in the gathering dark. They were sitting in their favourite window seat at Quaglini's. The seafood pasta was delicious, as always.

The open-necked sports shirt and white T-shirt only added to the all-American boy look. One or two people had given Danny the once over across the cannelloni.

'Do you fancy me?' he said, nudging her leg under the table.

'Of course I do. But only because it's you. Like I said, I don't fancy him at all. I don't go for these clean-cut types. They're too wholesome for me. I like men who look dangerous.'

He laughed, and speared a fragment of squid.

'The agency were pretty chuffed, I can tell you. They're going to see what they can come up with. It should mean a lot more money.'

'So you're a marketable commodity?'

'Lesley and Charmayne seemed really hyped up, you know. They're going to do a lot of ringing around. Something good will come of it, I can feel it.'

'Sure it will. But you want to be sure of what you're letting yourself in for, don't you?'

Their knees touched again under the table. He really had the hots for Chantal this evening. He knew she had the occasional dalliance outside their relationship and she hadn't been especially bothered about what he'd told her concerning Amelia. It was what they meant to each other that mattered most, not petty jealousies. Their relationship was strong enough for that.

'What about your work? I mean, your real work?'

'I can handle it. It's just another option, isn't it?'

'I guess so. Oh, I forgot to tell you. We got a new job today. Or rather I did.'

Chantal was retained by one of the big agencies but she clandestinely handled quite a bit of work on her own. She had studied film at college, worked on a couple of big commercials, knew the right people. She had a growing sideline as a consultant.

'What was that, then?'

'Another video, opportunities for kids, that kind of thing.'

'So what's new?'

'This is good. I can believe in it. It's helping kids do what they want to do – make records, dee-jaying, dance, make videos even. The Arts Council are co-funding it and there's some lottery money as well.'

'So it'll pay well?'

'No. Nothing that good ever does. Bit it'll be a good thing to do.'

'Sure. Maybe you need a Tom Cruise lookalike to introduce it, you know what I mean.'

She laughed. She had a very expressive smile, it made her whole face light up like she was really pleased. She had masses of dark curly hair that she wore pinned up in all kinds of crazy ways, never the same twice.

Danny had his hand on her knee. She was wearing a simple summer dress, Ghost or Monsoon or something, very gauzy. He could feel her bare flesh through the fabric. He fancied her like stink. They didn't bother with coffee.

He paid their bill and they made their way out into the night. It was almost dark outside, just a faint trace of colour in the sky, not a great deal of traffic about. The air was warm and the stars were incredibly bright, high up there between the buildings. They held hands as they walked through the night-time throng.

Danny was parked where he always parked when they ate at Quaglini's, on the long curling avenue next to the park. It was next to impossible to find a spot in the centre and out here, among the big houses where the well-to-do doctors and lawyers lived, there were always plenty of police cars doing the rounds. He knew his car wouldn't get stolen. It was an MG, British racing green, nice. And unfortunately very vulnerable.

They fucked against a tree over towards the bandstand. It was kind of weird being out in the park at eleven-thirty at night, with the wrought iron columns of the bandstand festooned with graffiti and the overpowering smell of night-scented flowers from the beds laid out all around them. It was a good park, well maintained, and it was always open at night. Did they lock parks up these days? he wondered. He would often come here at night to think, driving out from home and walking three or four miles or more around the winding paths.

He heard the distant sound of a car moving along the avenue. Chantal hoiked her dress up and he was sucking hungrily at her tits, lovely and round and fleshy with nice plump nipples.

He slipped his hand down inside her pants. Her pussy felt like it was on fire.

'Come on, Danny,' she whispered, stroking his reprofiled hair as he nuzzled her. 'Or should that be Tom?'

His fingers were slick with her secretions, the inside of her pussy opening up for his fingers like it was some species of rarely and ultimately exotic orchid. He had one finger right inside her and she seemed to be getting wetter and wetter and wetter, like she was really panting for him.

They broke, breathing deeply the still night air, and then she quickly stepped out of her pants. He pressed her against the tree trunk, cold and surprisingly rough against their naked flesh. Her dress was up around her hips and Danny was busy with his belt. For a second or two they looked at each other in the darkness, the distant lights of the houses reminding them where they were. An owl hooted. They were barely able to see each other's flesh in the gloom.

And then she stood up high on her toes and parted her legs and he was pushing inside her, hot and eager. She came almost immediately, tonguing him like mad, and then again as he pumped his strong, masculine backside up and down, up and down, his cock seeming to fill her completely until she was oblivious to everything else.

She hadn't seemed to be in an especially raunchy mood in the restaurant but she had such a mercurial temperament, it was one of the things that drew him to her. It was the mood of the evening that had been the most powerful aphrodisiac, this overwhelming feeling of optimism and hope. He hadn't felt as good as this in a long time, at least not about work.

He could feel the strain on his hamstrings, crouching down slightly so he could get his cock into her. It never occurred to either of them to do it lying down on the baked, sun-bleached turf of the park. There was something about a genuine knee-trembler that other forms of spontaneous intercourse always seemed to lack.

He pushed up and she pushed down and the both of them hoped to hell nobody was out there nearby, because they were making more noise than a rugby scrum and laughing at the same time, this crazy laughter that was born out of their happiness and fulfilment, laughing and fucking and licking and gasping like that beneath the stars, two grand a week and all the pussy you could manage, it was brilliant.

When he came into her, it was like a big shuddering spasm for both of them. He rammed himself right up into her so hard that she almost cried out with the pleasure of it all, and then he became, for a brief and ecstatic moment, absolutely still and silent. At that precise moment something right at the root of his cock seemed to contract and his spunk came flooding out like a dam was breaking. He came so hard and with such intensity that he could even feel his asshole pulsating in perfect synchronisation. It seemed to go on and on until finally the feeling subsided and he realised his legs were getting incredibly stiff standing like that.

They lay pressed together against the tree, until Chantal felt the come running down the inside of her thighs and then Danny withdrew and they went back to the car hand in hand.

'In the dark I can pretend you're anyone I like,' she whispered to him, laughing.

'And who am I? Or rather who was I?'

'Not Tom Cruise, that's for sure,' she replied. 'I'd have you any time.'

'What do you think, then?' asked Lesley. It was gay and lesbian night at Pussycats and the place was packed.

'I think we should go for it, you know,' replied Charmayne without a moment's hesitation. 'It's too much of a coincidence. I think it's a sign, or something.'

'You've been reading too many horoscopes, that's your trouble. But I think you're right. Fancy one for the gutter before we go?'

They got the barman's attention, ordered their usual – brandy and coke for Charmayne, dry-white-with-ice for Lesley. Then they continued their discussion of the day's events.

'When Danny came in I nearly wet myself. I mean, he looked so much like him, you know. He had these dark glasses on and when he whipped them off I thought, my God, who is this?'

'I know. I couldn't believe it myself. To be honest, I'd never really noticed it before, you know what I mean?'

'Neither had I. Neither had he, for that matter. He was saying some woman on that shoot in Leicestershire mentioned it to him first.'

'And what about that other one, you know, you met in Birmingham, who looks like *The X Files* woman? She left a message on the answerphone, didn't she?'

'I know. I got the feeling she wasn't satisfied with where she was. It was just this two-bit agency, you could tell from the way she spoke about them, really provincial.'

A tall black woman in spike heels and leather came by, gave them the glad eye. Her eye make-up was stunning and her breasts were huge beneath their straining zipper.

'Can I buy you lovely ladies a drink?' she breathed in a deep, husky voice, running the tip of a provocatively pink tongue along fuchsia lips.

'Later, Richie,' said Lesley. 'We're talking business.'

'At eleven at night?'

'At eleven at night. And your eleven o'clock shadow's showing too. You need a shave, Richie, it shows through your make-up.'

Richie teetered away on unfamiliar four-inch heels and they resumed their discussion.

'I thought she was really good too, even with a fag on in the ladies'. I had a hunch something would come of it. I'll call her back in the morning.'

'So what are you saying? That we go in for this lookalikes business in a big way? But we can't go very far if we've only got an Agent Scully and a Tom Cruise. Not much of a double act, is it? Unless we start some rumours, that there's a bit of partner-swapping going on.'

'I know what you mean, but it's a start. The thing is, you only need a couple of really good ones. You can get Elvis Presley impersonators down at Tesco, they don't need to be that good, just as long as they have the white rhinestone jump-suit and wiggle their hips a bit. *There's a guy works down the chip shop swears he's Elvis,* and all that stuff. Actually, there was one last year at Roger and Simon's do – you know, when they had the cabaret turns – and he must have been all of sixteen stone, didn't look a bit like Elvis, and his wig fell off in the middle of *Jailhouse Rock*. It was a regular riot . . .'

'So what do we do?'

'Put feelers out. Advertise. Talk to a few people. The same way as we do anything in this game. You never know what you might find.'

A tall, dark girl in a micro-mini passed right by them. Lesley and Charmayne looked her up and down, from the top of her hair – piled up high in an extraordinary Bardot-esque beehive – to the tips of her high, pointed boots, and looked at each other and smiled. They'd seen her before at Pussycats. They wondered if she'd be interested in making a threesome one night . . .

'I'd really like a Cliff Richard lookalike,' said Charmayne, when the vision had passed.

'Cliff? Why on earth?'

'Well, everybody knows him. He'd be brilliant at the clubs.'

'What about Shirley Bassey?'

'Yes, her too. And Dusty. Dusty'd be dead easy, wouldn't she? It'd just be hair and make-up.'

'And Marilyn. You get a lot of Marilyn lookalikes.'

'What about Madonna?'

'Nobody really knows what she looks like. One minute she's dark, the next she's this blowsy blonde. Anyway, she'd probably sue us. She's not supposed to have much of a sense of humour.'

'The Spice Girls?'

'Done to death. The second they came out, you had all these lookalike bands, don't you remember? The Spicy Girls, The Spicy Boys, the whole thing was dead as a doornail even before their movie came out. The Spice Girls were last year, dearie.'

'What about blokes? Who could we have?'

'I don't know. Who do you think?'

'A Mulder would be useful, But Tina says it's her they're really interested in. She's done a few gigs on her own.'

'What about the one she works with?'

'He's not very good. He doesn't really look like him, to be honest. And he's a bit of a boozer, not very reliable. He isn't a patch on her.'

'Something other than showbiz, maybe. It's always singers and things, isn't it? and movie stars. How about footballers, maybe? Or politicians?'

'Who'd pay money to hire a politician? You could probably get the real thing cheaper. They'll do anything for money – especially the Tories.'

'Yes, you're right. But Ryan Giggs, though. I'd love a Ryan Giggs. And that French guy, what's his name, the one who retired, the one who used to do the ads.'

'I know who you mean. Yes, I could quite fancy him myself.'

'You could get a lot of money if you had the right face.'

'In the right place.'

'That's it. The right face in the right place. Christ, I feel half pissed. Can we go home now?'

'Sure. Do you know, you can get a thousand a booking easy for a good Her Majesty? Do two or three shop openings in a day and you're laughing. I looked into it.'

'How much does your Scully make? Gina, whatever her name is.'

'Tina. Bugger all, really. Two or three hundred, more like, certainly not three thousand. And that's what her agency charges, she'd be lucky if she got a hundred. Her agency's ripping her off something rotten. That's why I knew she'd call us.'

'Maybe we should have a special name. Set up another business or something.'

'Yeah, I'd thought of that. Got any ideas?'

'Buy me another drink and I'll start thinking.'

'You just said you were wanting to go home.'

'Yes I did, but look.'

She nodded. Lesley turned round. The tall girl in the micro-mini was sitting about four or five stools down the bar. She caught Charmayne's eye and smiled.

'Brandy and coke?'

'What, as the name of the agency?'

'God, you are pissed. No, to drink. I'll get these.'

They spent ten minutes or so brainstorming each other, writing the better ones down on a paper napkin. Double Exposure – sounded too much like a porno movie. Double Trouble – didn't mean anything. Seeing Double – that was more like it, even if that would be what Charmayne would soon be doing if she had another brandy and coke.

Which, of course, she did. Picking up the tall girl was as easy as pie and they took it in turns to suck her tits all the way home.

Chapter Three

'I want you to try and think,' said Dr Leonie Swallow, in her clear, confident, well-paced lecturer's voice, 'about what it must have been like to go to the theatre in Shakespeare's day.'

Sixty-odd assorted students – some local and some from Namibia, Canadians rubbing shoulders with Bangladeshis, their numbers including two blind people and one Easter Islander – listened at her from the gently ranked seats of Lecture Theatre B. All of them were science and technology second years, doing a one-term contextual course in drama to show them something of the world. From the look of them, *Riverdance* was about the limit of their cultural aspirations. It was a hot afternoon and a few of them had been in the union bar through most of lunchtime.

'There were no purpose-built playhouses in Britain,' she began, 'until James Burbage opened The Theatre in Shoreditch in fifteen-seventy-six. And despite – or perhaps because of – the fact that few people could read, live performances of plays were extremely popular. Strolling players travelled the country, performing on makeshift stages at fairs and markets. Their dramas were often staged in the courtyards of inns, where people could watch either from the yard or from the surrounding galleries. In fifteen-seventy-seven we find records of performances, the earliest known in London, at the Boar's Head in Aldgate and the Saracen's Head, Islington.'

She looked around. At a rough count, perhaps about thirty per cent appeared to be paying attention. She glanced down at her notes and resumed.

'The first permanent theatres were built in the last quarter of the sixteenth century and the early years of the seventeenth. They were among the first buildings ever to have been designed specifically for entertainment. They closely followed the design of bear pits and bull-baiting arenas, with an open yard or ring surrounded by a covered area for standing spectators. From the inn courtyards came the idea of the galleries, where you would have seats for the well-to-do.

'So how did things look and sound from in the audience? Any ideas? What do you think?'

A bright girl near the front put her hand up.

'You probably couldn't hear very well. With it being in the open air and things.'

'Well,' said Leonie, 'that probably wasn't true. The design of the theatre brought players and audience close together. They were very – how can I put it? – intimate places.'

A giggle went round the lecture theatre. The couple sitting by themselves on the back row stopped snogging for a moment to see what the fuss was about.

'Naughty ladies sold oranges and things in the audience,' someone said in broad Glaswegian.

'That's right,' said Leonie. 'Naughty ladies. Actually it's a bit of a myth that the orange-sellers were hookers, but people were pretty broad-minded in those days. And with food and drink freely available, performances would have been lively affairs. People liked to join in – the idea of watching a performance, like we do, in reverential silence is not one the Elizabethans would have found very appealing. It was like pantomime at times, a great spectacle, a laugh. There were lots of rude jokes—'

'Even in Shakespeare?' someone asked, perhaps naively. Maybe there weren't any blue gags in the physical sciences.

'Especially in Shakespeare. It was no big deal going to the theatre, you know. It wasn't a sacred kind of place, it was more like going down the dog track than Royal Ascot. All kinds of people went, all kinds of tastes. Once you get an ear for Shakespearean language, you'll find all kind of smutty innuendoes.'

'What's that?' some kid asked.

'What's what?'

'Innuendo.'

'An Italian laxative,' she said, quick as a flash. She was like that, lecturer or no lecturer, doctorate or no doctorate. She didn't care. A big roar of laughter went up and it seemed a good note on which to finish.

She looked at her watch. It was twenty to four – she'd already over-run ten minutes and she was dying for a cup of tea.

'Okay then,' she said. 'We've got one more lecture before we go to London to see *Henry V* at the Globe Theatre so we'll talk next week about the actual design of the theatres, so you can understand what you're looking at. I'll see you all a week on Tuesday, then.'

The scientists and technologists weren't ones to hang around and ask questions at the end. They shot out as if they were rocket-propelled and in two minutes the cavernous lecture theatre was empty. It was pretty much the same story with her English students, who were doing a crash course on electronics, and the sociologists studying calculus. Someone had the idea of education broadening the mind, and this was the result. A bunch of bored kids listening to a lecture on something they had no interest in, however hard she tried to awaken it. Still, she got paid for it and it looked good on a CV.

Some of them were quite bright, though, the ones who answered her carefully planted questions. And there was always Tom Aspinall, a second-year computer sciences genius who seemed to get a lot out of her course. Sometimes they'd carry on talking afterwards in the bar, or in her office, just the two of them. It got so that she rather expected it.

He was waiting for her at the door of the lecture theatre when she'd finished gathering up her notes and stowed them in the big wicker basket she used for transporting things around the campus. They called it a campus now but to her it was still 'the site'. The local people remembered it as 'the park' and there was still a lot of resentment, despite the jobs that had been created for porters, cleaners and suchlike.

Three years ago, when she'd first joined the English faculty, the place was just a jumped up tech but now it was called a polytechnic university, whatever that meant. Well, it did signify to her a handsome salary increase and a significant rise in student numbers, if not always in quality.

'I thought that was really interesting,' said Tom as they made their way down the long corridors of the Arts Building. Polytechnic university or no polytechnic university, it was still the same depressing dump she'd always known – horrible beige walls, carpets on social security office brown and cheap plywood doors from the 1950s. There was a smart new logo on the sign by the main gate and some very swish stationery festooned with mission statements and similar hallmarks of the late twentieth century, but the place itself had hardly changed.

'I'm glad you liked it,' she said. 'But you've got to go to the Globe to get an idea of what it was really like – or at least, as near as we can recreate it.'

'I'm looking forward to that,' he said. 'It'll make a nice day out.'

She unlocked her door – they'd become very security conscious these days, what with all the computer equipment everyone had stashed away – and motioned Tom to step inside.

'Hey, Jack,' she called to a tall, bearded man who had just put his head round the door from the office opposite. 'Did you give me back that book on Elizabethan theatre design?'

'The one you lent me? Yes, I left it on your desk, last week I think it was.'

'Of course you did, I remember now. I was just going to lend it to Tom here. Is Spike in?'

Spike Bailey had the office next to hers – she had the last one in the corridor.

'No, no, he teaches on Tuesday, you remember.'

'So he does. I'll be forgetting my head next.' She knew already, but she just wanted to check.

She closed the door, rummaged through a pile of papers and found what she was looking for.

'Here, take it,' she said, offering him the book. 'I had to think of something. He's got such a suspicious mind, that guy.'

And then she was in Tom's arms, a good-looking, thirty-year-old lecturer with a good-looking, nineteen-year-old student, her tongue seeking his, and her heart beating wildly as it always did in these licentious moments.

She ground her breasts against him, luscious pneumatic 36Cs topped by suckable raspberry-red nipples that just called out for a good spunking. She undid a couple of buttons on his shirt and tugged it back over his shoulders, exposing his hunky pecs. His nipples were small and hard and nut-brown and she licked them greedily with the tip of her tongue, wishing he could do the same to her at the same time.

She'd been fucking Tom Aspinall for three or four weeks now, sometimes after her lectures and sometimes at her flat. They weren't going out together as such, although they'd had a few meals together and once they went to see some Czech film. This was primarily a physical relationship rather than a meeting of their minds. That, Leonie decreed, was reserved for the lecture theatre and the seminar. Her social life was more concerned with sex.

His hand was busy under her skirt, cupping her ass as he pulled her towards him. She could feel his erection hard against her thigh. God, she'd been longing for this for the past hour or more, all the way through that talk about Shakespearean theatre. She had felt herself getting damp at the thought. Her nipples always stuck out involuntarily when her erotic thoughts started to reach a certain peak of intensity and she was sure that Iranian guy in the second row had noticed it, the way he stared at her throughout without seeming to take in a single word of what she said.

Tom's cock was hard and insistent. She sank down to her knees, busy with his belt and zipper. His dick came flopping out over his jockeys, the skin already pulled right back, the big purple glans looking as inviting as a ripe plum. She sucked on it greedily, took all of it straight into her mouth at one go, hungrily slurping, driving him nuts. Lines of Shakespeare kept running through her head as she did so. Well, here was an invisible baldrick on which she would hang his bugle all right. They may not have often known the heat of a luxurious bed but the scratchy carpet of Leonie Swallow's study would serve them well enough for the moment.

Neither of them had time or patience to get fully undressed when she finally finished blowing him and broke off, gasping for breath. She slipped her tights and pants off, he pulled down his jeans and then she was lying on her back, her legs spread wide for him, and he was inside her.

Oh God, that was good, she loved it as he slid into her. She was over ten years older than he was, and she liked the way these young studs could fuck. There'd been quite a number of them, over the years – best of all she recalled an English student from Washington, then there was a handsome Saudi, followed by the son of a famous rock guitarist with whom she'd had a six-month fling the previous year (and got to have a tilt at his famous pop too).

Tom was really romping into her. She could feel his excitement.

Once, about the second or third time she and Tom had slept together, they must have done it six times in a single night and he'd shot his load off each time. He said his balls were sore for days afterwards and she wasn't in the least surprised. After a while, it had been wall-to-wall orgasms for her too, through the small hours and into the dawn.

This one would have to be a quickie, though – she'd barely have time to make a few phone calls and throw a cup of tea down her throat before the departmental meeting began at four-fifteen. It was an important one for her – she wanted to get better funding for the study courses for the next three terms and she reckoned she was in with a shout.

Shouting, though, was out of the question for the immediate future. It was part of the excitement of doing it in her own office that the walls were paper-thin, an exercise in 1950s civic architecture that placed little premium on privacy and laid every emphasis on economy. She could hear every match struck by pipe-smoking Spike Bailey in the next office and no doubt he'd be just as attuned to what she was up to – if she allowed him to be. Fortunately she was careful to arrange her amorous rendezvous at times when she knew he'd be teaching.

As it was, she snogged Tom and thrust up her hips to meet him and was aware of how deliciously huge he was, as well as having the stamina of a long-distance runner. She raised her legs up and wrapped them around his bare backside, pulling him even deeper inside her even as the first throes of orgasm began to course through her.

Leonie hit the button almost every time, even on a two-minute quickie on the carpet, and even before she noticed the yellow ball-point pen lying under her desk – so that was where it had got to. She'd spent ten minutes looking for it yesterday, long enough to fuck Tom Aspinall three or four times. She began to shake and tremble inside and then it all happened at once, the familiar quivering rush.

She could feel Tom spurting away as she milked him dry of every last drop of his copious juices, and then they were getting to their feet and he was tucking his denim shirt back into his jeans while she struggled to her feet as elegantly as she could in the circumstances and got busy with her hairbrush and make-up bag.

'There's an early Truffaut at the Film Theatre on Thursday, if you want to see it,' he said kind of sideways as he put the book she'd given him into his bag.

'Is it on any other night? I'm busy Thursday. Can't get out of it. You know how it is.'

'It's on Saturday late, I think. No, that's the horror double bill – *Curse of the Mummy's Tomb* and *Bride of the Werewolf.*'

'I'd rather see that, I think. Are you asking me out?'

'It sounds like it.'

'Maybe we can have a meal first.'

'I'd love to, but I'm skint.'

'Poor student, eh? No, I'll pay. What do you fancy? Pizza? Indian? There's a nice Thai place I know.'

'Whatever you like. I'd like to go to that Greek place again, it doesn't have to be anything fancy. Shall I stay the night with you afterwards?'

She kissed him on the cheek. 'We'll have to see how the evening goes first, won't we? I don't give myself to every man I buy dinner for, you know.'

He laughed. He had a lovely smile, expressive dark eyes. He knew she would.

'Something the matter?'

'Don't stop. What?'

'I just get this feeling something's bothering you.'

'Nothing's bothering me. I was almost there. Do it again the way you were. It felt great.'

'No, I've lost it now.'

'Oh, come on, sweetie. Do that thing with your tongue, the way you were twisting it about.'

'No. No. Look, we've got to talk.'

'Don't talk. Just lick.'

'About the business.'

'Fuck it. Suck me instead.'

'Are we doing the right thing?'

'I thought you thought something was bothering me, not that something was bothering you.'

'Well, it set me off.'

'What set you off?'

'This lookalikes thing. I mean, we've done pretty well out of the agency as it is. Don't you think we're taking a risk?'

'No I don't. It'll be fine, I'm telling you. Just believe me. Everything will be fine.'

'You don't think it's too much of a step all at once?'

'No, no.'

'I mean, six weeks ago we didn't know anything about lookalikes. Now we're signing them up left right and centre. We've got Tom Cruise and the Queen and the Gallagher brothers, not to mention that awful bitch who does Cilla Black. But it all takes up time. What's going to happen to the rest of the business?'

'It almost runs itself. Lou can handle it – she practically does that anyway. We'll promote her to operations manager or something, make it official. Christ, she's been doing the job for two years now, she ought to know better than we do how it works.'

'I'm still not sure.'

'Listen, you can't stay still in this business. You've got to change. You've got to grow. You know that as well as I do. It's not as though we're taking much of a risk – it's the bank's money, not ours. Just believe me.'

'Okay.'

'Say it with some assurance then.'

'Okay.'

'That's better. Now eat me out. You do it divinely, my dear. Much better than that girl in the mini skirt we picked up the other night. Mind you, she was good with a dildo.'

Charmayne stood up and took off her dress. Lesley did the same, without a word. Then they went upstairs and into the bedroom, their arms around one another, their nipples almost touching, one pair pink and firm, the other small and brown. Slowly, almost imperceptibly, their mouths and tongues met. The first kiss was slow and long, a gentle indication of pleasures to come. Lesley pressed her vulva against Charmayne and she was aware of the soft white lace that brushed against her naked skin.

She knelt down, hooked her thumbs around Lesley's pants and pulled them down far enough to insinuate her tongue once more into the gap between her legs. Lesley sighed and ran her fingers through Charmayne's hair. She always came when her beautiful blonde lover licked her pussy.

Charmayne eased the pants down and off, tossed them to one side. How clean and fresh Lesley smelt down there. Now both women were completely naked together. There was no hurry. Both of them felt calm and relaxed, though Charmayne's heart was fluttering with anticipation. She used her hands to part Lesley's legs and then she ran her tongue experimentally around the other girl's lips. She tasted as clean as she smelled, and slightly tart.

Still crouching, with her face barely leaving Lesley's vulva, Charmayne moved around until she found the edge of the bed. She sat down on it and pulled Lesley on to her lap until the two girls were face to face, Lesley sitting with her legs around her, her pussy already damp against Charmayne's thighs.

Charmayne reached up and put her arms around the dark-haired woman's neck, pulling her face down to meet her probing lips. Their tongues played together, breast touching breast, Lesley gently rubbing herself against Charmayne's lap. Charmayne broke off their kiss and applied her lips instead to Lesley's breasts, circling the areolae with her tongue, feeling them tense and pucker up beneath her caresses as she gave her attention to each one in turn until they stood up as hard and brown as little acorns.

Then she took each of them into her mouth, sucking deeply, nibbling them with her teeth until Lesley quivered and ground her sex against her. 'I want you up me,' she murmured in Charmayne's ear, a flourish with her tongue on her earlobe acting like a signature.

Charmayne slid her hand down over Lesley's warm, flat belly, feeling the luxuriant pubic hair against the palm of her hand. She knew what the other woman wanted, three or four fingers that would give her the feeling of a nice big cock in there, but handled with the sensitivity that only one woman could show to another. Charmayne might have liked a cock too, at that moment, in her pussy or even up her ass, but Lesley's tongue and fingers would have to do instead. At the weekend, perhaps . . . She rubbed her hips expectantly.

Still sucking Lesley's breast, Charmayne slid her hand into the warm, wet cleft and was surprised at how wet Lesley already was. There was an urgency about her now that had been lacking in the seductive languor of their post-prandial conversation. She knew what was expected of her. She pushed one, then two fingers into her friend's welcoming sheath, feeling its walls closing over her, the secretions that slowly seeped from her innermost chamber.

Lesley gasped, brushed her hands over Charmayne's own breasts and kissed her passionately on the lips. At the same time, Charmayne slipped a third and then a fourth finger into her, the ball of her hand rubbing against the clitoris that stood out as firm and hard as a little walnut. When she got close to orgasm, Lesley became a noisy lover. She gasped, and moaned, and whimpered, and Charmayne knew she was soon going to shipwreck herself on the reef of her desires.

'Get it up me,' she almost hissed, quite red in the face

beneath her summer tan, the words enunciated with surprising clarity.

Charmayne withdrew her index finger, rubbed it against the hard button of Lesley's clitoris and then, twisting her wrist around, managed to insert its tip into Lesley's tight little bum.

'Oh, that's it,' murmured Lesley. 'Just give it to me there.'

Afraid that her long nails might hurt her, Charmayne merely stroked the outer rim of that second little hole. But it had the desired effect on her lover. Allied to the three fingers tight inside her vagina – Charmayne could almost pinch her fingers together through the thin membrane dividing vagina and anus – she quickly brought Lesley to a short, shuddering orgasm, their tongues playing little twisting games with each other, their breath coming in ragged gasps until they were still.

After that, Charmayne lay down on the cool, flat sheets of the bed and Lesley lay down on top of her. They rubbed their pubic mounds together, aping heterosexual intercourse. Charmayne wrapped her long, elegant legs around Lesley as, with her heels, she urged their bodies closer together. She wished, for a moment, that it was a man who was on top of her now, a woman to lick and caress her perhaps but a man to penetrate her deeply, a man with a long, thick cock that would fill her to the hilt. A woman like Lesley, though, was fine enough. She loved her, madly.

Their bodies undulated gently against each for some while, thigh against thigh, breast against breast, lips against lips. Slowly their movements became more urgent. The grass they had smoked after their meal ensured that their skins were becoming one flowing receptive surface that told of pleasures given and experienced, the sheets a cool, smooth and pleasurable sensation against their flesh. The phone rang a couple of times but the calls were answered automatically. Here, in the luxurious home they shared together, they were living in a magnificent cocoon, a world dedicated solely to the senses of touch and taste, smell and sound.

They opened their eyes and looked at each other. Lesley's hands stole down into the wetness between Charmayne's legs, and then traced their way back up her sternum.

'Do me again, just there,' Charmayne murmured, without breaking her gaze.

'Want me to tongue you?' said Lesley. Charmayne nodded.

Her loins were as warm as the day. Lesley's tongue flickered out again and sought Charmayne's labia, opened up before her like an oyster revealing its treasure. It felt good, the way she played with her. Lesley certainly knew what to do. She had a finesse and delicacy about her that was extraordinary.

Charmayne parted her long, colt-like legs to make it easier for her, and to bring more of her body into contact with Lesley's probing tongue. Again she lay back and relaxed, letting her feelings flow through her, her thoughts and urges merging into one delicious stream of desire. The effect of the grass was beginning to wear off, and she was feeling warm and drowsy.

Her hips moved on the tangled quilt in a slow, easy rhythm, mimicking the movements of Lesley's tongue. She looked down at her, crouched at the foot of the bed, the way her firm pear-shaped breasts hung down like little pears ripe for the plucking.

Charmayne was aware of her own nipples, of how hard and firm they were. She ran her fingers over them, large and rosy-pink, aching for the touch of Lesley's tongue and teeth. She took each of them in turn between finger and thumb and pinched them, quite hard. The sensation of exquisite feeling, half-pleasure, half-pain, served only to enhance the urgings of her loins, made her push her hips up against Lesley's mouth, until she felt the dark girl's tongue pass along the furrow of her labia and gently insert itself into her vagina. She could see her now, wide-mouthed, her hair spilling out on to Charmayne's thighs, both girls naked.

So they lay there on the bed long after the distant church tower chimed midnight, sometimes changing or reversing positions so that Charmayne could lick her friend's pussy, each of them from time to time tonguing the other's breasts and nipples. It was a delightful feeling, the infinite tenderness of touch. As Charmayne rolled the firm, brownish nipples between her lips Lesley's hands were between her own thighs, moving in synchronisation, rolling her clitoris with practised ease. Then, quite suddenly, Charmayne felt herself aware of a butterfly fluttering deep within her stomach and knew that she was about to climax.

'Lick me out, darling,' she murmured. 'I want to come in your face.'

Lesley disentangled herself and slid down the bed. Charmayne opened her legs for her, aware of how wet her pussy was. She felt her familiar, expert tongue run along the furrow of her labia, probing and cherishing, seeking out those secret spots that gave her so much pleasure.

'Harder,' she hissed and Lesley, who knew a woman's needs, pressed her tongue into her with renewed urgency. It was like a weapon now, a penis, something with which to penetrate her fully, like she might do some nights with other means. Charmayne wanted her tongue up her, to put her own tongue into Lesley, to taste her salty essences, the reality of her pubic bush against her face. And then the flutterings grew imperceptibly into a tremor and she felt herself going over the edge, almost in slow motion, her nipples now absolutely rigid between her knowing fingers, her body arched and expectant as the first wave of orgasm hit her with the impact of a gale-driven sea.

They lay together in each other's arms, sated at last. Finally Lesley stirred, put on a thick white towelling robe.

'You really needn't worry about anything,' she said. 'I've got a new act lined up and you'll want her from the moment you set eyes on her.'

On Thursday evening Leonie sat at her make-up mirror. It always took ages but she actually enjoyed it, this ability to submerge herself in someone else's identity, if only for an evening at a time. On a good day she might go from Leonie to Marilyn in an hour but it could take longer. She always took the precaution of making-up at home if at all possible. Some of the pubs and clubs she worked in, the changing room was the ladies' loo and she didn't fancy an hour crouched in front of a cracked mirror while the cisterns flushed and other women gave her a baffled once-over.

It had started when she was a postgraduate student, six or seven years back. She'd always liked dressing up, even as a child, and one day she'd acquired a blonde wig, brand new, that a friend of hers who was a bit of an actress had given her when she was having a clear-out. 'It makes you look just like Marilyn Monroe,' Kiki had said. It still stood her in good stead.

Just for a laugh, they'd done the make-up together one night when they were a bit pissed. Of course, once she'd got over the shock, Leonie had immediately launched into 'I wanna be loved by you' and Kiki clapped like mad and said she really was the business. Leonie had a nice voice, had been the singer in a student band at one time, felt easy on stage. She always liked showing off, her mother said.

There was a fancy dress a few weeks later and it was her finest hour. There was an agent there who took one look at her and wanted to sign her up on the spot. One thing led to another and, from being a party piece, Leonie actually began working as a Marilyn clone. She refused a contract – she didn't want anything that would bind her – but was happy to work on an occasional basis. Doing Marilyn around the pubs and clubs very much took second place to her academic work, especially when she got her position at the Poly – sorry, polytechnic university – but it was a great way to let off steam and relax and be paid for it, into the bargain. It was more of a hobby for her, really, but she took it seriously. She might only do a couple of gigs a month, if that, and with a lecturer's salary the money wasn't that important, but she really enjoyed being Marilyn Monroe for an hour or so, instead of Dr Leonie Swallow, author of *Shakespeare's Plays in Performance* and *The Elizabethan Mind*.

Her friends and close colleagues were in on it but she didn't broadcast what she did. At first she used a backing tape but then at a party she'd met up with Jerry, a professional French horn player who played a mean nightclub piano as a sideline, and a new double-act was born. He had his black evening clothes that he wore with the orchestra – right down to the black silk socks and mirror-glass shoes, very natty – and she

66

had three or four Marilyn outfits made specially.

Tonight she and Jerry were playing somewhere rather swish, not her scene at all – she preferred music in smoky upstairs rooms – but it was three hundred cash between them for an hour's work. What made this especially interesting was that two women from some quite swanky-sounding agency were coming down to see her and Jerry play. She'd seen their ad, liked the sound of it, and sent them a videotape of her act. It wasn't great quality but they seemed impressed by it when they rang and were keen to see her work. She had half a mind to ask them to come to one of her lectures but she didn't think that was quite what they had in mind. She kept very quiet about her day-job – people, and women especially, could be intimidated by a female PhD with a growing list of academic publications to her name, even at the age of thirty. Of course, not many in the groves of academe had a clue about what she did on her nights off.

Jerry picked her up promptly at seven and they had a good journey and everything was absolutely fine at the gig, the piano was freshly tuned, the PA worked without a hitch and they got through their set without a single snag except that she sang one verse out of sequence in 'Diamonds are a girl's best friend'. They did exactly fifty minutes, timed to the second, and came back for 'Do it again' and a final encore of 'My heart belongs to daddy'. One hour, on the dot, three hundred cash and no, I don't need a receipt, let's keep it between ourselves and not trouble the VAT inspector.

They had quite a nice little changing room out back and it was while she and Jerry were relaxing here drinking white wine – Jerry, being the driver, was on Appletise – and eating smoked-salmon sandwiches, that these two broads from the agency came in.

They were incredibly complimentary about what they'd just seen and heard. Leonie could tell from the start that they were lesbian but they didn't look it, glammed up but not too glammed up, and anyway Jerry was gay and she had no problem with it, but it was surprising how unenlightened some of her colleagues were – and his – even in this day and age. If academics and classical musicians were stuffy about someone being queer, what chance the rest of society.

They talked generally at first, about how long they'd had the act and what kind of places they played and all this stuff. Jerry told them about being a 'proper' musician and everything but Leonie kept quiet about the day job.

'Do you have an agent?' said the dark one, Lesley.

'Sort of,' said Leonie. 'I mean, he gets us the gigs and he takes a percentage, but it's all on a very informal basis. We don't have a written contract or anything.'

'I do have a number of commitments,' Jerry added. He named a couple of orchestras who retained him, the studios he did session work for, everything from Borodin to advertising jingles.

'So if we were to make you an offer, we wouldn't be treading on anyone's toes?' Lesley continued.

'Not really. Like I said, nothing's cut and dried. Nobody owns us.'

'Yet,' said Jerry, with a laugh. Everyone joined in. There was a good mood in the dressing room.

'I know that you work as a double act, but I wonder how would you feel if Leonie did some appearances just on her own?'

'Not singing,' Charmayne intercut. 'This would be just Leonie on her own, as Marilyn. Just kind of being there. Like an actress.'

'Opening supermarkets and things?' asked Leonie, with a smile on her face. 'Sure, why not? What do you think, Jerry?'

'Fine by me. I hate the bloody places, to be honest.'

'It probably wouldn't be supermarkets, as such. But you know the kind of thing – sales promotions, presentations, guest appearances, a little modelling work perhaps. You have a great figure, if you don't mind me saying so.'

'Thanks. But I'm not too sure about the sales conferences, to be honest. That kind of thing turns me right off.' She knew all to well what academic conferences were like and to spend three days in a hotel surrounded by salesmen with attitude sounded like hell on earth.

'Of course. You need only do the things that appeal to you.

But I would say that there is a lot of demand from the commercial sector and it can be quite lucrative.'

'Maybe we'll see how it goes. I've only ever really thought about it as singing, to be honest. Anything else is a whole new ballgame for me.'

'Do you have a regular job, Leonie?'

'I work at the Poly.' She thought it best to leave it at that. They'd think she was a secretary or something. Luckily they didn't ask any more specific questions.

'You two are not, you know—?' said Lesley, very quietly.

'You know? Oh, heavens no, none of that. This is just a professional relationship – or rather strictly amateur.'

'No, I understand that. It's just that sometimes there's more to it than that, you know what I mean? It can be difficult, at times, believe me.'

'I'm sure it can.'

'And the hours might be tricky. Lots of late nights, that kind of thing.'

'I do have a lot of engagements,' said Jerry. 'And I do tend to get booked up pretty well in advance. But a lot of it's all a bit last-minute. Things get delayed, put off, you know the kind of thing. To be honest, I never say no to anything. You're never sure what's going to happen unless you've got something absolutely certain, like a concert tour or something.'

'Of course. No, I do understand. It's a bit like that with us, to be truthful. You try to arrange things so they're as firm as you can make them, but they have a habit of changing. How about you, Leonie?'

'Well, I do have commitments and I don't have a lot of free time. Some times are a lot less frantic than others.' She was thinking about the holidays, of course. 'But I can swing things with admin, if you know what I mean?'

And that was about it, really. Everybody seemed pretty happy with the way it had gone and while nobody had said anything definite about anything, Leonie had the feeling that things were going to happen. Lesley said that either she or Charmayne would call her as soon as they could, and in the meantime they'd post her a copy of their standard contract, and they thanked her for the loan of the video and could they keep it a little while longer because they had someone quite important who might be interested in it, and then they were gone. Jerry drove Leonie home and she was so excited she found it difficult to get to sleep.

She didn't go to see *Curse of the Mummy's Tomb* and *Bride of the Werewolf* with Tom after all. She was going to, but on the Saturday morning the draft contract arrived and when she saw the kind of money that was on offer, she decided she felt like celebrating. She rang Tom, asked him to come over to her place for dinner instead, and then hit the super-market.

All through the meal – there was just the two of them – she could hardly contain her excitement. Even Tom noticed she seemed unusually bright and happy with things. Things were getting pretty mellow between them. After the meal, Tom rolled a spliff and things got mellower still.

They'd been talking about movies, like they often did. Especially comedies – they were both of them in the mood for laughing.

'Anything with Jack Lemmon in it,' said Tom. 'I love his stuff.'

'You see *Some like It Hot*?'

'Half a dozen times. It's one of my real all-time favourites. And Marilyn's brilliant. She really could act, you know.'

'I know she could. And sing too. You want to hear a Marilyn Monroe album?'

'Sure, why not? As long as it's got "Diamonds are a Girl's Best Friend" on it.'

She put the CD on. It was exactly the right thing to play. Tom closed his eyes, took a big hit and smiled dreamily.

She stood up, kissed him lightly on the forehead. 'I'm just going upstairs,' she said. 'I'll be right back.'

Tom heard the door close and languidly opened his eyes. The sight before him was little short of astonishing. He thought, for a moment, his senses had been scrambled.

On the CD player was Marilyn Monroe breathily

mouthing 'Happy Birthday, Mr President'. He stretched, yawned and there she stood before his very eyes, wriggling her hips and miming the words. Then she winked at him and blew a big pink bubble of gum. It was astonishing. He didn't know quite what to think. He hadn't done acid in eighteen months but even white snake fever didn't give you hallucinations like this.

He knew, intuitively, that it was Leonie but the effect was uncanny. She was dressed just as Marilyn had been in one of her films – *Bus Stop*, was it, the one where she was a night-club singer? Tight black skirt and a black lace top, worn off the shoulder. The way she'd done her hair was sensational.

'You look like you've seen a ghost or something,' said Leonie. 'Pour me another glass, will you?'

She came over and sat next to him, teetering on four-inch heels, and ran her fingers across his shoulders as she did so. It sent goosebumps down his spine and he realised he had an erection.

The skirt was so tight she had difficulty sitting down in it. She was wearing black fishnets, he noticed.

She leaned across, planted a big kiss on his cheek.

'What's the matter, honey?' she said in Marilyn's baby-girl-lost voice. 'Ain't you glad to see me?'

Tom felt confused and aroused and baffled all at the same time, but his head was beginning to clear. He looked hard at her as she squeezed his knee, took in the generous curve of her bosom outlined against the thin black lace of her top. Marilyn was no sylph, of course, and Leonie would never be a size ten. 'I'm built for comfort, not for speed,' she used to say.

His eyes took in the red slash of lipstick and the skirt riding up over her thigh and then he'd taken her in his arms and was snogging her for all he was worth. Their tongues met and he could feel himself sliding off down that long, familiar slippery slope of lust.

The two of them were grunting and breathing heavily as they kissed, pulling away at each other's clothes. Even as she tore his Levi shirt out from the top of his jeans, he had pulled

71

the black lace top down and her tits came tumbling out, ripe and full. He grasped one in each hand, surprised at how firm and heavy they were, felt the nipples stiffen up against the flesh of his palms.

And then he began to nuzzle and lick them as she ran her hands through his hair, feeling those spectacular ruby nipples against his lips, running his tongue over them, wanting to spunk and bite and suck and fuck all at one and the same time.

Leonie almost tore his shirt off his back – luckily it had press studs rather than buttons – and then they were sinking together on to the thick rugs that covered the wooden floor of the room, still kissing passionately. She lay down beside him and he half-covered her, thigh against thigh, only too aware of his straining erection against her soft and welcoming body.

'What's all this about?' he gasped when they broke for breath but she wouldn't tell him.

'Later,' she murmured, and got busy with his zipper.

She had to stand up to take her skirt off, it was so tight. It dropped to the floor and he was entranced to see black suspenders tight against her shapely thighs, and her dark pubic bush looking naked and inviting.

'Marilyn didn't wear panties a lot of the time,' she said in answer to his unvoiced question. 'Or a bra, for that matter. I read it in a book somewhere.'

She took off the black top and then knelt down again, straddling him, her legs gaping to reveal the coral gash of her pussy. His cock lolled hugely on his stomach, growing in size by the second – or so it felt. She took it in her hand and guided it expertly into her wet and welcoming sheath. Almost immediately he began pumping into her, forcing his muscles upwards, his hands running up and down her naked thighs and the wicked black net stockings. With the blonde wig and all the make-up she was wearing, she looked sensational, and he told her so.

'Really?' she said, as though no one had ever told her that before.

He became mesmerised by her breasts as they swung above

his chest. He had always had a thing about big-breasted women and had fancied Leonie from the moment he first saw her in the lecture hall. She didn't flaunt them – not in public at any rate – but then she made little attempt to hide them either.

'Ever been titty-whipped?' she said. He hadn't a clue what she meant but he soon learned. She made him lie down flat and she hunkered down over his hugely distended cock. Then, slowly at first but soon with increasing vigour, she began to swing her boobs from side to side. She knelt down over him still further and then, as her nipples began to brush against his mightily swollen gland, he realised what titty-whipping was. Soon they were fairly slapping against his cock, firm and heavy, and it was all he could do not to shoot off there and then.

'That's enough for now,' she said at length, easing herself up to sit on his lap. 'I get sore if I do too much of it.'

He raised himself up on one elbow and managed to suck one tit into his mouth, his tongue playing around the nipple. He couldn't move his hips too well like this but Leonie began to move up and down on him with practised ease, varying the pace as she took her own private pleasure.

'I want you to spunk my tits later,' she said in an undertone. 'Do it up my cunt now.'

His response was almost instantaneous, and he was inside her almost before the words were out of her mouth. He loved her lack of inhibition, and even as his tongue froze on that succulent, engorged nipple he arched his back and shot his boiling essence deep into her body, a sequence of eight or nine heavy pulses in steady rhythm that seemed to open up the universe for him.

Almost at the same moment she came off herself, squeezing him between those tremendous fishnet-clad thighs. He could feel the wetness of her all over his abdomen, could sense his come streaming out of her, loved the very idea of this mutual exchange of bodily fluids, so free and deliciously wicked, so very un-English.

Later, while he fucked her from behind in front of the fireplace as they watched themselves in the big old mirror over the sofa, she told him about the lookalike business.

'Who do you imagine you're screwing?' she said. 'Me or Marilyn?'

'I'm not sure,' he gasped. His cock felt like it was on fire and his balls were full to bursting. 'Both of you, I guess. It's like it's both of you all at the same time.'

'I don't mind which one it is,' she said, a half-smile playing on her lips. 'I just like that lovely thick cock of yours up my slit.'

Later, in bed, he tit-fucked her as she had asked. When he came in from the bathroom she was sitting up in bed, still with the blonde hair but this time wearing a red lace Wonderbra as well.

'Did you know Marilyn used to sleep in her bra?' she said as he pushed his cock between those two delicious globes. 'She didn't wear one during the day – at least not often – but she felt she ought to wear one at night, if only for the sake of her figure.'

'You're kidding me,' he said, standing next to her so she could lick his cock and press it against her tits. He loved the feeling of the lacy fabric against his balls, but he wondered how much he had left in him.

Her tongue flickered out and she took the end of his cock into her mouth, teasing him. At the same time, she squeezed her tits around his balls. It was awkward kneeling over her like this but Tom's senses were on fire and he had long since lost the dividing line between pleasure and pain.

'Tits, cunts, spunk,' she murmured. 'Arse. Fuck. Cock. Do me now, you sod.'

Then she took him deep into her mouth and he knew, as her lips and tongue swirled around the distended length of his shaft, that he had enough come left in his balls to go on all night if she wanted him to. She sucked him deeply and hugely and then, when he could hold back no longer, he withdrew his wet, slithering cock from those succulent red lips and poured a torrent of white seed all over her breasts, just as she'd asked him to.

In the morning, when he awoke at seven-thirty, she was still wearing the red Wonderbra, just as Marilyn would have done. She seemed just as randy as she had been the night before.

This time, though, she got him to do it up her ass. At nine, she took a class on Sheridan and the English Tradition.

Chapter Four

'Hi, Danny, it's Charmayne. How are you?'

'I'm extremely well, thank you. How about you?'

'Oh fine, fine. I just got back from Milan. Went to see a client.'

'How very glam. Have fun?'

'Not really. Just business, really. Look, I'm sorry to call you so late in the evening but I was wondering, are you busy right now?'

'Right now? No, I'm just watching TV.'

'No, I mean workwise. Lesley's just called me from town and it seems like she's met this guy and there might be something for you.'

'Depends on what it is. I'm doing a new logo for one of the cable sports channels and it's getting a bit mega.'

'Sounds interesting. I was just wondering if you could do a job for us.'

'Depends what it is.'

'Weathersealing ad.'

'Forget it. The last time I did that, I got soaked through and they were six months paying.'

'Only joking, Danny. No, this could be good. I just want you to be you-know-who for a day.'

'When? I'm pretty busy.'

'Next Saturday.'

'I guess Saturday's all right. Whereabouts?'

'Suffolk.'

'Suffolk? What's that got to do with your man?'

'You know I told you he's making this movie over here?'

'Right—'

'Well, he's meant to be going to this big splashy wedding –

or at least that's what the rumours says.'

'It's not true?'

'Well, it is. The thing is, one of our clients knows where he's going to be staying.'

'Who's the client?'

'I can't really tell you that.'

'Of course you can.'

'Oh all right. He's a journalist. And he wants to get some exclusives on this one.'

'Using me?'

'No, using the real one.'

'Where do I fit in?'

'We want you to put the others off the scent. They all think he's staying somewhere else. If you show up there on Saturday, let them catch a glimpse of you, they'll all go chasing off after you instead. Or so he thinks.'

'Leaving the field clear for your man. Devious sort of bugger, isn't he? Tabloid, is it, or is he from the *Financial Times*?'

'I'll give you one guess. Look, all it needs is for you to be driven round in a car for a few hours, let them see your face from time to time.'

'How much?'

'Five hundred?'

'The phone went funny, Charmayne. It sounded like you said five hundred.'

'Seven?'

'A grand.'

'Oh come on, don't you know what things are like these days?'

'Fifteen then.'

'I'll see what I can do about a thousand. That's not bad for a day's work, you know, just sitting in a car showing your face from time to time.'

'Yeah, but I've got to get there, too. Suffolk's miles away. Where do I stay?'

'Don't worry. We'll lay on a car. And we've fixed up somewhere splashy for you. I'll be coming along too. I'll be your minder if you like.'

'What about the wedding? Am I supposed to show up there too?'

'No, that's private. But this chap from the *Daily Bleat* thinks he might be able to smuggle you into the reception, which will confuse them even more.'

'But that's going to be embarrassing, isn't it? I'm going to get chucked out of there, once they've sussed me. I'm not sure about that.'

'That's what we want for a thousand, Danny.'

'I dunno. It all sounds a bit fishy to me. I mean, some of the things I've done have been okay – the launch parties and stuff – but this one sounds a bit off, somehow.'

'It could be good, though. For you and for us. Lesley's been trying to get in with the tabloids for a long time and this could be just the break we need. Don't let us down, Danny, please.'

'Oh, all right then. But if anything goes wrong, I'm out of there, you know what I mean.'

'Oh, lovely. Actually, I think you'll enjoy it. I will too . . .'

He still had a sense of misgiving, even half an hour later when Chantal came back from the late-evening supermarket shop. They opened a bottle of wine and he told her about it. She didn't see anything in particular to worry about.

'I'd say no, but I need the money,' he said reluctantly.

'But you've been incredibly busy.'

'I know I have. But companies are getting worse and worse about paying. There's stuff I did six months back that I haven't been paid for yet.'

'Remind them about it.'

'I do. But short of threatening to take them to court, there's not much I can do. I know the money will come eventually but in the meantime I don't want to lose the client by being too pushy about getting paid.'

'Seeing Double are okay, aren't they?'

'They're very good. They usually pay within the month. But they're small – it's the big companies that take their time, and they're the ones I do most work for.'

'It's the same for everyone,' said Chantal. 'We have exactly the same problems. Mary, our accountant, spends half the day chasing people. But then she's just as bad herself when it comes to paying people who invoice us.'

'It's a vicious circle, I know. But it pisses me off sometimes.'

'I really wouldn't worry about it. How much is Lesley offering you?'

'A grand.'

'Take it, for God's sake.'

She took his hand, stroked his fingers. Their first kiss was inevitable as he pulled her on to his lap in the big armchair. Her tongue felt firm, strong and pointed as it played around his lips. He breathed in her perfume, soft and fruity, with a sensual hint of musk. Arabesque, he thought, or Cold Metal. He was pretty good on perfumes.

He forgot about money and clasped her closely, a burgeoning desire vipering through him. He stroked her shoulders, the soft bare flesh of her upper arms. Her tongue roved over his face, his neck, his ears. He felt her breasts crushed heavily against him, and could feel the warmth rising from her body, bringing with it a muskier edge to her perfume.

Her hair was thick and lustrous as he played with it, their lips pressed together still, their tongues snaking and intertwining. She had, he had always noticed, incredibly sweet breath, though she seemed to live on foreign food that was rich in garlic. Her teeth had a slightly uneven quality that he found oddly appealing.

She grunted softly and squirmed a little, as if to seat herself better. She reached for his hand and placed it on her breast. Its point was hard with desire. Through the tight lycra of her mini-dress he could feel the lacy fabric of her brassiere. He took the weight of her breast as she leaned forward slightly and it seemed to spill over into the palm of his hand. He stroked, pressed, squeezed, cupping it as his tongue again sought hers. His penis was stiff and, with her body lying half on top of him, it felt horribly uncomfortable, like a spring trying desperately to uncoil itself.

She had her hand inside his shirt, running under his arms, across his chest. She raked her long, red fingernails across his nipples and bit his earlobe. 'Come on, lover,' she breathed.

'Let's see what you've got for me.'

They stood up, went through into the bedroom. Chantal unbuttoned his shirt, running her hands across his chest, cupping his pectorals as though they were female breasts. She was not more than five-feet-five or six – Danny stood well over six feet tall without shoes – and she needed only to bend her knees a fraction to be able to take his nipples in her mouth by turn. As she did so, he shucked off the shirt, tugging his hands through the cuffs, heedless of the button that sprang off – he never did find it – and tossing the garment aside.

He sat on the bed and kicked off his shoes. Chantal stood there watching him, her eyes aflame, her chest visibly panting. He was surprised, looking at her this way, by how long and colt-like her legs were, accentuated by the spike-heeled boots she wore.

'Perhaps I should have brought that wine in,' he said. 'It tasted pretty good.'

'We'll finish it later,' she responded. 'After you've finished me.'

Still not shifting her gaze, she tugged the tight lycra sheath over her head. Her breasts wobbled noticeably as she did so. They were magnificent, large and full, tantalisingly separated into two luscious globes by an uplift brassiere of intricate black lace that plunged low at the front. She caught his gaze and came over and straddled him, pushing her superb bosom almost into his face.

'Fancy a little suck, Danny?' she breathed in a husky whisper.

He reached up, slipping his fingertips inside the cups, easing those marvellous tits out into his hands. Unbounded, they were heavy and pear-shaped, the nipples a delicate raspberry pink, long and inviting. He licked each one in turn, like a wine expert tasting a new vintage. And then with an audible sigh he took as much as he could of her breast deep into his mouth.

His tongue swirled around her nipple just as Chantal's had with his, nipping and teasing, caressing and cajoling. She threw her head back, her hands steadying herself on his strong shoulders. He released the nipple from his mouth and saw it glistening and swollen to twice the size of the other one. She looked down at him through her mane of hair and smiled encouragingly.

'Suck both my tits,' she murmured.

He repeated the exercise, licking and lapping, feeling her strong back muscles with his hands as she pushed her chest forward towards him. She seemed to be pulling him to her breast like a mother with her baby, urging him to suck, offering him not just pleasure but life itself. He unhooked the bra with practised ease – never a fumbler, even as a teenager, he had always rather fancied himself as a natural with hooks and eyes – and cast it aside.

They rolled over to lie side by side on the bed. She tugged at his belt, unzipped him, and all the while her tongue and lips were hungrily seeking his body. He took over and struggled out of his chinos, pressing his full erection against the softness of her thigh, naked now and feeling strong and proud. His hand slid under the waistband of her pants, feeling the thin, wispy material, and then his fingers could touch the soft, crinkly fur of her pubic mound and the lips that gaped so invitingly. He closed his eyes, alive only to the experience of touch.

She was incredibly wet even before he touched her. Her panties were soaked, just as he had anticipated. He wondered if – it wasn't beyond the bounds of possibility – she had already come. He ran a finger experimentally along the warm, slippery groove of her sex, the film of lust coating his finger-prints. She moaned softly, and spread her legs more for him. He stroked her gently, fingers delicately exploring the sensitive folds, his knuckle brushing against the erect clitoris.

He opened his eyes and saw she was looking at him again, willing him on. He pushed a finger deep into her vagina, and then another, and her gaze never faltered. Her tongue snaked out and sought his, one arm around his shoulder, the other lying crushed and immobile between them. His hips moved slowly and easily against hers, in a long, low, loping rhythm, sensuous and easy. He felt good.

When she came, his fingers still wriggling inside her, it was without obvious display. She sighed, drew in her breath, held him tightly and stopped moving altogether. Her eyes, for the first time, were tightly closed. Then she let out a great, shuddering breath and flopped back on the quilt, a smile playing around her lips.

They lay together, soundlessly, for several minutes. Then he got up – acutely aware of his erect penis bobbing up and down – and pulled off the rest of her clothes. Underneath she was wearing shamelessly transparent panties, so brief as to barely cover her pubic mound, whose curls showed through the gauzy black fabric like whorls of lace. He could smell her vaginal secretions, muskily bitter-sweet. She hooked her thumbs under the filmy garment and lay there as naked as he.

Her pussy, when he entered her, was tight and welcoming. He felt enveloped and embraced at the same time, as though she were urging him ever deeper inside her. Chantal hiked her legs up over his own and it seemed to draw him in even further. Slowly he began to move in the primordial rhythm, swaying and sliding, an inaudible beat pulsing through his blood like the deepest of deep bass notes. She matched his every move, pushing up against him, drawing away, her hips pressing up to meet his every urgent thrust.

He drew his penis out almost to the glans and then, with deliberate slowness, slid it all the way back in again.

She cried out. 'Oh, yes,' she hissed in his ear. 'Do it like that.'

He pulled out again, and in, each thrust like an entry into her vagina. She raked her nails across his back, more than playfully – it inflicted a sharp and momentary pain that only served to heighten his awareness of the sensations that were running riot through his body.

Slowly, consciousness of everything else began to ebb away. The room, the tangled bedcovers, the bedside light, even the breeze that had played through the open window – all slowly drifted away, unheeded and forgotten, until there was only the two of them, lost in a world of muscle and flesh, of fluid and feelings, wandering alone through the darkness of the senses.

There were no formed images now in his mind – not even

of the girl beneath him, her lustrous hair and stupendous breasts. they clung on for a while, bobbing around like drifting branches in a stream before being swept away by a greater and more irresistible force.

Stripped of any need other than to do what he was doing, his body seemed possessed of inordinate strength. He powered himself up from his elbows, taking the full weight of his torso on to his wrists, and thrust hard into her. She squealed – audibly squealed – but he was almost heedless, driven by his own biological urgency, his senses aflame. Their rhythm built up in intensity, each in turn adding a new twist, a different way of pushing, one's tongue from time to time seeking the other's and then pulling away, trailing across cheek or shoulder, soft wet trails of saliva invisibly mingling with body sweat.

Until, finally, he threw himself forward over the edge of the precipice, gliding freely in flight as he had done so often in his dreams, aware only of the tumult in his mind, the pressing urgency, the contractions and spasms and pulsing outburst of energy that preceded that great and final stillness in his loins.

'Just think of the money,' Tina told herself.

She leaned forward over the cushions and pulled the crotch of her creamy-white G-string aside, affording the guy with the camera an excellent view of her cunt.

Of course, she was on an exclusive contract with Seeing Double and she knew Lesley and Charmayne would go absolutely spare if they knew what she was up to. Still, a thousand quid was a thousand quid and the guy was just doing it for his own amusement. It wasn't as if he were a professional and would sell the snaps on, to grace every sleaze mag on every top shelf from Tokyo to Torquay.

He might have been an amateur but he had all the gear, right enough. He had his own studio on the top floor of his house and it was bigger than many of the professional studios she'd been in. He had so many strobes and spots and floods and fills, the lights across the West Midlands must have dimmed when he switched everything on.

She didn't fancy him but he was a nice guy, all the same. He was a lawyer, he told her, had been married but it had broken up about six or seven years back. His name was Anthony, not Tony, and he didn't mention his surname. She'd met him at a charity do where she'd been on duty, they'd got chatting and he'd made her the offer very discreetly. She said she'd have to think about it but she already knew what the answer would be. A grand cash would be a big help for her new car, but she wanted to play him along just to see if she could get more out of him. When she rang him a couple of days later at the number he'd given her, she was hoping she might be able to bump him up to fifteen but he wasn't going to budge, it was a grand or nothing. But they settled on it amicably, which was fine.

He seemed to be some kind of connoisseur of erotica. He showed her lovely albums of the photographs he'd taken of girls. They were really good, he obviously knew what he was about. And he did them entirely for his own amusement. He said he wasn't interested in selling to magazines or anything like that. Maybe, one day, he might do a book if he could find a publisher who was interested, but for the time being the pleasure would be his alone.

'Could you lean forward just a little more,' said Anthony. She did as she was told.

'Now just look round at me and think of a nice cool ice cream on a hot summer's afternoon. Imagine you're just licking through the coating to the ice cream beneath, your tongue's scooping up that lovely creamy filling.'

Involuntarily Tina smiled and she heard the lights pop three or four times in rapid succession. It was quite warm even beneath the modelling lights and she was glad she wasn't wearing many clothes.

The outfit had been his idea. She'd started off in a black two-piece with tight-fitting skirt – luckily she had just the thing in her wardrobe at home, bought last year for her cousin Jackie's wedding – but now she was down to the bare essentials, the little G-string and a cream satin basque with white stockings. Did the real Scully wear this kind of stuff, she wondered? She doubted it. It would be pretty expensive, lovely material but a bit plain perhaps, somehow virginal. See-through red quarter-cup bras and crotchless panties were definitely out at the Department, she reckoned, as were high-heeled mules with pom-poms.

Actually, Tina wasn't entirely new to this kind of work. A few years back, long before the Scully thing, before Ray even, she'd done a few piccies in a studio over a motorcycle showroom in Redditch and some more in the little courtyard behind. She still had a copy of the magazine at home, hidden from prying eyes. Fifty quid she'd got for the job but she discovered that she quite liked it, after she'd got over her initial embarrassment.

It was when she'd been working as a traffic warden, before the kids were born. This guy she'd been about to warn off had given her the glad eye and one thing had led to another. Before she knew it really she was being photographed in her uniform – with all the identifying marks removed, of course – except when she was on duty she didn't wear tiny little black lace panties and seamed black stockings and high heels, which was the way she was got up for the camera, bending over to write out a ticket so that her skirt rode up and all was revealed and then stripping off in the studio so that she was wearing just suspenders and her traffic warden hat, waving her notebook at the world.

Things were a lot different in the lawyer's house. She was lying on this expensive couch and the furnishings of the room wouldn't have disgraced a royal palace. There was a glass of wine for her and he'd already topped it up several times. She could tell he was turned on by her but he wasn't trying to get his leg over her and she was glad of that.

Now he got her to turn over on to her front, with her boobs spilling out of the basque. He gave her a cube of ice and she applied it to her nipples to get them to stick up nice and juicy. She was reading some glossy fashion magazine and eating plums as she did so and the guy must have done a whole roll of film just on that one image alone. She reckoned he must have liked it.

At no stage did she get completely undressed, but the last ones they did were just of her wearing the basque and the stockings, nothing else apart from her high-heeled shoes. She knew Scully usually wore something a little lower, for all the chasing around in darkened buildings she had to do – but the heels looked good. Of course they ended up doing the shot of her with her legs apart and fingering herself – she knew he'd want to do it – and he got in close until his camera was right in on her cunt and she was frigging herself for real in the end, she was so turned on by it.

He was too and though she hadn't really allowed for it, she ended up by giving him a bit of a blow-job and then she let him spunk off all over her tits. He had quite a big one and he was good-looking in a straight sort of way, but a bit too much of the sandy-haired Charles Dance type for her, a bit too public school, and she didn't want to ball him for real. She managed to stop his come running down on to her basque, it had cost her seventy odd quid but he gave her the money for it and said she could keep it.

She didn't want any more of the wine because she was driving, so he went off and made them both a pot of coffee. He left her alone while she got undressed out of her sexy stuff and back into the clothes she'd arrived in. She put on a simple white cotton shirt and blue jeans and did her hair in the mirror and pretty soon she looked like the familiar Tina again, not the bedroom fantasy she'd just been acting out on the couch. Anthony complimented her on how effective she was, and asked her about her work and things. Seeing he was a lawyer, she didn't put any questions about her contract arrangements but, seeing she'd just broken it, she reckoned he was merely being discreet.

He handed her an unsealed envelope which contained ten newly minted £50 notes, to go with the £500 he'd given her earlier as an advance payment. She thought he would get her to sign the usual agreement waiving any rights to the photographs – typical of a lawyer, she reckoned – but he didn't do this.

'No names, no pack drill, this is simply between us,' he said and for a thousand pounds for a little over two hours' work, she could hardly complain. And such a gentleman too, she reflected, as he opened the front door for her and she made her way to her car, nice and shiny and new. Maybe she might have let him make love to her, after all. She drove home through the late-evening Friday traffic to pick up the kids feeling happy with herself, as she often did these days. When she'd been with Ray, she sometimes wouldn't feel happy for weeks at a time.

Saturday morning, very early, found Danny in the back of a laundry van outside Parminter's Hotel. It was exactly the kind of place he would have expected a Hollywood superstar to stay in, and his means of gaining entry carried the shade of Tinseltown too.

At the given signal, he climbed into a laundry basket, the shutter doors opened and he found himself trundled round to the service entrance of the enormous Tudor pile, once a manor house but now a five-star entry in every guide worth its salt. A quick scramble through the kitchens and through the enormous entrance hall and then he was in a three-hundred-pounds-a-night suite with Charmayne and a grade-A tabloid creep called Rex Wagstaffe.

He made to look out of the window to get his bearings but Wagstaffe caught his arm.

'No, don't do that just yet,' he said in his forty-a-day voice. 'They'll see you and that's too soon. I want to play with them.'

So Danny sat in an armchair away from the window and contemplated the distant view. He could glimpse well-manicured grounds, some handsome trees and an ancient brick wall. At intervals he could see figures – presumably standing on stepladders – wielding powerful lenses. More of them were clustered around the ornate gates to the hall. They were the dreaded paparazzi, out for blood and the hope of an exclusive.

They'd got wind – care of Rex Wagstaffe's carefully planned disinformation – that the movie legend was staying here and, moreover, wasn't with his wife. It was part of the scenario that, at the right moment, Danny would appear briefly and apparently indiscreetly in public with Charmayne. It would be all over the front pages and the tabloid rivals to the *Daily Bleat* would have egg on their faces as soon as R. Wagstaffe revealed the true identities of the 'star' and his alleged lover. He, meanwhile, would have the real dope on the inside story.

Charmayne poured coffee for the three of them. 'They know you're in here,' said Wagstaffe. 'They had the place staked out all last night. I had a limo arrive just before midnight and they just creamed their fucking pants. Flashguns going off all over the place. It was empty, of course, ha, ha, fucking ha. Thanks, love, three sugars, please and pass me them chocolate biscuits.'

Danny didn't know precisely why but the guy gave him the willies. He looked mid-forties but was probably younger, had a voice that had more than a hint of Essex or Sarf London about it, wore an expensive suit and a silk tie and had terrible dandruff. He had the reputation of one of Wapping's finest.

His mobile beeped. 'Wagstaffe,' he said in his flatly accented monotone. 'Oh, hi, Jimmy. Nothing stirring yet, is there? Good. Okay, look, I'll be over there in about an hour, maybe less. But let me know if anything looks like happening, okay, or I'll be playing ping-pong with your fucking nuts, you know what I mean, ha, ha, ha.

'Photographer,' he said by way of explanation. 'He's up a tree smack opposite your man's bedroom.'

'How do you know he's there?' asked Danny.

'Oh believe me, son, he's there all right. Jimmy's got a scanner in the car and he picked up a couple of calls.'

'Where is this?' asked Charmayne.

Wagstaffe looked at her as if he were a royal equerry and she'd just asked him to get his dick out at a Royal garden party and flourish it in front of the Queen Mother.

'Oh come on, love, I'm not going to tell you that. They don't know where he is, where the wedding is, where the reception is. I'm the only one who knows. If word got out, before you knew it, all those pillocks out there would be up his arse.' He indicated the distant pressmen with a dismissive wave of his hand.

'And besides,' he went on in a conspiratorial whisper, 'it's not where he is that's the interesting bit, but who he's with, you know what I mean? That's why you're here, mate,' he said to Danny. 'To draw those fuckers off the scent.'

He demolished the biscuits. He hadn't bothered offering the plate to anyone else.

A half-hour or so went by in which nothing whatever happened. But Danny was used to this, through the work he'd done on commercials, 'waiting for the light'. So Danny and Charmayne watched television, while Wagstaffe kept vigil by the window.

Danny's mind was just starting to drift back to the things he'd done with Chantal last night when Wagstaffe's phone shrilled.

'Okay,' he said at length. 'Just show yourself for a couple of seconds.'

Danny stood up and walked over to the window.

'What do you want me to do?' he asked.

'Christ, do what everyone else does if they've just got up. Yawn, scratch your arse, fart a bit. Let them know you're around.'

So Danny stood there for a moment, casually dressed in an open-necked shirt, letting the sunlight fall on his face, advertising his presence.

'Come on, you dozy fuckers,' breathed Rex Wagstaffe. 'Wakey-wakey. Ah that's better, they've spotted you now. Count to five – one, two, three, four, five. Right, that's enough. Come back in now.'

Danny was distantly aware of the commotion over by the wall as the waiting photographers swung into action. Wagstaffe looked on sideways round the curtain and then motioned Danny and Charmayne to come to the window together.

'Just for a second, this time,' he hissed. 'Stand together, let them see your faces, right, that's fine. Now get away from the window. Oh, sweet fucking Jesus, just look at that – no, on second thoughts, don't. They loved that. They bit on that bugger hook, line and sinker. What a fucking laugh, eh, ha, ha, ha.'

Danny was back drinking coffee again while Wagstaffe made a clutch of phone calls. A couple of big guys in track-suits came into the room.

'Right, Danny, put these on now, will you?' he said, tossing him a T-shirt and a pair of sweat pants. 'You're going to go for a jog before breakfast. That's what he always does, you know. They'll be expecting it, our friends with the cameras.' Danny looked at Charmayne. He wondered just what else was going to be involved in this scam. But he did exactly as he was told, all the same.

Danny and the heavies did a quick circuit of the lawns at the rear of the house, trying to keep close to the trees so as not to let the big lenses get a really good view of him. The gorillas' conversation was limited and their faces were slab-like and impassive. A day in their company would hardly amount to much. They were the kind who communicated best by grunts, interspersed with the odd friendly blow to the back of the neck.

Danny jogged around the grounds without much enthusiasm. He was beginning to feel distinctly unhappy about this whole performance. He wasn't too keen on Charmayne's involvement, either – she seemed all too willing to go along with whatever Wagstaffe wanted. Even though it might not have been outside the Marquess of Queensbury's rules, it wasn't strictly by the book either. Still, he told himself, it all boiled down to money in the end. That was why he was here, for the sake of the grand he was going to make on top of the retainer that Kirtley Carmody paid him – except they weren't called Kirtley Carmody now, of course. They'd relaunched that side of the business at Seeing Double and he'd been feeling a bit pissed off that they hadn't asked him to design their new identity for them. Probably can't afford you, Chantal had told him, but that wasn't the point.

When they got back to the room, having hardly been out there long enough to raise much of a sweat, Rex Wagstaffe gave them their orders. Once everyone had got changed into their posh wedding togs, they were to drive off in one direction, hopefully drawing off the newshounds with their scent, while he went the other way to where his quarry was laid up with Nicole. That was his big exclusive – she was said to be too busy to attend but he knew that she'd flown in the previous afternoon. He'd known this for weeks, this was what gave him the idea for the scam. They had word, though, that she wouldn't be spending long at the wedding – immediately after, a chopper was going to take her to a private airfield near Thetford where there was a jet waiting to whisk her back to filming in North Africa. Still, it was a great story.

They had a spare car waiting for them in the forest on the far side of Bury St Edmunds. With a head start, they could get there easily, switch motors and meet up with Rex and Jimmy ready for the reception, leaving the rest of the press wondering what the fuck was going on.

The BMW took off as if it had afterburners with Heavy No 1 at the wheel. Danny and Charmayne sat in the back with Heavy No 2. 'Get right down in your seat,' he said, 'like you're trying to avoid them. But make sure you look right at 'em, all the same.'

They scorched down the drive, spitting gravel, and barely slowed to turn into the lane at the end. But it was enough for the car to be momentarily surrounded by photographers. Enough flashes went off to illuminate Wembley stadium on a black November night. As the car turned, the wing mirror caught one guy and sent him spinning into the roadway. Fortunately there was nothing coming in either direction, which was just as well because Heavy No 1 sure as hell wasn't going to stop for anything.

By the time the pressmen had got their wits about them and raced for their own cars – lined up two deep along the road – the black BMW was a mile away. They scorched along narrow country lanes rich with white cow parsley, under great hanging oak trees. Mercifully, at eight-thirty on a quiet Suffolk morning, there was little other traffic about. While Heavy No 2 read the map, his colleague hurled the speeding car from B road to unmarked road, twisting and turning around the sleeping countryside on a carefully planned journey to nowhere.

'I'm glad of the seat belt,' said Charmayne, looking distinctly green around the gills. 'I used to have a boyfriend who did rallying.'

Danny hoped his surprise didn't show. Charmayne was a real looker all right but he was sure she was lesbian, albeit of a distinctly lipsticky persuasion. Lesley Carmody, on the other hand, he knew to be almost totally gay but Charmayne, well perhaps he could see something there after all. He'd always rather fancied her himself. She had nice tits and big hair.

Inside ten minutes they'd lost the last of their pursuers and the car slowed to a normal pace.

They reached the forest. A red Jaguar was parked there with a chauffeur at the wheel. Rex Wagstaffe was sitting in the back seat, smoking, looking like he'd just won the lottery. Another guy was standing by the car, looking uncomfortable in a smart suit. This was obviously Jimmy, the photographer.

'The bike's just gone off with Jimmy's photos. He done brilliant, the lad. Our friend came walking out of the house with his old lady and before you could say, all right, mate, Jimmy'd shot off a whole roll of film. We'll scoop the lot of them tomorrow morning, I can tell you. They'll be splashing with Danny and Charmayne here and we've got the real thing to prove they're a bunch of arseholes. Ha, ha, fucking ha.'

'Why do you want to gatecrash the reception as well?' asked Charmayne.

''Cos his missus will be there, won't she, just for a few minutes. She's flying off right after. No one else is expecting that. They're all thinking she's stuck in Timbuctoo and hubby makes hay while the sun shines with your lovely self. If I can get pictures of the two of them and you as well, I'll be laughing. That'll be a double scoop, won't it? But I thought we'd take Danny along just to see what happens. Then there'll be four of you, what a fucking laugh that's going to be.'

Danny didn't feel too comfortable with this idea. It struck him that he was being set up for something and he didn't like it.

'But if they see me and him together, that's sunk your story, hasn't it?'

'Not a bit of it, sonny. There is no way any of them pillocks can get into that place, not unless they've got a lookalike of their own. So no one will know, apart from us.'

'How d'we get in?' asked Charmayne, who was also beginning to have misgivings. Rex Wagstaffe, it seemed, was as much a stranger to moral scruples as he was to discretion in the use of after-shave.

'We go straight in the front. There'll be security on the

door but they'll take one look at Danny boy here and we'll be waved through. They know he's coming. They know there'll be people with him. It's only a five minute drive from the church. My only hope is that we get there before he does – if we don't, we're up shit creek. Still, the wedding's at eleven and the reception's at twelve, so if we're there slightly early, we should be okay.'

'What happens then? What do you want us to do? What's the point of this, apart from getting your pictures?'

'The point, my dear girl, is to get me and Jimmy in the fucking place. Once that's happened and Jimmy's got a shot we can use, you and Danny can piss off home and bung us your invoice. You don't have to do anything. Jimmy's car is parked by the post office in the village and the keys are under the front seat. It's a white Xantia. You can take that.'

A little before twelve, the Jag pulled up outside the Hartlesham Hall. As predicted, the place was swarming with security, even though the whole wedding and the reception after were strictly hush-hush. God alone knew where Wagstaffe got his information from but the men with suits and portable phones took one look in the back of the car and waved them into a parking spot. Danny, Charmayne, Wagstaffe and the heavies all got out and made for the door. Surrounded by burly men in shades, crouching so he looked shorter than his six-foot-two, they took the door at a rush and got clean inside.

'Bride's father's place,' said Charmayne to Danny when they got inside and took a look at them. 'The wedding's at the church in the village.'

The main hall was already beginning to fill up. People turned and stared, but Wagstaffe grabbed a glass of champagne from a passing tray and steered his party into a small room off to one side.

'We'll hole up here for a couple of minutes,' he said. 'When he comes, we'll feel the buzz. Go easy on that bubbly, Jimmy.'

Danny was conscious only of a sinking feeling in his stomach. They'd bluffed their way into one of the stately homes of England and now heaven only knew what was going to happen. He wished he was back in his studio, working on corporate identities.

He sure as hell wasn't going to do anything like this again, that was for sure. There had to be an easier way of making a living. Still, he thought of the thousand quid that was going to buy him and Chantal a Barbados holiday, and then he thought of the other perks like that girl Amelia he'd screwed a few weeks back on that ad shoot up in Leicestershire. They'd scrapped the whole thing, he subsequently learned, and shot something entirely different with different models in a tropical waterfall that had been dummied up for the occasion in a studio in Reading. A pity about that, he was rather looking forward to seeing Amelia again, even if only on the screen rather than in her somewhat ample flesh.

'Oh shit, we're on,' hissed Wagstaffe, peering round the door. 'He's here now. Where's Nicole? Don't tell me she's pissed off already. Oh fuck, she has. Oh no, there she is. Thank Christ for that. Okay guys, go go go.'

He all but pushed them out of the small chamber. In the hall the scene was total chaos. Obviously the real Mr C had had problems at the gate. Now security men were screaming into phones and minders were milling around looking at one another as if to say, which one of you assholes fucked up this time. They were just about getting their heads together when this six-foot-two Tom Cruise lookalike burst on to the scene with a blonde in tow, with a couple of heavies virtually frog-marching them through the throng and right up to the man and his wife.

Jimmy's cameras spat light and, as Danny later recalled, it was just wild. For a couple of seconds he stood right next to the guy – he really wasn't very tall at all – and then Heavy No 1 manhandled him out of the way and hit some guy who tried to stop them. Heavy No 2, meanwhile, jammed a top hat on to his head and Danny remembered to put his shades on and then he was being hustled out of another door. He hadn't a clue were Charmayne had got to.

With his beefy minders clinging on to him for dear life he burst through a couple of doors and then they were in a large, empty room with just a couple of suits of armour and Rex Wagstaffe for company. Charmayne was with him, her hair tousled and looking none too pleased. Wagstaffe, on the other hand, looked like he'd won the lottery two weeks running.

'All right,' said the pressman, toasting them with a glass of champagne that he'd somehow managed to snatch a hold of during the confusion. 'That was brilliant. Now why don't you and Charmayne find the back entrance and me and the boys can lose ourselves.'

He grasped Danny's hand, gave it a quick wet squeeze. There was a door leading off the room they were in. It led, presumably, to the outside world. Beyond the grounds of the Hall was the village and Jimmy's Xantia, and beyond that were many miles of open road. He was determined to put as many of them as possible between himself and Rex Wagstaffe.

'I've got to find the little girl's room first,' whispered Charmayne. 'It must be all this excitement. I'll see you outside.'

Danny nodded and dipped quickly through the door. As instructed by Charmayne, he took his jacket and tie off, dumped them on one of the heavies and made sure he still had the sunglasses and baseball cap that were to disguise him from prying eyes.

He made his way along the corridor but the only exit he could find was locked. He turned around, climbed a staircase and found himself in a large, empty room directly above the room where he could hear the reception was starting to fill up.

He looked out of the window. A police car came scorching up the drive and there were security men all over the place. Oh God, he thought, and dodged back into the corridor. There was another set of stairs at the far end. He ran down them, feeling more than a little alarmed, but they gave out on to a half landing with another corridor running off that.

He tried a door, found it unlocked, went through it. The noise from below had all but vanished now. After all the ancestral paintings and heavy furniture this part of the house seemed to be more homely. He had found himself, he guessed, in the guest wing. He hoped he might find a servant or someone who could tell him where he was.

He stood at the end of the corridor, looking down through the elegant oriole window on to the old courtyard below, wondering how the hell he was going to get out of there. That shit Wagstaffe! He might have known something would go wrong.

There was no way he could get out that way, unfortunately. He tried a couple of doors but they were both locked – security, presumably. The third one he tried opened and he found himself in a luxuriously appointed bedroom. Mercifully, the sash was open too, and a soft breeze caused the curtains to flutter. He looked down into the elaborate formal garden at what was, presumably, the back of the building. There was an outhouse directly below and it would be easy to drop down out of the window where he was standing to the ground.

He heard a noise behind him, turned round, and there was a woman standing there looking at him. She was wearing a dress of peach-coloured silk and a broad hat liberally festooned with roses. She was also quite stunningly beautiful, in an expensive, sun-tanned, rich man's mistress way.

Her eyes perceptibly widened and then she gave him the most brilliant smile he had ever seen in his life.

Full consciousness returned in a rush. 'I'm sorry,' he said, temporarily grasping for words. 'I was just looking to see if I— Look, I know this sounds ridiculous but . . .'

Again the smile. She acted as if it were the most normal thing in the world to find men trying to climb out of her bedroom window. Especially ones who looked uncannily like a certain party whom she had been studying intently in church only a few moments before, only not looking quite so flustered.

'I'm here for the wedding,' he said as she took off her spectacular hat and tossed it casually on to a sofa. 'I'm just trying to find a way to – well, you know.'

He trailed off into silence. He didn't know what to say.

'You look stunning,' said the woman, with total honesty in her eyes and the most devilish smile playing around her lips. She had a heavy French accent. 'Just as stunning as I'd always imagined.'

The simple peach-coloured silk seemed moulded to her body, clinging where it needed to cling and swinging elegantly loose where it didn't.

Danny could feel himself blushing. Surely she couldn't be confusing him with—

'I like the hat,' he said at length, with stunning banality.

She didn't reply.

'Listen,' he began again, moving towards the door. 'I got to, you know—'

She stepped across, reached for the key and locked the door. 'Why all the hurry?' she said. There was a zee in the 'the' and 'hurry' didn't have much of an aitch. 'My name's Gabrielle.'

Danny had always had a thing about French women. He felt a strange erotic thrill course through him, trapped in a bedroom with a beautiful women he had never seen before in his life while downstairs, presumably, security men combed the building for him. Was this how it always was for film stars? Surely she could tell by his northern accent that he wasn't who he seemed to be? But then, he reasoned with himself, she didn't speak English all that well herself. Maybe she couldn't tell.

And yet he felt undeniably aroused by her. He could tell, too, that she knew it. What he didn't know was that those heavy, uplifted breasts, with the deep cleavage designed to excite, had been prepared for him that very morning, for the opportunity of a chance meeting. Her dream, it seemed, was about to come true.

He stood there, unsure of what to do next. He smiled, his slow lazy reptile smile that so many women had found irresistible.

They looked at each other in silence.

'Pour me a drink, would you?' she said. 'There's champagne by the bed.' He did as he was told, heard the sound of a zip and then the rustle of something soft and silky. When he turned round, Gabrielle was standing by the locked door in her underwear.

'I've been longing to meet you,' she repeated. 'We've got half an hour. How would you like me?'

Lust shot through him like the motion of an express lift. Direct propositions from women had always had this power over him. He felt his erection rising as fast as his misgivings were falling away from him and in that sweet moment he knew that, once again, he was lost to his bodily lusts.

For a few tantalising seconds he stood there transfixed, just looking at her. Gabrielle was quite tall, five feet eight or nine, and with her hair up it made her look even taller. She stood there on the carpet in ridiculously high heels. Her silk knickers were the same shade of pale peach as her Laroche suit. Her underwired bra was a froth of lace at the front where her breasts hung heavy and full. She wore matching suspenders and sheer, glossy stockings in smoky grey. In a room like this, with its antiques and books and mellowed furniture, the summer sunlight drifting in through the heavily leaded windows, the effect was like a photo-spread from one of the upmarket lingerie catalogues that were advertised in the Sunday broadsheets.

The suddenness of his movement surprised even him. Without consciously thinking about it, as much a slave as ever to his earthy desires, he crossed the room and took her in his arms, crushing to him her fleshy body in its sheaths of warm silk. Her tongue sought his, tracing its way over his neck, her hands all the while pushing up under his shirt.

Blood roared through his head as they paused for breath and then kissed again, with ferocious intensity. Time stood still. Down below, the wedding reception was getting under way and the security men – outraged at being hoodwinked – were moving in for the kill.

Gabrielle slithered to her knees and pressed her head against his groin, with its burgeoning erection. Oh Christ, he thought. Then she was busy with his zip, roughly yanking his trousers down as he pulled his shirt off over his head. His cock lolled there, stiff and ready. She took hold of it in one hand, gently stroking it as she licked around the top of his thighs, her cheeks brushing against his thick pubic hair. Then her lips closed over it and he felt himself transported into another realm.

He opened his eyes to see Gabrielle looking up at him, a wicked twinkle playing around her eyes. She nibbled around the tip of his glans, her tongue gently playing with the slit at the end of his cock, before swooping down and taking as much of him as she could into her mouth. She did this repeatedly, an exercise calculated to tease him into madness, the pause after each suck becoming an aching void of anticipation that was immediately gratified.

He glanced down at her deep cleavage vanishing into a mysterious fleshy darkness, her breasts swelling full and ripe, her nipples pressed hard against the thin gauze of peachy lace. God, he wanted to suck her, to press his cock against the warm fullness that seemed to invite him to nestle there. He could see how tautly her suspenders were stretched against her thighs, the legs slightly parted so that her knickers were moulded tight against the fleshy lips of her pussy. He could see her touching herself with her fingertips, openly masturbating while she fellated him. For some reason this excited him uncontrollably. He liked the idea of sexy women bringing themselves off while they thought of him.

He took hold of her shoulders, urging her on, thrusting his cock into her mouth. She seemed the type who liked her men to be forceful and dominant with her. Here in this sunlit room, with birdsong in the grounds outside and a heavy sultriness in the air, he abandoned himself to the realm of the senses.

As he felt his seed rising within him he took hold of her head with both hands. Her cheeks were engorged, her heavily made-up eyes closed as though she were dreaming. There was a wildness in him now, a red mist seemed to be descending on him, a delicious lewdness of thought giving way to a total surrender to the sensations of his body. He caught sight of her buttocks straining against the silk, her high-heeled shoes, her breasts swinging as he leaned forward. Here he was, being sucked off by a deeply sensual Frenchwoman in a strange bedroom at midday under totally false pretences – and he didn't care.

He let out his pent-up breath, made a sound that was half-groan, half a cry of triumph, and then his seed boiled over into Gabrielle's mouth in thick, succulent pulses of pleasure. He closed his eyes and it was like he had gone shooting off beyond the planets, never to return. He seemed to come into her mouth for an aeon.

He opened his eyes once more and almost at the same time he could sense her tensing up. As though she had been waiting for his signal, he was aware of the movement of her hand between her legs becoming more urgent, more insistent, more immediate. Her swollen clitoris responded to her own expert touch and she moved back away from him, letting his cock flop from her mouth. As she did so, he saw a little dash of semen overflowing on to the perfectly applied lipstick. With her free hand she grasped him round the buttocks, pressed herself forcefully against his muscular thighs and came in shuddering waves of sighs.

'I think I'll have that drink now,' said Gabrielle at length, when she had had time to compose herself.

He sank down on to the bed, suddenly drained. It was all too much, on top of all the excitement and tension of the morning. He lay back, as consciousness slowly returned.

He felt so strangely relaxed after the high drama of the morning's events that he dozed off for a couple of seconds. When he came round, Gabrielle was now as naked as himself. She handed him a glass of wine, lay down next to him with those stupendous breasts right next to his face.

They sipped their wine, lips nibbling at each other, making small talk. He was safer here than anywhere, he found himself thinking over and over again while his cock renewed its potency. Still, he reasoned, he could spend the next half-hour with the willing Gabrielle while his pursuers ran themselves silly around Hartlesham Hall.

Slowly, almost languidly, they found themselves in each other's arms again. This time the kisses were stronger, richer, less frenetic. With practised ease, Danny's hand snaked down towards the warm slickness of Gabrielle's sex, the outer lips already engorged and puffy, her clitoris aroused by his touch.

'God, you know how to do that to me, don't you, you bastard,' she breathed. He licked her neck slowly and sensually. She liked that, he discovered. She liked him to tongue her ear, too, until she squealed and wriggled like a schoolgirl.

Her hands moved up and down his flanks, across his chest, down his back. She proffered him her breasts and he licked hungrily at the plump raspberry nipples and the dusky areolae.

'More slowly,' she breathed. 'I like it slow.'

He did as he was bid, his tongue moving in gentle flicks, his fingers continuing to caress her pussy. Almost without effort the two of them moved off the bed and on to the floor, the polished wood cold and hard against naked flesh, the smell of the antique rugs mingling in their nostrils with the muskier scents of sex.

She nudged him with her hips and then he was on top of her, his cock perhaps not entirely erect as yet but sufficiently hard enough to penetrate her easily. She gasped slightly as he slid inside her. His cock, she told him, was huge and his come was sweet to the taste.

Though he was on top, it was Gabrielle who was doing most of the work. Her hips ground against his in slow, sensuous circles, flesh pressing flesh, her big bare nipples brushing the hair on his chest. She nipped his shoulder with her teeth, licked his own nipples with the tip of her tongue in a way that made his cock stiffen appreciably and then he was away, falling into rhythm with hers, intoxicated with the mixture of perfume and sweat that rose up from her gorgeous body.

She looked up at him, big eyes wide, the make-up smudged now, an unmistakable flush of colour in her cheeks that was not entirely due to the summer heat. His hand slipped under her buttocks, slightly lifting her up as he forced himself into her. She spread her legs more, bringing them round and up over the backs of his thighs.

'Fuck me, you sexy bastard,' she breathed. 'I love you up my cunt.'

Danny liked a woman who talked during sex. Gabrielle did, more than most. What she was doing, what she wanted to do, what she had done in the past – it all blurred into one long, deliciously pornographic monologue of abandoned sexual fantasy, conducted partly in English but for the most part in a soft Gallic tone that bore little resemblance to what he'd learned in school.

When he really began to hit the note, though, she looked him straight in the eye. 'That's good,' she breathed. 'Oh, God, I can really feel that. Squeeze my tits – don't you like them? I love it when guys come all over my tits. I love to lick spunk, I want your spunk all the time. I want it all over me.'

Locked in a familiar rhythm of desire, Danny slowly and surely brought her to orgasm. She came with quiet, almost sobbing yelps, her long polished nails digging into his back, her eyes squeezed tight shut, her mouth open. He wasn't long in following her. As he rolled off her and lay looking up at the heavy beams on the ceiling, he felt a strange contentment.

Both had taken – and given – exactly what they wanted, nothing more and nothing less. Afterwards, he lay there naked and watched as she made herself ready to face the world again. Back on, like a striptease in reverse, went the stockings, the silk underwear, the Laroche suit, the heels. Out came the make-up bag and mirror. The adjustments were carefully made, the hat at just the right angle. It was like she was armouring herself against the world. He saw her glancing from time to time at her watch as though for assurance. Ten minutes, and she was bright as steel again. This was a woman on whose voluptuous body men erected their fantasies, a vehicle for other people's ideas. And she'd used him in exactly the right way.

She walked over to where he lay on the bed, still naked.

'It's best if we leave separately, don't you think?' she said. 'I can't be too long or my husband will wonder where I am.'

She leaned down and kissed him lightly on the lips and then, lingering a little longer, on the end of his cock.

'You're taller than I thought,' she breathed, still believing he was Cruise. 'But your cock is just as beautiful as I'd imagined.'

In a waft of perfume, she was gone.

As soon as the door had closed behind her, he dressed quickly. He checked himself in the mirror, combed his hair back over his temples, put the shades on. The disguise complete, he climbed out of the window. A new-model MG was parked around the corner, engine running, a guy about his own age in the front seat, formally dressed.

'You're not going to the village, are you?' he said. 'My partner seems to have gone off without me.'

The guy indicated the seat alongside him. He climbed in

and tugged the cap down over his eyes. They shot past the security men on the gate with a wave.

'You know this part of the world?' asked Danny.

'Sure,' said the driver. 'I own the restaurant in the village.'

'Where the hell have you been?' asked Charmayne when he finally tracked down the car in the side street where it was parked. 'You've been gone an hour.'

'Is that all?' he said. She looked at him quizzically.

'I got waylaid,' he tried to explain.

She gave him an even more quizzical look.

'I'll explain later,' he said. 'Can we go now? I want some lunch. I met a guy who says there's a very good restaurant just over the way.'

Chapter Five

Things had only got better for Tina Richardson since she'd dumped her previous agent and signed up with Seeing Double. The money was great, for a start, and the gigs were really good. Where once she might have been stuck for an hour or more at the special-discount opening of yet another branch of some awful tyre and exhaust company, being ogled by hairy-arsed mechanics and greasy execs called Kevin and Warren, now she was doing big conferences and product launches. Only last week she'd managed to ship the kids off to her mum and taken three days at a ritzy health hydro in Somerset – that wasn't the kind of thing she'd ever have been able to do in the past. She'd given a short talk that was kind of *X-Files*-ish, all about loyalty and determination and truth-seeking and stuff, but mostly she just had to be there, answering questions and putting on the Californian accent which these days was rilly rather neat.

Sure, there was a downside to it all – wasn't there always? There were guys who seemed only to want to get in her pants, who wanted her to put on the Scully voice and do the pout and toss her famous red hair and talk dirty to them, all that kind of thing. This usually happened when the booze had been flowing. She hated those cocksure sales guys with their tans and aftershave and their endless talk of 'leveraging' and 'downsizing'. They weren't interested in her at all as a person. Still, it was better than being a traffic warden, which was what she'd been before *The X Files* thing had first started, back with the crappy agency she'd started out with. But it all seemed such a long, long time ago now.

Things were looking up in other areas of her life. Her estranged husband Ray, mercifully, seemed to be leaving her alone for now. He'd got himself a new job – which was some going at his time of life – and he had to spend a lot of time in Germany on company business. Better still, he'd found himself a woman out there in Dusseldorf and that seemed to keep him occupied.

She'd been seeing at lot of Christopher Francombe, the guy she'd met the same day as she met Lesley Carmody from the agency. It seemed now like that had been her lucky day, one way or another. Christopher was a nice guy to be with – funny, caring, intelligent, not in the least bit vain although he was good-looking and dressed well. He was great in bed, too, which made him even more attractive to her.

Sure, there was the Scully thing but with him it was a fun thing to do once in a while. It wasn't what he was really interested in her for. They'd done it a couple of times with her pretending to be you-know-who and then that seemed to satisfy him and they didn't bother with it any more. When she was off-duty, as she liked to think of it, she used to do her hair differently and her make-up as well, so that the resemblance was really quite slight. Once or twice she'd even gone out with her hair coloured quite dark, just to be different, but Christopher – and he was a Christopher, not a Chris – didn't like that much and neither did she. So she went back to being herself.

In some ways her work was beginning to grate on her. She liked doing it and she loved all the publicity but there was a downside too – people staring, people getting their cameras out, the endless autographs and 'can you pose with my husband, he's a big fan of yours'. Sometimes she wondered if Scully were taking over her life, all the videos she had to watch to check every last detail, the books and mags she had to study to make sure of her facts.

But she was herself tonight, Tina, the one with the naturally red hair who had existed long before Scully and Mulder. Tonight it was Tina and Christopher, very definitely. They were having a good evening, a little French restaurant they'd discovered, very intimate and not too expensive – she wasn't in that price bracket yet. It was discreet, too – once or twice in the half-dozen or so occasions they'd eaten there she'd sensed someone, usually a woman, giving her the once-over but this wasn't the kind of place where someone would come weaving unsteadily across the floor and say, in a broad Stirchley accent, ''ere, 'as anyone ever told yew 'ow much you're like that woman on the telly.'

She felt confident with him but she hadn't told him about that evening with the lawyer and the photographs. It was none of his business, anyway.

There was a real chemistry between her and Christopher and already it had led her into areas she'd never been into before. No one had ever had her in the bum before, for a start. She remembered the first time Christopher had done it to her that way. She had been at his house, listening to music, the old soul and R&B records that both of them liked, upbeat and funky and yet kind of sensual all at the same time. Then, when the moment had seemed right, he'd led her by the hand to the bedroom. They undressed each other, slowly and deliciously, as was their habit. She loved the moment when she would pull his shirt over his shoulders, see his nut-brown nipples there, give each of them a teasing little suck.

When both of them were naked she'd run her hands over his body, the muscular rugby-player's back, the broad shoulders, the powerful thighs. He didn't look like a muscle guy with his clothes on but bare-ass naked he did, not like some guys, all bulges and twisty slabs of meat, but in a strong kind of way, very masculine. His body didn't look like it had been worked on.

She lay down on the bed and he was beside her. He had his head propped up on his elbow and with his other hand he was gently running up and down her torso, caressing her belly button with butterfly fingers, taking his time and making it seem like it didn't matter at all whether or not he made it down to her sex, not like some guys who'd be groping her while she was still bone-dry.

They were looking at each other, their eyes all innocence, trying to see what was there for each of them. Without even realising it, she felt his fingers on her vulva and then his thumb was gently pressuring her clitoris. She felt herself relax, giving way to his ministrations, as the gentle, circular motions of his fingertips gave way to something more intensely rhythmic. And then he had two, three, four fingers into her and she was starting to feel wild and abandoned, wanting him to do it harder, wanting to push her bodily sensations to the limit.

She was pushing up her hips against his hands, wanting his whole fist in her, his dick, his tongue, anything, anywhere, just so long as she was penetrated. He had that effect on her, he could switch her circuits on faster than any man she had ever known. With other guys she'd come to think of herself as a bit of a slow burner but with Christopher, she was quickly at the edge.

She still didn't know quite how it had happened. She was on fire but suddenly he seemed calm, firm, authoritative even.

'Turn over and kneel towards me,' he said.

She reached up as she rolled over and tousled his hair, caressed his ear. She'd wondered what was going to happen – rear entry, she assumed, or perhaps he was going to spank her or something like that. She liked all the different things they did that she'd never wanted to do with Ray and any of the others, not that there'd been all that many, not really.

He stroked her backside for some while, running his fingers along the crack, cupping each soft, fleshy buttock in his palm. At one time he had his hand right down deep in her cleft so she could feel the heel against her labia. She rubbed excitedly against him, anxious for the moment of penetration.

'Do me, Christopher,' she breathed. 'I want you up me.'

'Arch your back,' he said, again in that firm voice of command, but still gentle like the way he was. 'And draw your knees up more.'

He was kneeling behind her now and she felt deliciously rude, with her coral pink genitalia exposed to his gaze. She wiggled her butt impatiently.

'Come on, come on,' she murmured. 'I'm dying for it.'

She was, she realised, absolutely soaking wet down there. He had been playing with her clitty for some time and her lips were engorged, inflamed, aroused beyond endurance. He was moving his hand up and down, all over her vagina and anal region, and she could feel his cock bobbing and dipping up against her bum cheeks.

They were right by the edge of the bed and he was standing up, right over her back, with his hands around her hips. She felt lost to him, absolutely in his thrall.

He had his cock between her legs now, moving it gently around and he continued to caress her buttocks. Now it was resting against her backside and he gave her a little gentle push. She could feel the tip of his glans right up against her sphincter muscle.

All of a sudden she realised what he had in mind. She felt excited, wanton. She'd never done this before. It was like losing her virginity for a second time. She felt excited and yet a little scared too, all at the same time.

'Do you want to?' he asked.

She didn't need to consider her reply.

'Yes. Oh yes,' she breathed.

'Really? You sure?'

'Oh yes. Oh yes.'

It hurt at first, even though he pushed into her as carefully as he could. He couldn't have been more than an inch or two inside her but the pain ripped through her like nothing she'd experienced outside of childbirth. For a second or so she almost called out for him to stop. Neither of them moved, just crouched there in the darkness panting.

'Okay, go on,' she heard herself saying. It was like her mind and her body belonged to two different people, as if she was watching herself.

He held more tightly on to her buttocks and moved slowly inside her, a fraction at a time. She felt agony and excitement beyond endurance, both at the same time. She was aware, too, of Christopher's own emotions, the sense of power that radiated from him, his own arousal, his gentleness and his power, even when he had her in his thrall.

After a while the pain began to subside and she felt a warm, dark glow begin to suffuse her abdomen. She couldn't take any more of him in but what she had was fine, he was filling her utterly, she felt violated and revered at the same time.

She took hold of his hand and guided it between her legs, could feel his heavy balls lying against her, then she touched his cock shaft where it was embedded in her arse. She made

109

him touch her clitoris, very delicately, and then she started to move her hips in tiny, almost infinitesimal circles, pressing gently back against him, a fraction at a time. Less was more, it seemed, when you had a nice big dick up your arse.

And then something seemed to open up inside her and he slipped right into her, vast and throbbing, and in that same second she felt his fingertips on her clit and a wave of pleasure started to pulse within her, rolling through her like no emotion she'd ever known before.

Her breathing became ragged and she started to pant and then she came in a low, steady wave while he pulsed his seed into her, standing behind her at the bedside, pressed tight up against her and – she noticed with pleasure – sighing out her name.

Christopher came back – he'd gone to call for a taxi – a smile on his face, snapping her out of her imagined post-coital reverie. He looked very handsome tonight in an open-necked blue shirt and cream linen trousers. He had a public-school type of face, a bit of the Hugh Grants about him but his features were bigger and in any case, he'd only been to a grant-maintained school.

'Be another half an hour, I'm afraid,' he said as his hand lightly brushed hers. 'They're busy tonight. I should have rung earlier.'

'That's all right,' she said, and meant it. They had a good two-thirds of their second bottle left and she thought she might even have a cigarette. Once she'd smoked ten a day largely to relieve stress but now she might only have one or two a week, purely for enjoyment.

He sat down and poured her a glass of wine. She nibbled a bit of cheese – she didn't bother with a sweet, she'd always had to watch her figure for professional purposes and these days it was the thinner the better. She hoped she wasn't becoming anorexic but she felt there was little chance of that – she'd always liked her food and these days she seemed to be enjoying it more and more, especially now that Ray was out of the way.

She leaned forwards towards him, aware of how his eyes travelled towards her cleavage. She was wearing a floating

110

white top from Ghost that came quite low at the front. Her skirt was new that very morning, white kid leather and really quite short, especially to wear with stockings. She'd never worn stockings and suspenders with Ray, even though he'd often asked her to, but with Christopher it seemed the right thing to do, just as it had been for the lawyer with his camera. She knew how much he liked it and she was happy to do it for him.

'Looking forward to getting back?' she asked dreamily as he lit her cigarette for her. Her hand caressed his knee for a second. 'I know I am,' she added pointedly.

She leaned back and exhaled smoke. Her skirt rode up over her thighs as she did so, exposing for a brief and tantalising moment the lace top of her stockings and a pink suspender ribbon. She smoothed it down hastily – she wouldn't have minded one little bit if Christopher had seen all but she didn't want anyone else to see anything. Really, she thought, perhaps this skirt is a little too short, at least to go out in.

Christopher knew all about Ray. He'd been so understanding about it and that was one of the things that had attracted her most to it. He seemed so much more sensitive than other guys, and yet he was far from being a wimp. He was still playing rugby every Saturday even at thirty-four, though he was in the second team now, but he wasn't really a bloke's bloke. A grade-A womaniser, that's what you are, she once told him, and he'd laughed. He could cook as well, very good Chinese and Thai, not like Ray who could just about manage bacon and eggs, blackened around the edges.

They chatted easily and comfortably for the next half hour while they waited for the taxi to arrive, but underneath it was impatience and an awareness of the growing frisson between them, the undeniable sexual tension in the air. She felt sure he had an erection, she could tell just by the way he was talking and the way he sat facing her, hands on the table. If this had been one of her practised night-time fantasies, rather than a sixty-pounds-a-head country restaurant surrounded by well-heeled Saturday-night diners, she would have dropped to her knees there and then and sucked him off under the table.

'How's next week looking?' he asked.

'I don't think I've got over this one yet,' she said, laughing. It was true. Her new lease of life may have been exciting but it was damn hard work. She felt guilty, too, that she didn't see the kids more than she did but she knew the childminder she employed well and she was only two streets away.

'Don't you have to go to Paris?'

'No, that's the week after. I think it is, anyway. After a while, it just becomes a blur.'

'Where are you staying?'

'I don't know. Lesley or Charmayne usually fix these things. Why do you ask?'

'I'm worried that you're seeing another man, that you're off for a sexy weekend.'

She looked at him, startled for the moment. Then he laughed. 'No, I've got to be in Paris myself for a couple of days. See a client, you know. I wondered if we might be able to spend some time together.'

It sounded so incredibly romantic, a couple of stolen nights together in some ludicrously expensive hotel, and someone else paying the bill for both of them.

'Actually, between ourselves this guy is more than just a client. I think he might be trying to head-hunt me. We know he wants to set up an operation on this side of the Channel and I think, from various little hints he's been dropping, that I might be the man.'

'Sounds good,' said Tina. Everything sounded good these days. It certainly made a change from the way things had been over the last eighteen months or so, with the uncertain work situation and Ray getting more and more unreasonable.

A waiter came over. Their taxi had arrived. She finished the last of her demi-tasse while Christopher settled the bill. Then they made their way out into the cold night air.

In the cab she could hardly stop herself seizing hold of him there and then. She wrapped her coat around her legs so the driver couldn't see up her skirt in the rear-view mirror. The journey to Christopher's seemed to take an age.

They held hands in the back seat, like teenagers. She thought of all the things they'd done together in the past few weeks, mostly round at his place while her mum looked after the kids. She'd introduced them to Christopher but she'd not let him stay the night with her yet, at least not while the kids were there. It was too soon after Ray and besides, she was afraid of what their father might do if he found out. He was over in Germany most of the time but she was scared what might happen if he turned up unexpectedly and found Christopher there with his wife and kids.

Last weekend had been brilliant. They'd been to a party – some of his friends from the rugby club – and it had been really wild. They'd ended up going upstairs together and fucked in someone else's bedroom like teenagers, surrounded by records and books and clothes. She hadn't done anything like that since Karen Plumseed's eighteenth birthday party and now she was doing the same thing, as a respectable woman with a growing career in the modelling business.

She'd gone to the party as Scully, not as herself. It was her idea, not Christopher's, and she'd done it just for a laugh. The guys thought it was great, as well they ought, and some of them had even said she ought to do it for a living. She does, said Christopher in his quiet voice, and she could sense the pride in the way he said it.

She was drinking quite a bit these days too, not because she was unhappy like she was in the last months of her relationship with Ray, but because she felt wild. During the working week she had to be sober and sweet but at the weekend, assuming she didn't have any bookings, she could really let her hair down.

It had seemed almost inevitable that they'd go upstairs together. They were dancing to loud, loud music and he was very close to her and she could feel his cock against her thigh. At one stage, when she was sure no one was looking, she gave him a squeeze and she could tell from his reaction that he was really turned on. As soon as they could decently manage it, they slipped off upstairs and found themselves a room.

It wasn't anything fancy, the way they did it – both of

113

them were too far gone for that – but there was an incredible urgency about the way they tore their clothes off and kicked off the various coats and things that were lying on the bed. When he entered her, urgent and monstrously erect, she started to come almost immediately. She was so wet she hoped her juices didn't soak through on to the bedclothes. No more than a dozen huge, powerful, passion-driven shoves later, Christopher came off inside her, a series of enormous rhythmic pulses as he shot what must have been a whole week's worth of thick, creamy come right into her. She'd never known a man who had so much come in him as he did. When she sucked him on to orgasm – which was something else she'd never done with Ray – she was half-afraid she would gag on his semen. And yet she loved to do it, loved to do anything with him. Having his spunk in her mouth and up her arse made her feel alive once again after years of being buried in a loveless marriage. If she hadn't been done after Kirsty, she'd have wanted to have a baby with him.

The taxi driver flipped his wipers on. It had started to rain, the first they had had in several weeks. As the first, fat drops spattered the speeding window, she ran her fingers up and down his thighs, leaned across and murmured something in his ear.

'Nearly there now,' he said, as if she were a five-year-old going on holiday. She was glad, she'd had quite a bit to drink with the meal and a couple of aperitifs beforehand, and she was starting to feel a little motion-sick. She wanted desperately to get back with Christopher and their nice warm bed but not perhaps with quite the urgency that the driver seemed to be showing, hurtling around bends and roundabouts in a way that made her stomach loop the loop.

She recognised the big Asda near where he lived. Thank God for that, she said to herself. She was aware of the dampness of her crotch.

They were making love even as they came up the steps off the street and he fumbled with the locks on his door. The ambience of the rooms – the pictures on the walls, the CDs and books that were scattered around the place, the sense of ordered disorder – seemed an extension of his own masculinity.

They went straight to the bedroom. He unzipped her white leather skirt and let it fall to the floor. She stepped out of it with elegant grace and his hungry eyes took in her long, stockinged legs, the silk suspender belt and the white lace pants. She was, unmistakably, dressed for sex. He crushed her against him, his need becoming more urgent with every second that passed.

Eyes closed, feeling she had to gain control over herself lest she go too far too soon, she breathed in the heady, intoxicating scent that arose from his skin, a mixture of expensive cologne and something deeper, muskier, so mysterious she scarcely knew if it were real.

She felt drunk – not because of the wine she had had but because of Christopher and of what she knew he meant to her and she meant to him. He covered her face and hair with tiny butterfly kisses but his groin was pressed against her, hard and urgent. He was excited by the very texture of her skin against his open mouth and wet, probing tongue.

For a couple of minutes or more his fingers delicately brushed across her skin, making it tingle, making her long for him. She could feel his erection against her belly, hard and urgent. She wanted his fingers there, his tongue, his naked penis. She wanted him to take control.

His fingertips moved down her body. She glanced around the room – it was okay, the curtains were drawn already, no one could see them. She felt reassured, and was able to relax. She parted her legs a little more, moved forward in her seat so that his fingers brushed against her pants.

He stroked her delicately, between her legs. He was looking straight into her eyes.

She was wearing delicate knickers of pure alabaster whiteness, with a deep lace trim. They were the kind of thing Christopher liked. She had been looking forward to him taking them off for her.

He sighed, and his fingers slid between her legs, against the moist lips of her pudenda, the palm of his hand cupping her pubic mound. She had to push herself up on tiptoe so he could reach her and then his middle finger was roving around her labia, probing between the folds, finding at last the entrance and slipping inside her. She had been really wet before but now she felt her juices beginning to flow, easing the passage of another finger and then another, until he had three fingers buried in her.

'Let's get into bed,' she heard herself say for form's sake but she wanted him to go on, to push on into her, to push her over the edge. With the ball of his thumb he found her clitoris and he massaged it with infinite gentleness, all the while his fingers twisting and sliding and turning inside her. It was so very different to the rough and uncompromising way most men had done it to her, even the more refined ones. Already she was pushing out to meet him, trying to force herself on to him, ready to be penetrated.

She could sense how fired up he was. She welcomed his immediacy, allowed him to melt into her until they were one burning, incandescent whole. With Christopher, she felt something was happening to her, something that had not happened between herself and a man for many years – but she didn't want to think about that now. Sometimes she had glimpsed it and it had evaporated before her eyes, before it had even reached tangibility. Now she knew it was for real, that he was for real, that she was for real. Even if she did make a living by pretending to be somebody she wasn't.

His tongue sought hers. The sensation of melting and merging became stronger. It was no longer the kind of heady, wine-fuelled rush they had felt in the restaurant, in the taxi, even on the stairs. Now their desire had become transcendent, their hearts were aflame.

She could feel the thud of hers beating fast and strong against his chest. Her breathing seemed to be short and ragged and she opened her eyes and looked at him, his lips half-parted, the eyes half-closed. She wanted him as she had never wanted a man in her life before.

Then she was looking straight into his eyes, going deeper and deeper until he felt his very soul was exposed to her. He knew what to do. Christopher always knew what to do.

He pressed her hard against him, his free hand roving over her breasts. He could feel how hard her nipples were, poking insolently through the lace of her bra, strong and sensitive.

'Do it now,' she breathed in his ear, but he sensed she was already a million miles away.

She tugged at his shirt and pulled it out of his trousers. She was busy with his buttons, pushing his shirt open, her hands roving over his chest. Then he was naked and they lay down on the bed together, their mouths together, legs and hips moving in unison, tongues probing, hands roving. She knew how much he liked the way her fingers touched the muscles of his stomach, seeking his erect and urgent penis.

He unhooked her brassiere and tossed it to one side. Then he stood back, his distended cock lolling there as she stepped out of her pants and unclipped her stockings. They, too, ended up on the floor, over a chair, under the bed, anywhere.

For a brief moment they looked into each other's eyes and then he was on top of her, feeling her breasts and nipples crushed against him, her thighs parting to reveal the warm slickness between them. She wanted him to take her body and plunder it, to take everything that she had.

Taking hold of her shoulders, he pressed her against the pillows and in that same moment she drew his penis deeper inside her. He thrust his pelvis downwards in a huge, hypnotic rhythm, oblivious to anything apart from his genital urges and the roar of blood in his ears. Tina's hips rose up to meet him, strong and confident, almost forcing him backwards, as if defying him and taunting him, threatening and maligning his masculinity through her own strength and prowess as a lover.

Her raw lust was more than he could take. He came inside her, powerfully and abundantly, as she called out his name and bit his shoulder hard enough to bruise. Sprawled underneath him, feeling the texture of her body against his naked skin, her head on his forearm, she realised his watch was right in front of his eyes.

No more than ten minutes, at most, had elapsed since they stepped out of the car. It surprised her.

They dozed. When she came around, extricating herself from a messy tangle of limbs and bedclothes, she realised they had been asleep for more than an hour.

Tina got out of bed, went to the bathroom. She felt as if

she was on fire, like she was someone else entirely. When she got back, he was sitting up in bed, the covers thrown back. His penis was erect again and he had sex in his eyes. She looked into them; they seemed bright and yet distant at the same time, dreamy. A half-smile played on his lips.

She knelt down on the bed, facing away from him, and parted her legs.

'Fuck my bum, Christopher,' she breathed. 'I love it when you do that.'

There was no need to speak. She indicated the jar of cream by the side of the bed. She gasped when he entered her.

It was another couple of hours before they finally got to sleep. She felt very damp and very sore and very happy, for the first time in years.

'I must say, Tina,' said Carole Chivers, 'you're the most convincing lookalike I've ever seen. I think you're even more like Scully than the real thing. What do you think, Paul?'

Paul Chivers nodded in agreement. 'Amazing,' he said. 'Wonderful. Brilliant.' The audience clapped like mad.

As she did the familiar pouting thing, Tina felt immensely flattered. She'd been watching Paul and Carole's afternoon chat show for years and now she was actually appearing on it, she could hardly believe her good fortune. She was there with Lesley from the agency, of course, and Leonie who did Marilyn, and their new Imran Khan lookalike, a dishy accountancy student called Ashwin.

The money from the telly, actually, wasn't that good, especially with three of them on the same budget. But it was great PR, said Lesley. It could be just the opportunity they needed.

Lesley had fielded a couple of tricky questions about the tabloid thing but she reckoned she'd got away with it. After all, they weren't doing anything illegal, she explained. It had exposed the tabloid press for what it was. People wanted to see film stars caught with their trousers down and that was the point of the operation. Every other paper apart from the *Daily Bleat* had printed FILM STAR'S LOVE NEST stories and they'd shown that the whole thing was a send-up. They were doing the public a favour. No, she didn't have any qualms.

In point of fact most of the questions had been directed at Leonie (mostly by Paul Chivers) and at Ashwin (by Carole). For all their experience – they'd had everyone from Tony Blair to one of the Great Train Robbers on the show – the husband-and-wife team seemed slightly fazed by Tina. But then people often were, like she really was an agent from the Department and not a thirty-two-year-old former traffic warden with two kids and a bastard of an estranged husband.

So she sat there in her dark linen suit, legs demurely crossed in the approved manner, and listened politely to the others' conversation. Close up like this, Paul and Carole looked older than she'd expected them to be. The make-up department and the lighting cameramen knew how to flatter them, it seemed. When she'd first seen them in the hospitality room, an hour before the show, she'd wondered whether they were lookalikes too, rather than the real thing.

Carole was very sexy, though, she had to admit that. She had this sensual quality about her but there was a delicacy, too, that you didn't really see on the telly. She was surprised how short she was. She'd been expecting someone about her own height but Carole was no more than about five-three, if that.

Paul, though, really was gorgeous. She found herself looking at that familiar profile as he asked Ashwin whether he, like Imran, harboured any political ambitions. Then, to her surprise, he turned to face her.

'What's the biggest difference being Agent Scully has made to your life?' he asked. She'd forgotten this question was in the script sequence they'd worked out in the hospitality room, but she'd answered it a hundred times and more in her busy double life.

'It's not the money, or the fame, or the recognition,' she said with practised ease. 'It's how it's made me aware of who I am. People only see this—' she indicated the hair, the make-up, the clothes '–but when I go home I change out of it and become myself again. I'm me, and my kids know me, and my mum and my boyfriend. They're the ones who're important, they don't think of me as the redhead from *The X Files*. Other people, the ones I meet in my work, they don't see that side of me so I value the privacy that it gives me.'

'Do the rest of you feel like that?' asked Carole.

'Tina's right,' broke in Leonie. 'I've met people in the lookalike business and they've started to believe they are that person, you know. They act all high and mighty and they can be incredibly rude sometimes. I won't mention any names, but I know one very well known lookalike and he is just famous for how awful he is to people. And yet, eighteen months ago this guy was a nobody, he worked in a shoe shop or something.'

'People can have difficulty adjusting,' said Lesley. 'We do have a counsellor on our team and she advises our clients on how to cope with the stresses of being someone else for five days a week, sometimes more. You must know what I mean, being on the TV every day and then you go home and you're yourselves again. You can't lose sight of that.'

'I try not to,' said Paul with a laugh.

'Actually,' Lesley went on, 'we do get asked if we can do a Paul and Carole.'

'Really?' said Carole, looking up from her clipboard. 'I'm not sure I'd want someone pretending to be me.'

'Oh yes. But we've never found anyone who quite fits the bill.'

'Maybe we should ask the viewers if they know someone,' said Paul, automatically knowing which camera to speak to. 'So if you've got a friend or a workmate who looks like me or Carole, why not drop us a line or phone or fax us.'

'I don't think I'd like to know what people think I look like,' said Carole, but she was smiling and Tina could tell she was really quite flattered by the idea.

A guy with a headset was making wind-up noises from the edge of the set. Paul took his cue expertly and with seamless grace steered the viewers into the story of the extraordinary talking tomato from Tadcaster.

'That was an ordeal, wasn't it?' said Ashwin when the show was over and they were back in the hospitality suite.

'I've faced worse, you know,' Tina replied, smiling. 'When I was a traffic warden, you really took shit from people. The bigger the car and the more expensive the suit, the worse they were. Compared with that, this was a doddle. Anyway, I'm going out for a smoke. I'm trying to cut them right down, but I think I deserve it.'

The hospitality area was no-smoking but she knew there was a room at the end of the corridor where smoking was allowed. The trouble was, once she'd negotiated three or four sets of double doors with springs that would have taxed a circus strongman, she realised the smoking room wasn't where she thought it was. She spotted a staircase that looked familiar, went down a flight and there it was – only it wasn't. She'd gatecrashed a meeting room where half a dozen execs in shirtsleeves were thrashing over audience ratings and schedule revisions. They looked up, thought they saw Agent Scully framed in the doorway and to a man stood to attention.

Feeling confused, she retraced her steps and found she was in another corridor entirely. God, this is ridiculous, she thought. Then a door opened and right towards her came Lesley and Leonie, with Paul and Carole.

'Hi, Tina!' cried Carole brightly. 'You look lost!'

'I am,' she said. 'I was looking for the smoking room.'

'Oh right, that's not hard to find. See that yellow door on the left there? That's our office. Go past there, take the next on the left and it's at the end of the corridor. You must have walked right past it. Actually, I could do with a ciggie myself. I might join you down there later.'

Actually, Tina had smoker's corner to herself, which was just as well given the reaction she might have provoked if some red-braces exec with his head in the clouds had walked in and found not The Cigarette Man but Scully herself in there stoking up on the B&Hs. 'Rilly, I only smoke them for the coupons,' she would say at moments like that in her best Californian, but people didn't seem to get the joke.

She looked out of the window. It was an amazing building all right, kind of inside out with all the plumbing and things exposed for all to see amid the struts and girders that held it all together. She was looking down on a kind of covered courtyard – didn't they call it an atrium or something? – where a fountain was playing and she could see right through the reception desk where they'd arrived a good three or four hours earlier. Why did everything on television take so long? she found herself wondering. The programmes were over in a flash but they seemed to spend ages just waiting around. Occasionally someone would come over and run through what was going to happen, and then Paul Chivers had appeared and chatted to them and they'd worked out what he and Carole were going to say. Then they'd waited another half hour or so before some other bright young thing with a clipboard came over and said that the new boy-band from Australia had cancelled and they'd had to reshuffle them and bring in the talking tomato, which was a story just breaking, so they'd be on sooner than they'd thought. Then everything was put back another half hour but they'd have more time, which meant Paul and Carole could run through some more chat lines with them – she'd thought it was all supposed to be spontaneous. By the time they actually hit the airwaves, she was pretty well exhausted.

Tina stubbed out her cigarette and made her way back down the corridor. Just up there on the left, wasn't it, past the yellow door? But it wasn't the staircase she'd thought it was – Tina had a lousy sense of direction, she knew, and she'd hated it when motorists used to ask her how to get to Cornhill or the Sun City Health Centre. There was no one about she could ask – the whole place seemed deserted. She retraced her steps back to the yellow door. There was no answer to her discreet tap but she could hear voices inside and so she pushed open the door and went in.

The sight that greeted her beggared description. Leonie, still in her full Marilyn Monroe outfit, was sprawled face down on a desk with her billowing skirts up around her waist. Paul Chivers was fucking her from behind, doggie-style, his Armani trousers round his ankles. His wife, meanwhile, was sitting in an armchair, legs apart, her dress hiked up to reveal stockings and black suspenders, while Lesley knelt in front of her with her face buried in her crotch and her tongue working overtime. A pair of black lace panties lay incongruously on a telephone. It was ringing but the people in the room sure as hell weren't answering.

'I'm sorry,' said Tina as she realised what she had

inadvertently stumbled upon. Paul glanced up at her and smiled but she was shocked into the next world.

'Come and join us,' he said, still thrusting in and out of the ever-willing Leonie. But Tina couldn't handle it. She nodded no, looking supremely cool like a good agent should, and made her way hurriedly back to the smoking room. She had two in quick succession and they made her feel vaguely nauseous. She'd been up since five-thirty and she'd not had anything to eat since. The whole thing was too awful for words. She felt a real innocent.

'Didn't you know?' asked Christopher over takeaway Chinese. 'Apparently they're real swingers.'

'I never knew,' replied Tina, back in familiar sweatshirt and leggings but still feeling slightly taken aback. 'How did you hear about it anyway? It's not the kind of thing you read in the TV pages.'

'Oh, some sales rep told me, you know how they talk. Apparently they go in for these wild parties and things, you know, partner-swapping and all that. They're pretty discreet about it but somebody knew somebody who knew somebody, that kind of thing.'

'But there was her and Lesley. I guessed Lesley was one, you know.'

'Sure, so had I. But Carole swings both ways, I gather, just like Charmayne. He doesn't, apparently, but they both had a thing going once with that weather girl, you know the one I mean.'

'The one you fancy?'

'Well, she is quite attractive. I love the way they jiggle when she waves her arms about.'

'Sexist brute.'

'It's not her fault if there's an area of high pressure approaching from the west, is it? She has to show where it's coming from.'

'I could see where Paul was coming from, right enough. He was doing it with Leoni right there in front of his wife.'

'She's the lecturer?'

'That's right. She teaches English at the Polytechnic

University. She's got a PhD, has written books.'

'Bloody hell. We didn't have teachers like that when I was a student. All the men looked like ex-hippies trying to be businessmen and the women had moustaches and wouldn't let you use words like "manual" and "management".'

'Why ever not?'

'Because it had "man" in it and that was a no-go area. Things like "spokesperson" I can handle but that was just getting ridiculous. Want any more of this fried rice?'

'Want any more of this champagne?' asked Lesley. 'I'd better go and get another bottle.'

Charmayne looked at her, eyes perhaps just a little blurry.

'I think I've had more than enough already. Yes, please.'

'How about you, Josh? Can you still work that magic calculator of yours?'

Josh was Lesley and Charmayne's tame accountant. It was the time of year when they went through the books. With most of his clients this was a desperately dull and pedantic process. Not so with the two principal partners in Seeing Double.

'I'll have what's left in that bottle, if that's all right.'

Charmayne poured it out into a flute of purest crystal.

'I could use some food too,' he said. 'This is taking longer than I thought. My head's starting to spin.'

'We've got a long way to go yet, sweetie. I'll go and get something from the fridge. Paté be all right for you? I've got some lovely Italian bread to help soak up the booze.'

With a surge of water and a wave Charmayne got out of the jacuzzi and wrapped a towel around her naked torso. When she got back, Josh and Lesley were fucking. Her lover didn't have sex with men very often – most people seemed to assume she was a hundred per cent lesbian but it wasn't true – Josh was one of the lucky ones.

Later, after still more champagne, they went through the last of the paperwork that Josh had brought with him. His laptop was in danger of disappearing beneath the waves as they splashed and sported but it was their way of paying him back for all the good work he did on their behalf. It was his idea and they were happy to go along with it.

The jacuzzi wasn't as big as they might have liked – now that they were rolling in it, they might look for something bigger and better – but somehow the three of them managed to squeeze in together, thigh against thigh, hip against hip. Josh made some pretence of soaping the two women but mostly it was just larking about, as he squeezed their breasts and put his stubby keypad-pressing fingers inside them.

'So you had it off with what's their names from the telly?' he said.

'Paul and Carole? Yeah, it was great. We're going to a party over at their place. I bet it's really wild, from what I've heard.'

'I'll never be able to watch their programme again,' he said, as he sucked Charmayne's elegantly proffered breast.

Somehow Charmayne managed to climb on to Josh's lap and spit herself on his cock. It was not an especially large one and, in the circumstances, with water slopping on the floor and Lesley laughing and trying to pour champagne, she was hardly aware of having it inside her. She bobbed up and down nevertheless, her breasts crushed against his hairy chest, and reassured him about how huge he was, and she thrust her nipples into his face and made him lick and suck them until they stood up hard and firm.

Slowly, Josh was slipping down the sides of the bath, the water up above his waist now as Charmayne rode on top of him, all three of them quite drunk.

'Hey, steady on!' cried Josh as Lesley tried to turn round in the water and succeeded only in forming a tidal wave that threatened to engulf them all. Charmayne laughed and squeezed his cock hard with her vaginal muscles. Slowly, with practised skill, she took control of the situation. She got him where she wanted him, lying flat in the bath so he could hardly move, and then she began to bob up and down on his cock, gently at first and then with increased vigour. She could sense him beginning to relax and to enjoy having her do all the work. Lesley was sprawled back drunkenly, sitting on Josh's calves, her legs splayed, her knees up against Charmayne's bottom cheeks. The whole situation was ridiculous but it was great fun and it saved on accountant's fees, that was sure enough.

Just when she had begun to despair of him, Josh gave a hoarse cry and grabbed hold of Charmayne's waist quite roughly. He buried his face between her breasts and then she felt his cock pulse three or four times in quick succession. Their bodies gently subsided into the surging water and his come slowly began to seep out of her.

Later, after they'd had something to eat, they'd signed their agreements. After that it was party time. Josh liked them both to wear high-heeled fetish boots and stockings while he had sex with them one after the other and then both at once. Although he didn't have the biggest cock the world had ever seen, he had more come in him than most. Six times a night was no trouble at all to him. He was good with his tongue, too, and his fingers. He also liked girls to dildo-fuck him.

Lesley and Charmayne climbed on to the bed together, naked apart from their boots and stockings. They could scarcely stop themselves from laughing at the expression of gleeful anticipation on the face of Josh, lying there on the cover, his dick sticking up like a flagpole and a glass of champagne balanced on his stomach, munching a bowl of hors d'oeuvres.

They kissed as he watched, breasts pressed together. The light in the bedroom was subdued and it was uncomfortably hot in there. Lesley was glad to be naked.

Slowly her hands travelled down Charmayne's body, running over the smooth curves of her ample hips, the dark cleft between her thighs, clad in smooth shiny leather that reached up almost to her pubis. Her skin was as smooth and soft as a baby's. Propped up on the pillow, eating and sipping champagne, Josh gurgled like a baby and called out ribald encouragement.

Lesley's tongue probed her lover's mouth, brushing against her teeth. Charmayne was cupping her buttocks, drawing her to her as they knelt on the bed facing each other. She was aware of how hard and erect her nipples were. She liked to perform like this, in front of an audience. It excited her.

They broke from their kiss.

126

'Pour me a glass of champagne, there's a love,' said Charmayne.

Josh rolled over and filled their glasses. His penis was still hard. Lesley knew no other man who could keep an erection going for so long. If he'd had a nine-inch dick, he could have been a porno star instead of an accountant, however successful he was at that – BMW 7-series, house in the Algarve, plenty of blue-chip clients. Because of his appetite and unusual ability, Josh almost always preferred to take his women in twos. Sometimes he'd go with hookers, although lately, he was showing more than an uncommon interest in Leonie in her Marilyn Monroe mode.

They sat on the bed, sipping the champagne. Refreshed, they redoubled their efforts. Lesley lay down on her back on the counterpane and parted her legs. Charmayne climbed on top of her. She could feel their pubic bushes as they brushed together. She pushed up her hips to meet her friend's gentle movements, her tongue flickering. Charmayne had an exquisitely furnished vagina, smooth and slick and tight. Sometimes Lesley would push two or three fingers inside her and wonder how it might feel to be a man in those circumstances, his cock pushed up inside her, squeezed exquisitely in the warm wet folds.

They rubbed against each other, both of them frantically excited by what they were doing. Their kisses hot and long and intense. They knew Josh was watching every movement, every ripple of muscle, with the intensity of a fox.

Still wearing her spike-heeled boots and with a large black vibrator inserted into her pussy, Charmayne slid down the bed and let her tongue make gentle ministrations to Lesley's body. Breasts, nipples, belly – all the time she was teasing her. They were doing all this largely for the benefit of Josh and yet Lesley found it impossible not to become aroused herself. It was one of the reasons why she was so good at what she did.

She glanced down at her lover's flowing blonde hair, spread out over her thighs. Oh God, if Charmayne licked her there she would come almost immediately, she knew it.

Slowly, inexorably, Charmayne began her work. Her tongue

probed Lesley's outer lips, giving up their secrets to her incessant searching. She could feel herself opening up like an oyster. Unconsciously her hands strayed on to her breasts and she caressed her nipples, each in turn, lush and raspberry pink. Her breasts were quite large and one of her most appealing features. Men liked to come off over her tits, because of their size. Josh certainly did.

There! She had it. Her delicate tongue-tip touch on Lesley's clitoris sent a shock wave coursing through her body. Charmayne's tongue was like a tiny finger, at once gentle and urgent. She always knew how to do it so delicately, not like a man, licking and lapping in that crude way they had about them, as if they'd never been weaned from the breast. Charmayne could do Lesley all night if she wanted to. Sometimes she did.

Charmayne's tongue was tracing little circles around Lesley's labia. The feeling was divine. She knew she shouldn't come – it would tire her, of that she was aware – but she couldn't stop herself. The feeling in her loins was too intense, the sense of abandonment that went running through her like quicksilver. She drew up her legs and felt those first flickerings of pleasure stirring deep within her, like a moth's wings fluttering in her womb.

The feeling grew, became more and more intense with every second that ticked by, and she abandoned herself to her senses, gasping out her pleasure even as she came in little purple rivulets of ecstasy, scarcely aware of Josh as he climbed up behind Charmayne and thrust his now rampant cock into her from behind, pumping so furiously that the bed shook.

When the tremblings had subsided she opened her eyes and winked at Charmayne. She was lying face down on Lesley's stomach while their accountant, red-faced and rampant, thrust inside her. His body was beaded with perspiration, glowing pink in the warm light of the room. On his face was an expression of perfect rapture.

With a hoarse cry he seized Charmayne's rump in both red hands and pushed as hard as he could inside her. At the same time, he took hold of the dildo and pushed it into Lesley's welcoming sheath. His eyes closed – was this pleasure or pain?

Lesley never ceased to marvel at how ridiculous most men looked at the moment of ecstasy. Charmayne lay on her stomach still, but on her face was an expression of perfect pleasure.

When he'd finally spunked her they flopped down in a heap on the bed. It was littered with empty bottles and party food. Dildoes and wispy panties lay in reckless abandonment among bowls of potato chips. One of Lesley's spike-heeled boots was peeping out from under a pillow. It looked like everyone had been having a good time.

Charmayne completed the final act of their arrangement. Josh must have been tiring now, for he took ages to come, sitting on the edge of the bed while Charmayne knelt before him and took his almost flaccid penis in her mouth. Her friend too was tired, Lesley could tell.

'Here,' she said at length, and knelt down beside them. Lesley was naked now. Charmayne still in her wickedly shiny spike-heeled boots. As Charmayne licked his prick-stem, Lesley's tongue played with his balls. Once or twice their tongues met. They squeezed hands. He wouldn't be long now, not under their double ministrations.

He had spent six times already in the past two hours and was in no hurry to come again. Lesley, however, was hungry, and sleepy, and had to go to London for a meeting in the morning. She wanted to flop down in her bed with Charmayne and sleep until noon.

Now the two women were sucking him together, their tongues curling wetly around him, the great purple dome of his prepuce beginning to seep the first signs of his seventh and final spend. It would be soon now, she knew. Her back felt stiff from the way she was kneeling but she stuck to her task. It was a challenge for her, sucking the last come out of a man. Most of them were. She was much better with women.

It was Charmayne who took him finally in her mouth. Lesley was sitting beside him on the bed now, frigging his cock up and down with increasing friction as he panted and muttered his lewd thoughts. Charmayne's tongue flickered in and out of her mouth, dabbing at the little oval eye at the end of his cock, while Lesley's soft and practised hand continued to move rhythmically up and down, squeezing him just the right way for him – for all men were different in the way they liked women to handle their cocks – and then finally she knew they were there.

Lesley quickly took hold of the vibrator and pushed it hard against Josh's arsehole, which parted to receive it. At the same moment she saw, actually saw, his balls contract and she let go with her hand as Charmayne took him fully in her mouth and his last, tired spurt of come came struggling out and dribbled into her mouth and down her throat.

Josh flopped down on the bed and seemed to pass out.

'There,' Charmayne said, swallowing hard and giving him a pat on the shoulder such as a child in the nursery might receive. 'That was nice, wasn't it?'

Eventually, when they could coax their aching muscles into making a move, all three of them rose to their feet, the business of the evening concluded. After Josh had gone, Lesley did the best she could to tidy the bedroom.

She found Charmayne in the en-suite bathroom. She was sucking her teeth vigorously, trying to dislodge something.

'I've got a pube stuck at the back of my throat,' she said. 'It's driving me mad.'

'It's an occupational hazard,' said Lesley, smiling. 'I wonder whose it is?'

Chapter Six

Her Majesty the Queen looked at her lobster canapé as though she had never seen such a thing in her life before and said in that familiar, slightly hesitant voice:

'Nero's Crown was never much good in the wet.'

The Duke of Edinburgh, mouth full of pastry, looked at her and raised his patrician eyebrows.

'He was always one for good, firm going. I saw him race at Ascot once and he was simply marvellous. But two weeks later, at Towcester, it rained before the start and he came nowhere. Didn't like the wet. He was out of Cottage Loaf and he never liked the wet either.'

'Didn't the Sheik of Qmpai buy him in the end?'

'Sirwali, I think. Yes, and he was very good out there. And in Hong Kong too. He went like the wind. But on a dull, rainy day at York or Liverpool, forget it. Money down the drain.'

'Who do you fancy for Sandown, then?'

The question was posed by a short, stocky man who looked like every inch the tabloid journalist he was. Her Majesty gave him a disdainful look but summoned every ounce of her composure to reply.

'It's difficult to say. They say the smart money will be on Two Can Play. But I'm not so sure.'

'The word is that Battery Boy could stand to clean up.'

'Battery Boy? At Sandown? He's never even had a finish there before.'

'So I hear. I know someone has an in at Kenny Maguire's yard, and they reckon he'll really do the business this time out.'

'Hmmmmmm. Still, you could be right. He looked very good at Newmarket, I have to say. Who's up?'

'Jackie Ramage. He rode him at Liverpool last week and came third behind Loose Suzie and My Boy Lollipop.'

'Jackie Ramage, eh?' said the Duke, dusting crumbs from his fingers and placing his hands behind his back in the familiar pose. 'Getting awfully thin, that boy. But he ran a good race at Exeter a couple of weeks back, I'm told. Came in third on Friar's Balsam on a hot day and that was pretty good. Friar's Balsam can be pretty lazy, you know. Who did you say you are?'

'The name's Rex Wagstaffe,' he said, handing him a card. 'I work for the *Daily Bleat*.'

'Oh, that rag,' said Her Majesty. 'We don't like that one at all, do we?'

The Duke was giving a passing blonde the benefit of his expert eye.

'What was that?' he said, slightly flustered. He had the mannerisms off pat but he spoke with a very slight trace of Lancashire in his voice, and no amount of coaxing by Charmayne could ever quite winkle it out of him.

'I said, we don't care greatly for the tabloid papers,' the Queen repeated, her vowels artificially plummy and rich.

The Duke glowered.

'Anyway, must dash,' said Rex Wagstaffe, taking the hint. 'I gotta see a man about a dog. But remember Battery Boy, all the same.'

'What a vulgar man,' said the Queen to no one in particular when he was out of earshot. 'As common as muck.'

At the other end of the marquee, Marilyn Monroe was explaining the basic tenets of chaos theory to a bemused-looking Ryan Giggs.

'Of course, it's old hat now in academic circles but I think it's becoming generally accepted in the mainstream.'

'Yeah, right,' said Ryan, looking none too sure. 'Where was it you said you worked?'

'At the Polytechnic University,' she replied. 'I teach the history and theory of drama. How about you?'

'I bin on the dole since I left school.'

'Does that make you feel frustrated? About not getting a job, I mean?'

'Not really,' he muttered. 'Me dad never had a job either. I think I'll go and get another beer.'

She let him go.

'Leonie!' a voice called out from the throng. It was Lesley.

'Lovely party, darling,' said Leonie, sipping chilled Chablis. 'And this wine is gorgeous.'

'Do you like the marquee? You don't think it's too big for the lawn?'

'No, not at all.'

'We've been looking for new houses, something a bit bigger. But I thought it would be nice to have the party here, rather than somewhere posh.'

'Oh, absolutely. But this is posh enough for me. I love garden parties and things.'

'So do I. I see you met Dave, by the way—'

'Dave?'

'Our Ryan Giggs. He's a very good likeness, isn't he? He was recommended.'

'Not much on the conversation front, though.'

'Well, what do you expect? He's a nice lad, though, and he looks the part. That's his natural hair, too, it doesn't need much styling. He gets a lot of bookings. He did three supermarkets last week alone but the big one's next month.'

'What's that?'

'A new chain of cut-price sports gear shops. Thirty of them, all over the country. There's a big launch in Manchester and we've let them have Dave for three grand. That's probably more than the real Ryan would get, which is a laugh.'

'Surely they'd go for the real thing, wouldn't they?'

'I don't know about that. It's getting so that sometimes people seem to prefer the lookalike to the real thing. I would bet you that our Michael Aspel's busier than himself these days.'

A big, big guy with round glasses came up. 'Can I get you ladies anything?' he said.

'Another glass of this would be nice,' said Leonie.

'Do you know each other?' asked Lesley.

'I know Leonie, of course,' said the newcomer. 'I'm Josh, Lesley's accountant.'

'Oh right,' said Leonie, offering her hand. 'We've not met, have we?'

'Not met, but I've spoken to you on the phone a couple of times.'

'That's right. The tax thing and outside earnings. That's all squared now, thank goodness.'

'Excellent. I'll get you that drink now. Your usual, Lesley?'

The party was Lesley and Charmayne's way of saying thank-you to all the people who now worked for Seeing Double. There were close on two hundred people there, in the marquee and milling around the garden. Most of the acts were there, and quite a few of the regular clients, and a few media types such as Rex Wagstaffe that were worth keeping in with. There were boyfriends, girlfriends, even a few children running in and out of the house.

Someone touched Lesley on the shoulder, very lightly. She turned and saw Tina. She'd been on holiday recently and her familiar red hair was much lighter – not permanently, Lesley hoped. She had bookings for her stretching clear through into next year.

'Hi,' said Tina. 'Look, I wonder if we could have a word sometime.'

'Sure. What about?'

'Well, it's just that I'm wondering how long I can cope with all this.'

Lesley's stomach suddenly felt like she'd dropped twenty floors in an express lift. *Oh, God, no,* she found herself thinking. *Don't tell me she's getting cold feet. She's one of our biggest acts.*

'I understand, I understand,' she heard herself saying. 'Do you want to come into the house and talk about it?'

'Well, I—'

'Or maybe we can have lunch – I'm having Monday, Tuesday and Wednesday off. Could we do that, have a nice heart-to-heart girl-to-girl?'

'Sure. Whatever.'

Someone called her name loudly. She turned round.

'Lesley, there's something wrong with the oven,' called

Charmayne. 'I can't get the door open and the salmon puffs are inside turning to a crisp.'

She glanced at Tina, her face full of frustration. 'I'll talk to you later,' she said, as friendly and sympathetic as she could, but by the time she'd got the kitchen sorted out, something else had cropped up. And then there was a call from Carole Chivers and in the end she forgot all about Tina and her problems.

Upstairs, in one of the bedrooms, one extremely famous film actor, who might better be identified as Sean, was pleasuring an equally famous television presenter, who could have been called Katy.

They'd met in the marquee, stuffing strawberries. They got talking. He said he had some coke and would she like to do a line or two with him. Katy liked nothing better than a line of coke and then to have some handsome stranger lick her cunt and then spunk all over her celebrated tits. She didn't say this to him at the time, of course. That came later.

They made their excuses and then, separately, disappeared upstairs to one of the bedrooms. She was in a state of elation, scarcely aware of the clothes and material possessions that were scattered around the place.

She watched like a hawk as he measured out the contents of the little phial on the glass top of the dressing table, did the necessary business with his little razor blade. Oh, she was ready for it, that familiar bitter taste, the tingling in the nostrils. She never did coke if she was going to public appearances but at weekends and at times when she was resting, the sky was the limit. The money she got from Seeing Double gave her a good lifestyle and she looked on her drug usage as a means of propelling herself still further into the realms of pleasure. Lately she'd even been doing a little smack. Coke made her confident but she craved the opiate's soft enveloping of her feelings and sensations, the new awareness of being swaddled in the softest down.

They took a couple of lines together, each silently lost for a few minutes in their own individual rapture. And then they looked at each other, and giggled like errant children. He really did think she was Katy, and she really did think he was Sean. In real life, he drove a delivery truck and she was a secretary – or had been, until she could afford to give it all up on the strength of what Josh said her projected earnings might be over the next eighteen months.

They tore on each other's clothes in their raging passion for one another, then fell naked into bed together, their bodies writhing and mingling on clean, fresh sheets, their spirits somewhere up among the clouds. He went into her straight away and she gasped as he took her, again and again as he pushed into her. She spread her legs out wide for him, aware of the way she gaped and the lewdness with which she welcomed him inside her. Oh, but he was strong. Her regular fuck, a sales manager called Gary, was an imaginative and inventive lover but this guy was all power and strength, a man more like a rutting animal. She knew it wasn't just the powder, even though it was good stuff and it hadn't cost her anything.

They paused, panting for breath. She had already come once, abandoning herself wildly to her passions. She could still feel the drug running through her veins, her senses beautifully numbed and distorted. She turned round on the crisp white sheets and looked at his dilated pupils.

'Put it up me again,' she murmured dreamily.

'Suck me first.'

She felt wild, reckless, daring. Maybe she might like him up her bum, even. What a way to screw a guy she'd only just met! Gary didn't fuck her there but she'd done it once or twice with other guys and kind of felt like she'd like to try it again, especially when she was as high as a kite. She slid down the bed, down his long and hairless torso. She could smell his arousal, the tangy smell of maleness that arose from his loins. With the bedclothes kicked roughly back she took hold of his penis in one hand and began to move her fingers up and down his shaft. She was fascinated by the way his foreskin drew back and forth under her expert touch, hiding and then revealing the domed purple glans with its mysterious little eye in the middle. What a strange shape the tip of a man's prick was, she reflected, looking at it with stoned eyes. It wasn't round at all, more a collection of curves and ridges going off in different directions. One way and another, she had looked at quite a few of them, as her mouth closed over the delicious plum-like morsel, and she didn't think any two of them were quite alike.

She swirled her tongue over him – how clean and fresh he tasted – and then took the whole length of his shaft into her mouth until she almost choked. He tried to push against her but she pushed back, bidding him resist. He might hurt her and she didn't want her pleasure to be over too soon.

Up and down she bobbed her head, lying there crouched over his body at the foot of the bed, and then she began to turn herself round, still with his penis in her mouth, so that her body was lying inverted by his side. Her pubic bush was now almost level with his face, pushing forwards at him in an unmistakable invitation. When she parted her legs for him, he showered her lower lips with kisses, his tongue flickering in and out until it found the little nibbly bud of her clitoris.

The shock was almost too much for her. His cock, in her own mouth, felt thick and potent. He licked her expertly, just the tip of his tongue at first. She loved the feeling of his tongue against her slick labia. It was ticklish though, it kept making her giggle. It made her feel jumpy and confused. She thought she was starting to lose it, maybe she shouldn't have had that last line, after all.

'Enough,' she sighed, and got – a little unsteadily – on to all fours on the bed, with her feet on the pillows. His cock lolled there, hugely erect after she had sucked him up to his full stiffness. His saliva and her own juices were running all over her pussy and arse.

He climbed up behind her, moistening the tip of his cock with his own spittle, though it was still wet from her ministrations. It was never difficult to get into her from this position. She liked to take control of her lovers, and soon she was arching round and with her hand steered his cock until it was pressed against her wet, slippery vaginal lips.

He fucked her hard and fast but it wasn't enough for her. She needed more, needed to slip over the edge, into that crazy borderland country where pain and pleasure met.

Expertly, she brought him to a standstill. His cock slipped out of her, still hugely erect.

'Guess where else I like it?' she breathed, her eyes closed, a smile on her lips.

His balls were bobbing lewdly against her backside. She took hold of his hand – how slippery it felt, slick from her secretions – and guided it until just the tip of a finger of it had brushed against her little rosebud.

He got the message.

'Now,' she said and he pushed his finger forward into her. Instantly she felt herself filled to repletion, that great distended cock in that tight little pussy of hers while her other channel was opening up for him right on cue. Everyone said how tight her slit was but her ass was something else. She liked guys to fuck her there, if she knew them well enough, and if she didn't she got them to finger her. If the guy was big and she wasn't wet enough, it hurt, sometimes, but not now, just a finger, the pure white cocaine loose in her veins making her reckless, and she urged him to give her another couple of fingers and to fuck her hard, too, right up her cunt. Gary's cock, she knew, would almost split her apart if she wasn't really wet and ready for him but this guy was a more reasonable size, better suited perhaps to her little games.

As he rocked backwards and forwards, his arms clasped around her waist, his cock rock hard up her pussy and his fingers probing her ass, she basked in the warm glow of the afternoon's triumphs. She'd met a guy who'd promised her a season in panto in Bournemouth, there were a couple of modelling assignments in the Caribbean at three grand a go, and any number of gigs doing fetes and parties and openings. She felt powerful and wild and free, fucking this man in the afternoon sunlight, her mind still reeling from the drug, an expensive new car parked outside. It sure as hell beat going down the Dog and Pheasant on a Saturday lunchtime before going with the lads to watch Rovers play.

Now it was time for pure fucking. His expertly probing fingers withdrew. They soon found her clitoris, and she parted her legs even wider to let him caress it, moving her towards orgasm even as he powered into her from behind, the gentleness of his fingers contrasting with the violence of his rearward attack – though to her it was all a part of the same sensation, inevitable and irresistible, her breasts swinging free as she pushed back against him, spreading herself right to the hilt on his cock even as she felt the little butterfly tremblings inside her building up into a steady fluttering roar of feeling. She was scarcely aware of the torrent of seed that came bursting out from his loins and into her violated body. Instead, she was lost in a dizzy kaleidoscope of her own senses, where pleasure and pain became one and nothing had any meaning any longer and everything was just feeling. The roaring rollercoaster of her sensations reached the very top of the track and then fell down and down and down, faster and faster, and the screams in her ears were her own.

Danny (Tom Cruise), Ashwin (Imran Khan), Tina (Scully) and Chantal (as herself) were deep in conversation.

'Do you ever get, you know, propositioned?' Chantal asked Ashwin. 'I know people come on strong to Danny sometimes.'

'There were a couple of gay guys came on to me only last week,' said Ashwin.

'When you were working?'

'Yeah. That cricket-club dinner near Cirencester. Very posh. A couple of guys came up to me in the gents and really gave me the hard sell.'

'What, they offered you money?'

'Not in so many words but it was obvious what they were about.'

'What did you do?' asked Chantal.

'Told 'em where to stuff it. Politely, of course. I ain't no bum boy. Mind you, if it had been a couple of girls, it would have been different!'

Everyone laughed.

'I've been offered money three or four times,' chipped in Tina.

They all looked at her. So far, she hadn't taken much part in the conversation. She seemed a bit distracted, like she wasn't really there with the rest of them.

'What kind of people?'

'Businessmen, the usual sort. The ones with money, think everything's for sale. One of them even had his wife with him.'

'Danny's had a few women after him, haven't you?' added Chantal. 'There was that woman up in Suffolk, for a start. And a lady who was very good with horses.'

They exchanged glances, very significant and knowing.

'One guy offered me five hundred pounds,' Tina went on, conveniently forgetting her lawyer who'd given her a thousand in cash. 'He was the chairman of a soft drinks company. I mean, I can understand people propositioning you but to offer you money outright, well that's a bit up front.'

'Maybe it's an occupational hazard.'

'I wouldn't say no if someone propositioned me,' a flat Lancashire accent proclaimed. It was Wally Gee, the greengrocer from Wigan who did the Duke of Edinburgh in his spare time and fancied himself as a bit of a lad, although he'd not see sixty again. 'Especially if they were offering me money. The trouble is, nothing's happened yet.'

He laughed, and went off to get himself a drink.

Tina caught sight of Lesley again but by the time she'd disentangled herself from the group she was with, she had disappeared. She really had to talk to her, she knew.

Pretending to be someone she wasn't was no real problem – actors and con artists did it every day of the week – but a couple of times recently people had thought she was the real person. Once she'd been photographed on the beach by some press guy while she and Christopher had sneaked a few days on Lanzarotte and the second time, coming back through Heathrow, it had been really embarrassing. More and more of the guys had come crowding round her and it had taken all of Christopher's force of personality – helped by a couple of security guards who came rushing over to see what all the fuss was about – to extricate her from the situation. She still had another week of her holiday to go – they were flying to Paris on Friday for a long weekend – and she'd had some tints put into her hair to make it lighter. It was all starting to get on top of her, that was why she needed to desperately speak to Lesley. She didn't want anything to spoil those few special days she had left with Christopher.

Rex Wagstaffe had what it took to be a tabloid journalist – a fevered imagination, a total disregard for people's feelings and a good pair of eyes. He saw things that others didn't. He had seen Katy and Sean sidling off, he saw the way Chantal was coming on to Danny, and it was making him randy. He wanted a slice of the action himself. In fact, he got more than he bargained for. A bit of a scoop, in fact.

He oiled over to a woman who had been on her own for a good part of the afternoon and, perhaps because of this, seemed to be a little the worse for drink.

It turned out she was the wife of the company's accountant and, as he quickly surmised, a bit of a goer. This was the first time she'd met most of them and she seemed edgy. A few lines of well-practised charm from Rex, though, seemed to calm her down. When she'd warmed up a little he gave her a few secondhand morsels of showbiz gossip, the sort that always got them interested.

'I wonder if Paul and Carole are coming?' he asked, quite casually.

'I don't know. It would be interesting to see what they're really like.'

Now Rex, like all the hacks, knew a thing or two about Paul and Carole. Of course, no one knew anything for definite about their supposed inclinations.

'Apparently Lesley and Charmayne are great chums with them these days, ever since they appeared on the show,' he said. 'They were at a party there last week.'

She smiled, dreamily and secretively.

'So I gather,' she said, a hint of mystery in her voice.

'I wonder if it's true, what you hear about them?' he asked very laid back.

'I wonder too,' she added. 'Josh, my husband, went and he says—'

But then she stopped. Rex, the professional, knew better than to pump her. So she maybe knew something, perhaps from the horse's mouth. He let the conversation drop, knowing he'd got himself a lead and could come back to it any time he liked. Instead, he concentrated on giving her a few more lines of the old well-practised chat and it worked like a dream.

It didn't take Rex long to steer her away from the crush in the marquee and down to the bottom of the garden, where there was a rundown summer house.

He tried to take her in his arms there and then but she resisted.

'They'll see us,' she hissed. 'From the house. There are people on the lawn, look.'

But something had stirred within her, triggered by his obvious interest in her.

The door of the summerhouse was open. No one could see them there.

Inside it was musty and damp. There was a broken plastic table, and some chairs. It didn't look as though anyone had used it in ages.

Rex had a monstrous erection already. The time for chat had passed. He kissed her neck, his hands cupping her breasts. They were firm and full, like ripe fruit. He could feel the nipples stiffening up under his touch. He put his hand under her skirt and felt her vagina warm and moist through her underwear. He rubbed it with the ball of his hand. She parted her legs for him.

She put her hands on his shoulders and looked up at him. He could smell the booze on her breath.

'It doesn't mean anything, this, you know,' she said. He was startled by the evident sincerity in her voice, in her look. What did she mean by those unexpected words?

What is she thinking? he found himself wondering. *That I want a relationship with her, or something? All I want is your cunt, love. I want to fuck you.* He was used to going with whores, could tell them a mile off. She was one too, underneath those expensive clothes.

'Of course,' he said. 'Let's just have a bit of fun, shall we? And no questions asked.'

The questioning look seemed to vanish from her eyes. He pushed an exploratory finger into her vagina, its folds wet and mysterious, welcoming him. She smiled at him. Her tongue traced a line along her lip. She knew what she wanted.

He knelt down and pushed up her skirt. She wore intricate panties of peach-coloured lace which he pulled down to her ankles. She stepped out of them with practised ease and then he pressed his face against the downy musk of her sex. Her pubic hair was surprisingly harsh and raspy, barely covering the mound. Like her whole body, it was heavily perfumed.

Tentatively he licked the outer lips of her vagina, breathing in the scent of her secretions. She tasted salty. It reminded him of a tart he knew, worked the Mayfair hotels, did it with rich Arabs – but he was on the free list. Funny how little details were so evocative like that. Sometimes he would go with his hooker right after she had been with another guy. Some women, he knew, liked to keep a man's semen inside them as long as possible, as a kind of keepsake or a talisman. Sometimes he would have sex with his regular tart soon after she had had another client and he was surprised by just how excited he became at the slippery wetness he encountered on such occasions. If he was pissed enough he'd lick her out, but usually he was content just to fuck in another guy's spunk. He half-wondered if this might mean he was queer or something but he didn't reckon so.

The moment passed. Quickly he found her clitoris and nibbled. Rex preferred cunnilingus to be superficial, concentrating on the outer nerve endings rather than the deeper, more hidden folds. He wasn't all that bothered about giving pleasure to the women he went with. He was in it for what he could get for himself and a well-licked woman would give him almost anything he wanted.

He sensed her enjoyment of what he was doing, though, just through the way she moved her hips, a slow undulating dance that brought her close to the brink of orgasm. Just when he thought she was about to fall off the edge of the world she pulled away from him.

'Do it up my arse,' she murmured dreamily. 'I like it up there, don't you? My husband fucks me up the bum all the time.'

This was a bit more like it, he said to himself. He liked a bit of arse every now and then. He kicked aside the chairs, pushed her face downwards on to the dusty table top. She sneezed. He hiked her dress up around her hips.

'Won't it be, you know, a bit tight?' he said hesitantly. 'We need some cream or something.'

'Just put it in a little way. You needn't push right in. It doesn't hurt that way.'

Her backside was spread out invitingly beneath him as he pulled up her dress even more, until her breasts were exposed. He admired the shapely globes of her cheeks, the pale whiteness of her flesh contrasting with the shimmering satin of her dress. It was ruffled up around her neck, exposing her wanton body.

He rubbed some spit over the end of his penis, then parted her arse cheeks. His heart was pounding heavily. He didn't even notice whether she was excited too. He could see her puckered little anus, the purple tip of his cock pressing against it. She took hold of his prick and guided it home.

'Wait till I tell you,' she breathed. His mind was on fire – buggery was always a delight for him, a pleasure to be indulged in only under auspicious circumstances. This was one of them. He felt almost ready to cream her there and then. He couldn't wait to tell the guys down the pub when he got back that he'd buggered a total stranger in a summer house and got a good lead on the Paul and Carole story out of her into the bargain.

'Okay,' she hissed and he pushed hard. After the initial pressure her sphincter gave way and then the tip of his cock was embedded inside her. She winced.

'God, don't go in any further,' she said, panting. His cock felt like it was being squeezed in a vice. Each time he moved, even if only slightly, she seemed to shudder beneath him. He looked down and saw that only a couple of inches were in her. But it was enough.

They stayed like that for some little while, scarcely moving together, just an occasional rippling movement of the hips. Then, gradually, he felt her muscles beginning to relax and he was able to slide further and further inside her. The pressure on the sensitive glans was incredible and he knew he couldn't hold out much longer.

She pushed her hand between her thighs and began to masturbate herself. He couldn't see what she was doing in any detail but her eyes were closed and her breathing became slower and more even. She began to rock back and forth a little, squeezing his cock with her sphincter muscles. Each minuscule movement served only to heighten his awareness and enhance his pleasure. She came with a half-sigh, half-grunt that was the trigger for his own climax. His seed boiled up out of him and afterwards he wanted to lie down and sleep. He reckoned it was the heat or the wine or something. He dumped her as soon as he decently could and went off to get some more booze. He'd already forgotten her name but he remembered that little hint about Paul and Carole right enough.

Carole Chivers wriggled her bum to get more comfortable and at that precise moment the guy she was with shot his come deep into her mouth. He'd already had her once in the missionary position and there wasn't all that much left in him, but it still came as a surprise and she swallowed it down as best she could. Guys got terribly uptight if you let them come in your mouth and then couldn't swallow it.

'Let's go and see what the others are doing, shall we?' she said with all the exemplary politeness of a Benenden girl as she got up off the bed. He was called Raoul or Ralph or something, she hadn't quite caught it and she wasn't that interested, but he'd done a couple of cola ads in the States and he looked gorgeous. That was enough for her.

She took off her ruined nylons and, still in her wickedly transparent teddy, did her face in the mirror. Raoul or Ralph or whoever he was pulled on his toreador pants and beat it, which was just as well because Carole could be a bit like a female spider after she'd been fucked.

It had been a good party. She'd also been in a threesome with a couple of friends from Los Angeles who were over and of course there were Lesley and Charmayne still to come – in the literal sense. Arrangements at the Chivers' private parties were always – and necessarily – a little informal but the intention was that she and Paul, after they'd had the fill of their other guests, would spend the night with the two lovelies from the agency. They'd driven over that afternoon with some interesting videos for them all to watch and both looked game for anything.

She brushed her hair the way her mother had taught her thirty-odd years ago, fifty on this side and fifty on that, and then she checked her mascara and put some lipstick on and studied the effects. Her tits looked good in the mirror, the teddy really showed them off to her best advantage, and it was cut high at the waist so her legs looked long. With spike-heeled shoes, she could have any man she wanted – or woman, for that matter – on their knees in a moment.

She went along the landing, paused at the top of the stairs. Leonie Swallow in full warpaint was coming up, hand in hand with a tall, black-haired guy. They exchanged glances. Carole could see the bulge in the guy's tight jeans. She quite fancied him herself. Maybe they could get something going once Leonie had finished with him.

She must have been gone with the guy from the cola ad for longer than she thought because when she came back to the room where most of the others were everyone seemed to have changed partners. Chrissie McSweeney, arguably the most lusted-after of all TV weather girls, had taken her top off and was sitting there on the sofa with her luscious melon breasts upheld by a black Wonderbra. Paul was standing over her pumping furiously on his dick and then, even as Carole watched he shot a big trail of come all over her exaggerated bosom.

The sight made Carole break out in a hot flush. She went and got herself a drink, took a joint that someone offered her, blew out smoke. The next thing was, Chrissie's partner Bill Davidson – a bright guy who had a company that designed computer games – was standing next to her, close right in her personal space, and suddenly she wanted him – like she really wanted him. She looked across at Chrissie who smiled as if to say, yes I know, and Carole didn't need to ask Bill how he was feeling. Their parties were notoriously wild but this time everyone seemed to have really loosened up. It seemed perfectly normal to have beautiful girls walking round the room in expensive lingerie but people usually – if not always – went upstairs to suck and fuck. Not tonight, though.

She stubbed out the joint – it was too strong, it was making her head spin – and she let Bill take her in his arms there and then, right there in her living room with her husband watching. She loved it when it got like this, when it was like the kind of fantasy you only read about in paperback novels and top-shelf magazines.

She and Bill flopped down into a big easy chair, tongue seeking tongue. His hands were working feverishly all over her black teddy. Carole had always been given to understand by Chrissie that Bill was pretty well hung but nothing could have prepared her for the sight that greeted her when she finally got it out. Bill's dick must have been a good eight or nine inches long and very thick.

'Let me take a suck on that,' she heard herself murmur. As she went down on him, she glanced across the room and she could see Charmayne from the agency with some guy whose name she hadn't caught. He had pushed her face forward over a low sofa and pulled her dress up over her hips and was tugging away at the white satin panties that Paul'd given her. She was wearing the matching brassiere as well, to get him excited later, when she and Lesley and Paul and Carole were alone together. Carole always liked to wear nice lingerie too and Paul certainly wasn't complaining.

Carole sucked him up to super-hardness and then lay down on the antique kelim rug in front of the fireplace. Bill felt real good as he slid into her and then she saw the guy she'd just been upstairs with come off all over Chrissie's 38Ds again, and she could see the come running down over the black lace bra she wore. Then Paul came over, lay down on the sofa next to Charmayne and started kissing her, and then Chrissie came over too and took off her skirt and her brassiere and her panties and knelt down so she could suck Paul's dick. Even though, in the natural course of events, it normally took him a good twenty minutes or so to get hard again after they'd done it, Chrissie seemed to have some kind of gift when it came to blowing a guy and in the blink of an eye Paul's dick was stiff once more.

Carole reached out and touched Charmayne's ample breasts, could feel the sperm on them. *Christ*, she thought, *this is just totally out of this world. Pinch me, someone, I'm dreaming. Better still, fuck me.*

Bill was pushing into her real hard from behind and she knew he would come soon, as she bucked hard against him and felt that familiar tingling from deep in her loins. A wonderful sense of abandonment seemed to fill her and with it, a sense that this was all okay. Sometimes she'd done things that had made her feel guilty, like when she first started doing drugs in a regular way or when she and Paul had first started swinging, at first with just another woman for company but later with couples too, but this just felt terrific. These were people you had supper with every few weeks, after all. It wasn't as though you were being fucked by a total stranger. She'd never even realised until now how sexually attractive she found Bill Davidson, until tonight.

Paul and Chrissie, both of them naked now, were laying beside them on the exquisite rug in front of the fireplace, their arms and hands roving every which way, and then Chrissie was straddling him, guiding his dick into her. Raoul had got Paul's video camera out – they had to be careful about things like that, for obvious reasons – and was prowling around the room shooting off footage of Chrissie fucking Paul and Bill fucking Carole, and then Charmayne licking Lesley out while she waited for a spare dick. *Don't get your come on the rug*, she hissed to Paul as he pumped away. *That rug's worth three grand, remember.*

Carole was almost there when Bill came off and then Raoul or whatever his name was took over, fucking straight into another man's spunk like it was the kind of thing he did every day. Carole's cutely pointed tits were spilling out of her brassiere and Bill was cupping them and doing wondrous things to her nipples but the best thing was that big fat dick of Raoul's stuck in her right up to the hilt. Fired up by what Bill had been doing to her, she came almost immediately Raoul shoved that big luscious thick thing of his right up into her and now she was going to come again. She could see Chrissie leaning forward with her big melon breasts only an inch or so from her husband's probing tongue and, with a voluptuous thrill that always came over her when she had sex with another woman, Carole moved over and began to suck the other one herself.

The thought of her tonguing one of Chrissie's gorgeous strawberry nipples while Paul licked the other brought on a shimmering wave of pleasure and then she was riding the wild surf again, away in a world of her own, free and unbound.

Later, in bed, just the two of them with Lesley and Charmayne, the feeling continued. Even as Paul climbed on top of her she seemed to be on the brink of perpetual orgasm. He pushed inside her and she felt as if she were peeling herself open, raw and urgent and slick with desire. And the pleasure of it all, this feeling of abandonment that she felt, the letting go. It wasn't any kind of big cataclysmic deal, it all seemed so natural to her.

The guys she had had sex with that evening and the girls too, their names were almost an irrelevance, Raoul or whatever his name was, his girlfriend Sophie, if that's what it was, who had turned up late when the party was almost over, they were now forgotten already, like so much superfluous and repetitive background material that she could comfortably shed. People came on their show and remembered it all their lives – she'd forgotten them half an hour later. All she was aware of was the wave of feeling that swept over her, the pulsing power of her own body and the tingling of her nerve ends. She felt free, lifted up and away from conscious thought. There was no specific detail in this love-making, no tongue seeking nipple, no hand on penis, no mouth upon mouth, chest upon chest, even when she sensed that Lesley and Charmayne were there with them too, the four of them in that huge bed.

It was all there for her, of course, and yet not there. Everything was a part of something so much bigger, something that she rushed out to greet as others wanted to greet the millennium or the second coming, her arms metaphorically open wide and her legs wider still, as her husband slammed into her, his body slick with sweat and effort as she mauled his back and bit his shoulders and thrust her pelvis up to meet his thrusting physicality, and the two girls tonguing her where it mattered and then his semen swelling up hot and urgent as though she could sense it a long way off, riding on the crest of her own shattering orgasm, an orgasm that wasn't an orgasm at all but a piercing entry into light and a new realm of being, beyond rational thought and analysis and muscle control and all the cloying instruments of consciousness from which, momentarily and majestically, she had finally managed to free herself.

Whether it had all been down to the drugs or whatever Carole didn't know but in the morning, though, it all seemed curiously empty. In the course of the evening she had had five or six lovers of either sex and yet she didn't feel truly satisfied, not even when both Charmayne and Lesley had made love to her together. She had done almost everything that a woman of her age and standing could have done and yet she was jaded, as if she needed to experience new thrills, to venture ever further into the black reaches of her imagination.

The answer came in a conversation begun by Charmayne and finished, over bacon and muffins, the following morning with Lesley. She knew the lookalikes must get propositioned and Leonie, pretty well tanked up on Paul's Chateau Yquem at an earlier soirée of theirs, had kind of hinted that she didn't always say no out of hand.

'We don't encourage it,' said Lesley. 'I mean, we're totally legit as a company. Anything that smacks of prostitution, even escort agency stuff, just isn't our scene. What the girls and boys get up to in their spare time is up to them but when they're working for us and pretending to be whoever it might be, then they keep their legs firmly crossed.'

'It's in the contracts,' added Charmayne. 'Anything they do in relation to that character has to be done with our approval.'

'That's right,' went on Lesley. 'What they do with their boyfriend or girlfriend is fine but if it's for money, we have to give our say-so. And if there's any jiggery-pokery going on, the answer's no, every time. We've got to cover ourselves.'

'But what about Leonie, that time she was over here? That strip act she did in the kitchen was sensational. There was nothing like that in *Gentlemen Prefer Blondes*, especially not with my best marble rolling pin.'

'That was different. That was just for us and besides, we were here. You wouldn't get Carly Morrissey doing that, I can tell you, but that's Leonie for you.'

Carly was the best of the Carole Chivers lookalikes to have come forward after the TV appearance. She looked the part but she was a bit of a cold fish and certainly not a party animal. She worked for the social services in Bishop Auckland and they'd teamed her up with a computer salesman from Chester who did a plausible Paul but was equally lacking in the personality stakes. They'd had quite a few bookings at first but when people got wind of what a pair of wet weeks they were, the engagements had started to tail off. In fact, Lesley was already thinking of dropping them from the agency.

'She was a bit of a dead loss, really, wasn't she?' said Carole of her double. 'I don't mind. Maybe our ratings are falling, I don't know.'

'I'm sure they're not. I think it's just that Carly might look the part but there's nothing more to it than that. No personality.'

'And yet, you know, they got asked loads of times if they'd, you know, stay around afterwards,' said Lesley.

'You didn't tell me that,' said Charmayne.

'Didn't I? Perhaps it didn't seem to matter. But no, you and Paul should be flattered. I mean, they never did anything, but the offer was always there.'

'Who's making the offer,' asked Carole, intrigued. 'And how do they make it?'

'Oh, you know, just the usual things – looks, gestures, nothing overt but enough so you know what's going on. Body language too, that kind of thing. It's the same for everyone, Leonie, Tina, Danny – all of them. They get these vibes off people. A lot of them are just fans, you know, people who've turned up. I know for a fact that Danny had it off with this absolutely gorgeous woman at a wedding reception once, but don't ever tell him that I know 'cos he thinks he got away with it and he's a nice bloke. And Leonie too, she gets some really dishy blokes coming up to her with the big come-on.'

'Big hard-on too, I should imagine,' said Carole, and they all cracked up. Amid the laughter, though, a seed had been sown.

'I quit,' said Tina, quite suddenly, that same morning.

She and Christopher were sitting up in bed in their hotel in Paris, drinking tea.

'You what?' he said, the *Sunday Times* open on his lap at the sports pages.

'I'm quitting.'

'Quitting what?'

'This bloody lookalike business.'

'It doesn't surprise me. I could tell you weren't happy.'

'It's nothing to do with happy, not really. I just feel it's taking over my life.'

'An identity crisis? Being someone you're not?'

'No, not that. Well, not really. Actually, I quite like playing at being someone else and I've got used to people thinking that's who I really am.'

'So what is it?'

'It doesn't leave me any time or space to be myself. Sometimes I only get to see the kids every other day. The thing at Heathrow was bad enough but last night was the absolute limit.'

Christopher understood. They'd been out together to a fashionable restaurant in the XIXeme arrondisement, very discreet. In a way, it was inviting risk, going to a place like that, but they'd been recommended by one of Christopher's friends and reservations were hard to come by. The food, of course, had been absolutely fantastic, it practically fell apart without the need for knives, and Christopher worked his way around the wine list with aplomb.

She was feeling excited as she always did, eating out with someone she loved, with the prospect of a long night of pleasure ahead. She almost felt herself to be at her happiest in such a situation. England seemed so far away at that moment, and all the pressures. She still couldn't believe who she was and where she was. Two years ago, and it would have been an Italian place and Ray getting steadily more and more pissed on the house red.

It wasn't like that tonight. Nothing in her life was quite the same as it had been. She felt at times to be strangely alienated from herself.

They didn't talk much through the course of the meal. But they were in constant contact all the same, through look and gesture and touch and all the other hundred and one subtle ways in which people who are in love can communicate with one another.

And that was when somebody'd seen her – even though Tina was dressed entirely as herself, with her red hair restored to its full coppery glory – and fingers had pointed and the next thing she'd known there were cameramen all over the place, and the maitre d' was trying not to shoo them away but to shoo them towards her, as if having a 'celebrity' would instantly confer even more status on his Michelin four-star establishment.

The meal, of course, was ruined. They just couldn't settle after that and what made things even worse was that Christopher had, in his jacket pocket, an exquisite diamond solitaire with which he was, that very evening, hoping to propose marriage. As soon as they could, they made their way out of the restaurant and back to their hotel.

It was a fine evening and they decided not to take a taxi. In the confusion brought about by the altercation, they found themselves walking by the Seine. Christopher felt angry over the incident – he felt he could have done more to protect his girlfriend but, faced with the determination and brute rudeness of the photographers, what could he do? It was hardly their fault, either, that she looked so like the character from whose identity she made a tidy living. Maybe they shouldn't have gone to the kind of place where Hollywood stars might conceivably show up – he'd noticed signed photographs of Sharon Stone and Nicole Kidman in the bar – but on the other hand, why should Tina's looks bar her from living her own life, the way she wanted to? She shouldn't have to go out in dark glasses with her hair in a headscarf, like Princess Margaret on a bad day.

They walked along in near silence, staring out at the bright lights twinkling on the black waters.

On a deserted stretch of the promenade, as far as possible from the nearest street light, they sat in shadow on a bench. He had his arm around her, drew her close. He realised she was crying softly.

'You want to talk about it?' he said.

'It gets to me sometimes,' she said at length. 'Sometimes it's fine, you know the money and the fun and everything, and then you get something like this. I used to think I could handle it, but I'm not so sure.'

'How is it when you're working?'

'It's fine, usually. I'm okay then, I'm doing a job and I know who I am. It's like being an actress or something. I come home and take the make-up off and I'm fine.'

She took a tissue from her evening bag and blew.

'I'm back being myself then. That's no problem. Sometimes I'm myself and sometimes I'm her. I can draw a line, I know what's going on.'

'So what's the problem?'

'Things like tonight are the problem.'

'It's only one incident.'

'No it isn't. There've been other times. At the airport the other week, and in Lanzarotte. But even when it was the small-time stuff, when I worked with that crummy agency, you'd get guys coming on to you with all their fantasies.'

'That's another issue, though.'

'Well it is, but it's just one more thing. But what gets to me is when the two get mixed up, when people come crashing in on my real life like they did tonight. It's awful.'

She was thinking of the time Ray had burst into her home. Something like that could happen again at any time and it wouldn't necessarily be Ray.

'You know, I'm there being me and then there are people all around thinking I'm someone else. One time I was shopping for clothes and this woman asked me for my autograph. I told her I wasn't really who she thought I was and she was like really angry with me, like she was asking me what right did I have to be someone else. What was I doing pretending to be someone else.'

'It must be tough, I know. But everyone makes mistakes.'

'What kind of mistakes?'

'A guy came up to me a couple of weeks back and said he was sure he knew my face, reckoned he was at school with me.'

'Were you?'

'No. I'd never seen him before in my life. I was in a pub with some of the guys after work. I'd seen this guy looking at me and then, when I went to buy a round, he asked me. But he was fine about it.'

'Okay, I see that, but it's different, isn't it? No one's forcing you to be that person, the one he thinks you are. But people are forcing me to be someone I'm not. It happens all the time, but I just want to be me.'

He held her close. She was calmer now, the sniffing ceased. He realised how beautiful she looked in the moonlight.

'Besides,' she said, 'I don't even like the bloody programme.'

'You never said that before.'

'I'm saying it now. Why can't I be somebody in my own right?'

'You are to me.'

'What?'

'A person in her own right.'

'Yes, but you have fantasies too, don't you?'

'Sure, but not often. And you encouraged me, at first.'

'That time when we ate out and we got the mini-cab home?'

'Yes. That was one time.'

'More than one time. But you enjoyed it?'

'Sure I did. Didn't you?'

'I guess I did. But not all the time.'

'That's it, isn't it? Every now and then is fine, but not all the time.'

'I know what you mean. Sometimes I like getting really glammed up, you know, even when we're staying in, and other times I just want to slop around in jeans.'

'Which one is tonight?'

'Pretty glam.'

He took her in his arms there and then, kissed her long and deep. They laughed a lot about nothing in particular. People passed by on the riverside, looking at this sexy couple kissing and laughing in the darkness, but they didn't care any longer.

She remembered the time as a sixteen-year-old when, for a bet, she'd snogged Gary Rose for a full ten minutes without opening her eyes. She noticed the time on the clock tower behind them and then she drew Christopher to her, her tongue seeking his, an endless liquid movement.

When she opened her eyes again, she'd missed her record by a good seven minutes. She smiled to herself.

A movement made her look round. There were guys with cameras all around her. She'd scarcely time to pull her skirt down over her thighs before the flashes started to go off, turning the Paris night into day.

That was it for Tina. The last straw.

Chapter Seven

'Rip my panties, you bastard!'

It was a line straight out of a porno movie, though she'd growled it with her own lips. But Katryn Davies still couldn't believe they were her own words or her own lips or her own panties, nor who was doing the ripping. It was a long story.

Katryn's boyfriend Tom had told her about this guy he knew down the pub – she reckoned it was Cloughie, but he wasn't saying – who had got hold of this video that was pretty hot stuff.

So hot, in fact, that it wasn't one of your regular releases brought in from Holland or Denmark, and certainly not the kind of thing you could rent from the video shop. It was a copy of a copy of a copy, until it had been copied so much it was like watching people fucking through a dirty window while snowflakes whipped the air.

There were movies about people fucking, and there were movies about people *fucking*. This was one of the latter. The way Tom described it, there had never been anything like it in the history of motion pictures. If it's so bloody good, she had said to him over a bottle of Rolling Rock, then why not get hold of it and we can see if what your mate says is true.

But Tom said that wasn't the point. The guy his mate had borrowed it off wanted it back and so his mate, Cloughie or whoever, reckoned he'd like a copy to keep. But he couldn't get the video he'd borrowed off his mam to hook up with the one he had to do a tape-to-tape, which was a bugger.

Then he hit on an idea. His brother was away (Cloughie had a brother who was in the army, thought Katryn, he was always coming and going so that narrows down the field considerably) and he knew he had a videocam he'd won in a raffle that he could borrow.

So he got hold of the videocam and set it up on a tripod all professional-like in front of the TV, and then he'd played the porno epic and filmed it off the screen. He was feeling pretty chuffed with himself and all the more so when he cottoned on to the fact that, if he hung on to the original and handed back the copy he'd just made, his mate would probably be none the wiser while he'd have something that was 100% better in terms of technical quality. This mate he'd borrowed it off, he was a boozer and half-blind anyway and he'd never notice the difference but he (who's he? said Katryn. The mate who borrowed the fucking video, said Tom) had an eye for screen graphics, on account of all the arcade games he liked to play.

So he took the copy down to the pub and gave it back to the guy and they had a few beers together and then he hoofs it back home to watch his video all over again. His mate, meanwhile, drops in at the offie to get a few more cans and while he's there he meets up with some more of his mates and he says, come back to my place, I got this killer video you gotta see.

So they went back to his place and put the video on and there for all the world to see is an hour and a half of his other mate sprawled on the sofa wanking himself off, reflected in the TV screen and faithfully recorded by his brother's video camera. You couldn't hardly see the action on the screen at all, all you could see clearly was the reflection of this guy sitting in his living room with his dick sticking out and his fist flying up and down, up and down.

They never let on, Tom had said. But it was a fucking laugh, all the same.

It made Katryn feel slightly guilty. Every other Wednesday and Thursday she did a late shift at the supermarket which meant she had time to watch Paul and Carole do their afternoon TV show. Katryn had had the hots for Paul for years, she only really went out with Tom because he had the same kind of eyes and hair, and sometimes he would pretend to be Paul when they were fucking and she would go absolutely crazy, would suck him off and let him fuck her in the bum and all kinds of things she wouldn't normally do when he was just himself. Actually she reckoned Tom had the hots for Carole but he wasn't letting on, even though she wouldn't have minded because she felt Carole was very fanciable with her short skirts and big tits and nice blonde hair. She would have quite liked Tom to pretend she was Carole while he was screwing her but he wasn't imaginative like that, not like her.

So on a Wednesday or Thursday if her mam wasn't around, Katryn would watch the big telly in the living room and play with herself and things. Sometimes she wouldn't wear knickers and she'd pull up her skirt and let him see it all, nice split beaver with a thick dark snatch of fur, all ripe and juicy for him. She could bring herself off three or four times in the course of one show and it was hard sometimes to get into her overall and go and do another shift behind the till at the local Kwikmart in Cwmbargoed.

The show was off the air – or at least Paul and Carole were, they were the only bit the mattered – for the next six weeks for their summer break. Someone else was doing the programme in their place and without her regular fix, Katryn felt deprived instead of depraved. But this morning, oh what excitement! Okay, it wasn't the real Paul and Carole Chivers who were coming to open the new vacuum cleaner factory in Llanwelty but it was the next best thing, a pair of lookalikes hired by an enterprising management from an agency in London or Birmingham or somewhere. Katryn's friend Betheny worked as secretary to the works manager there and she had fixed things so Katryn could be smuggled in. It was meant to be employees and invited guests only but Betheny had snaffled a couple of invites and so Katryn was in.

She had worn her new top bought the weekend before in Cardiff especially for the big occasion, very expensive but almost completely see-through in cream, and under it a white underwired bra deliberately chosen for being a size too small so her generous 38Cs all but spilled out of its frothy lace, and then a pair of incredibly tight black trousers that cut right up the crotch and hugged her bum so she could only wear a G-string under it, normal pants would show and if there was anything Katryn hated it was a VPL.

And when she saw him, oh bliss. Of course he was only a lookalike, the same as Carole, but he really did look like him except he seemed a bit older close to and he wasn't as tall as she'd imagined. Carole too was a bit shorter and a bit plumper, too, especially around the bum. But you didn't see her bum on television.

You didn't see Paul's dick either. She hoped it was like his double's, though, because it was huge.

The Paul and Carole lookalikes had done the opening ceremony really well – they even spoke a lot like them – and then they'd done a quick tour of the factory with a chat with selected employees and there was the reception afterwards and it was there that Katryn made her move. It didn't take her long to get up close to him – crowds part remarkably quickly for a tall, pretty girl with blonde hair and big tits in a see-through blouse – and in a surprisingly short space of time she'd smuggled him into the ladies' lavvy and was giving him a blow-job.

'Oh Paul, Paul, Paul,' she murmured between slurps. She knew it wasn't him, of course, but she didn't let a little detail like that spoil her fun. She could imagine what she wanted to imagine and having a real live spunky dick to suck on was a lot better than dreaming in front of the TV.

She took him deep into her mouth and washed her tongue around the big domed helmet, licked around the ridge behind his glans. He was moving his hips rhythmically as she did so, gently fucking her in her mouth, and she'd have been happy for him to have come off but she wanted to have him inside her as well.

So she sucked and sucked and sucked and then she unbuttoned her top so that her breasts were exposed in their tiny half cups, and then she pressed her warm flesh against his hard, hot dick, and she could hear him gasp. Men liked Katryn's nice big titties and this guy was no exception. She didn't even know his real name – Paul Chivers was good enough for her.

She knew they'd have to be quick or he'd be missed, but at

the same time she wanted to give him the works or at least the concert version of her full repertoire, which meant the blow-job followed by tit-fucking followed by having that nice meaty cock stuffed right up her. So she rubbed his cock between her tits – she hoped he wouldn't come off, it would be embarrassing to have spunk stains all down the front of her near-transparent blouse – and then she eased one succulent breast out of her lacy bra and pressed a hard, raspberry nipple against his dick.

She could hear him breathing all the more heavily and he was running his fingers through her hair like he was going to start pulling it out in handfuls. She put her arms round his hips – he had a lovely bum on him, whoever he was – and drew him too her, crushing his cock in pneumatic passion and really squirming those sensational tits against him, his bollocks hanging firm and heavy in her cleavage, the smell of male musk in her nostrils as she took him in her mouth again for one last time.

And then she was up on her feet and snogging him, her tongue all over the place, and she was busy with her tight black pants at the same time, trying to get them down over her thighs. In the end she managed it, though not without a certain difficulty, and they broke from their clench and she stood before him in just her wispy white G-string and her tits falling out of her blouse, which mercifully was non-iron and didn't show the creasing everything else had taken.

He looked at her eye to eye and she could see the desire there, the raw naked man lust that she had so often coveted, so often imagined on the sofa in front of the television show. He was still in his dark suit with his trousers loosened and his dick sticking out between his shirt tails – she thought men looked incredibly sexy like that. He had his hands on her hips and they were pressed together so she could feel his erection against her body, the tip of his cock still wet from the sucking she'd given him.

'Rip my panties, you bastard!' she growled. This had always been a part of the fantasy for her.

He reached out, grasped the tiny wisp of white lace, and tore it from her body. Then his hands were between her legs and she parted them slightly as he cupped her, pressing her warm lips against his palm. He got the hint and inserted one, then two, then three fingers into her and she was bobbing up and down against him while, with her free hand, she frigged his big sexy cock and wished he'd push it into her.

She knew he found her wetness exciting because he was kissing her like crazy now and then he kind of scooped her up with one hand cupping each of her delicious buttocks, and pulled her on to him, still standing up, how strong he was to do that like in the movies, and she somehow managed to reach down and guide his dick home. She wrapped her legs around him and he leaned against the cubicle wall for support and pumped up into her as she pushed down, as hard as she could without causing them both to overbalance.

Oh Christ, it was too wonderful for words, being held like that with her arse spread wide and his big thick cock spearing her right to the hilt. She knew she couldn't hold on long and neither could he. With a hoarse cry, he thrust right up into her and sent a half-dozen or more thick creamy jets of spunk into her, right at the moment when a tidal wave of pleasure swept over her. She both felt it and heard it, and then she realised that she'd flushed the loo with her foot, and then she came back to earth.

They disengaged, not without a certain difficulty – screwing is hard in a toilet barely three feet square – and he struggled back into his trousers while she struggled back into hers and did up her top, fingers trembling, noticing her ruined panties lying on the floor. She kicked them behind the pedestal, out of sight.

Luckily there wasn't anyone else in the ladies' room as they slipped out and made their way back to the reception. Katryn checked her watch – they'd only been gone ten minutes so they could hardly have been missed. The Carole Chivers clone was standing right inside the door, clutching a glass of white wine in one hand and a canapé in the other.

'Hello darling,' she said as her lookalike husband joined her, her eyes twinkling, a smile on her lips. 'You've been gone a long time.'

Her gaze rested for a second or two on Katryn and – before

she disappeared into the throng – Katryn could have sworn that she not only knew what her make-believe husband had been up to but, in some strange way, actually approved.

'Don't you think,' said Lesley as she adjusted the harness on the black dildo she had strapped to her hips, 'that you're running a bit of a risk?'

Carole couldn't answer because she had one of her nylon stockings pushed into her mouth but her eyes, just visible through the leather mask she wore, suggested that she didn't.

She lay flat on her back with her legs and arms spread wide manacled to the bedpost. She was completely naked apart from one sheer nylon stocking and Paul had just finished filming a glorious close-up of her pouting pussy lips.

He stood back, the expensive pro-quality video camera to his eye, as Lesley climbed on top of his wife. She too was naked apart from the large black thing that bobbed wickedly between her legs. Carole knew it wasn't the same as a real prick but she wanted to be fucked by Lesley and to fuck her with it in return. And so the thick black vibrator with its sexy harness was the answer.

Lesley liked screwing her friends like this but, as she rocked to and fro with it buried deep inside her – and all the while Paul filming them silently – she would have preferred it if Carole hadn't been tied up. She could have responded a lot more but still, it was her whim and she was her friend. She thought back to how things had been only three or four years ago, before she and Charmayne had met and while she was still only assistant manager of a two-bit model agency in Leicester, and thought how far she'd come on. Now she was in bed with one of Britain's most popular TV personalities and had a brand-new Mercedes convertible and an eighty-thousand pound diamond ring to slip through her newly pierced nipples.

With the girth of that monstrous black thing allied to Lesley's vigorous humping, Carole soon came off. As her shudders subsided, she made take-it-off gestures. Paul stopped filming and removed the stocking and the mask. Then he masturbated, rapidly and effusively, all over his wife's bosom.

'Don't you think,' Lesley repeated, 'that you're running a bit of a risk?'

'No, I don't believe so,' said Carole as she rubbed his spunk into her ample flesh. She believed semen was an excellent skin cream. 'I mean, they all think we're the lookalikes, don't they?'

'So why do you do it then? I mean, you're hardly sex-starved. Why risk screwing complete strangers?'

'Because I like a bit of rough sometimes. So does Paul. That girl at the vacuum cleaner factory. Very sexy – I could have had her myself – but dead common. Did you see her nails?

'No, it's a game really,' she went on, pouring champagne. 'Pretending to be someone you're not.'

'That's a laugh. As far as they're concerned, you're pretending to be someone you are. Is there any more of that coke left?'

'Christ,' said Paul, looking into the empty box. 'I bought five grammes only yesterday. Don't say we've got through it already.'

While they were off the air, the Chivers were certainly making hay. There would be parties almost every weekend, as usual, and a couple of times a week they would dress up and pretend not to be themselves for an hour or two. No one ever guessed. Sometimes there would be sex, sometimes not. Anyone they picked up – always individually, never together – would never have guessed that they weren't Carly from Bishop Auckland and Jess from Chester, even though the resemblance was uncanny.

'You ought to go on the real Paul and Carole show one day,' said a beautiful red-headed assistant manager as Paul screwed her one afternoon in his rented Ford Mondeo amid the articulated trucks parked outside the loading bays at a newly opened DIY store in the Manchester suburbs.

'Your eyes are a different colour to hers, though,' the handsome birthday boy said while he performed cunnilingus on his Carole Chivers kissagram girl in a hotel room, while his friends and parents celebrated his eighteenth birthday downstairs.

It was a laugh, right enough, Paul and Carole agreed. A regular hoot.

'So tell me,' said Rex Wagstaffe in that unctuous drawl of his, 'what finally made you decide to quit?'

Christ, thought Tina. *I've been out of it a month and they're still crawling round me.* Charmayne had got in touch with her – they'd been really understanding at the agency and it made things a lot easier for her – and said that this guy had wanted to do a follow-up story.

She'd refused to meet him in person but she said, after a bit of gentle persuasion, that she'd be willing to talk over the phone. Not her own, of course, or her mum's, or Christopher's, but from a hotel room in Bristol. She didn't want anybody chasing her, although Seeing Double had always been very good about confidentiality. Scully would have been proud of her concern for secrecy. She wanted to give nothing away.

'Being hounded by the press was what finally did for me,' Tina replied. It was good to drop the Californian voice at last.

'Yes, but that wasn't because of you, but because of who they thought you were. A simple case of mistaken identity.'

'Sure, but it amounts to the same thing. In the morning, there were photographers outside our hotel. Christopher, he's my boyfriend—' she hated using the word fiancé, '—he tried to explain the situation to them but they wouldn't listen. They wanted me to be Gillian Whatshername and that's who they decided I was.'

'How did you feel?'

'Very angry. Wouldn't you?'

'I'd have thought the whole thing was a scream, personally.'

'Would you now? Well, I didn't. That's why I quit.'

'Can you just walk away from it like that? What about your contract?'

'It says the agreement can be terminated by mutual consent at any time, I checked it out.' With her lawyer friend – she knew he'd be useful one day, over and above the thousand in cash he'd paid her for the photographs. It was amazing what some men would do for a glimpse of stocking.

165

'What happens now? You were a traffic warden, weren't you?'

'I was once, but I'm not going to go back to that. I've got money, I'm going to have a holiday and think about things.' Like becoming Mr and Mrs Francombe, she added to herself, as soon as I've got unhitched from Ray.

'So what was it like, the lookalike business?'

'It was hard work but good fun. I enjoyed it, the actual work. It was the hassling and the harassment I didn't like.'

'What kind of harassment?'

'People wanting a slice of you, wanting to own you. We paid two thousand pounds for an hour of your time, we deserve everything we can get.'

'Did anyone ask you for favours?'

'What do you mean?'

'Come on, Tina. That kind of favours. What other kind is there?'

'Men are always going to try it on with you.'

'So you were propositioned?'

'I didn't say that.'

'Yeah, but that's what you implied. Men trying it on. Did you encourage them?'

'No, I certainly didn't.'

'Some women do, I gather, in your line of business. Some people can be very obliging.'

'I'm sure Seeing Double are above that kind of thing.'

'Are you now? But anyway, let's not get into that. Did you know Paul and Carole Chivers very well?'

Tina felt a cold flush steal down her back.

'No, I didn't.'

'You were on their TV show a couple of times.'

'Yes, but that's as far as it went. I don't expect to get a Christmas card from them.'

'Did you ever go to their house?'

'No, never.'

'You might have missed out there. I gather they're a right pair of ravers, Paul and Carole. You hear anything about that?'

'No, I didn't.'

'You don't sound too sure.'

166

'Look, what is it you want from me? Surely you've got enough to write your article with?'

'Sure, sure, I don't want to upset anyone. I'm just curious. Just things you hear, things you pick up, that's all. But that's fine for now, Tina lovey. I'll get back to you if there's anything else I need.'

He rang off. She thought he was the biggest slimeball she'd ever some across in her life. Thank God she was out of that business at last.

Danny Kirkpatrick, however, was very glad he was still in it. Very much so, in fact.

He had done his number at the launch of a new TV listings magazine and it had gone down really well – mingle, chat, meet the people who mattered, press flesh, chat up the pretty ones and the not-so-pretties. Afterwards he went out for dinner with a few of the publishing people involved. Everyone else from Seeing Double had gone home but Chantal was away in Germany on company business and he didn't fancy returning to an empty house and spending what was left of the evening alone.

The food was great and the conversation a sight more intelligent than it usually was at these things. He got into conversation with the MD of the publishing firm, a tall blonde woman called Chloe.

'Do you do this full-time?' she asked, intrigued.

'No, I don't,' he replied. 'I could do, but I don't want to put all my eggs in one basket.'

'So what else do you do?'

'I'm a designer and illustrator.'

'Really? Who do you work for?'

'I have my own studio.'

Her arched eyebrows rose perceptibly. 'I'm impressed. Look, I'm sorry but I didn't catch your name. Your real name, I mean.'

'Danny Kirkpatrick.'

'Not the Danny Kirkpatrick?'

'Well, I'm certainly a Danny Kirkpatrick but I'm not sure I'm the one you mean.'

'I mean the guy who did the identity for the SportWorld channel.'

'That's me.'

She looked suitably dumbfounded. 'I thought it was brilliant,' she said simply. 'We've got cable interests, maybe I should talk to some of our people. What else have you done?'

He reeled off the names of a few well-known High Street stores he'd done design work for. In truth, a lot of his clients these days came from the financial world but he didn't think she'd have heard of many of them, even though they were big in their own field.

'Oh wow,' she said. 'So how did you come to be doing this, then? This lookalike stuff.'

'I just kind of fell into it. I'd done a bit of modelling work – really just to help out a friend who was in the business – and I'd been with an agency. It was just odd things, really, but for a time I was doing more modelling stuff than the design.'

'But hadn't people always thought you looked like you-know-who?'

'No, not really. It just kind of came out. I used to have my hair very different, quite long in a pony tail. Then someone said something and it all started from there.'

'There was that business with the real one, wasn't there? The thing in the *Daily Bleat*?' There was a smile on her face. She wasn't checking him out.

'Oh that? I prefer to forget that kind of thing. No, that was a bit of a bummer, I wouldn't do that again in a hurry.'

His mind, however, went back to that house in Suffolk and the gorgeous Frenchwoman he'd screwed in one of the guest bedrooms. What was her name? Camille or Gabrielle or something. But this was Chloe he was talking to, though they were a similar type – even if she was ten times brighter than Gabrielle.

Chloe laughed, poured more wine. The party was beginning to break up.

'It must be interesting, though,' she said. 'And it makes a change from corporate identities.'

One of her colleagues leaned across to have a word in her

ear. Danny didn't talk to her again until they were ready to leave. He was standing by the door when she came out of the ladies' room, a big smile on her face.

'I just had a word with Mike, our design director. Maybe we can put something together for you.'

'Wearing which hat?'

'The designer. The computer graphics, you know, the stuff you were telling me about. Here's my business card.'

She laughed again. He really liked her, he realised, as he looked briefly at her card and tucked it away in his top pocket.

'And this is for you as well,' she added, tucking something else in after it. 'Look at it later, not now.'

'Chloe, the cab's here,' someone called. She pecked him on the cheek and was gone.

Danny got home later than he thought to find a message from Chantal on the machine. Oh God, he remembered, she was going to have news about some upcoming project in Germany for him and he'd told her he'd be back by ten. But it was long gone midnight and there was no point in ringing her now. Besides, he didn't have her hotel number.

No, this was important, he told himself. He knew she'd be travelling the next day and he didn't want to call her on her mobile in case her colleagues got wind of what was going on.

He got the number from international enquiries – thank God he remembered the name of the hotel. His German was pretty rudimentary, left over from school and rarely used since, but he managed to make the night clerk understand.

Chantal sounded sleepy.

'Who is it?' she asked, still in a dream.

'It's me, honey.'

'Oh, it's you. Where were you?'

'I was out. That magazine launch. It went on later than I thought and then we went out for dinner.'

'Who's we?'

'Some people from the publishers. There might be something for me there, I've got a number to call. I'm sorry I was out when you rang.'

'That's okay,' she said. 'Nothing much has happened, really. The German people want you to do it still but they're still waiting to sign a deal with their own production company, so it's going to be a couple of weeks yet. I suppose I could have said that in the message but I just wanted to hear your voice.'

After a while, inevitably, they began to talk about more personal things, as he would with someone he'd been living with for the past year. Now he was on his own again, alone in the night, and he didn't greatly like it. He'd been feeling horny all evening and the supper with Chloe hadn't helped.

They fixed to eat at Quaglini's the following Friday, at eight, the day she got back. It was the place he'd just eaten. He said she'd like it. She'd never been there.

'There is one other thing, though,' said Danny, when they'd run out of practical subjects.

'What's that?'

'Talking to you, just hearing your voice, gives me the most incredible hard-on.'

'I'm turned on too. I wish you were here with me, in bed.'

'Me too.'

He felt like he'd just dropped out of a window fifteen floors up. His arms and legs suddenly seemed very prickly.

'Is that right?' she said. She sounded breathless, her voice suddenly seemed to drop an octave.

'I mean, I just keep going back over that afternoon in the Cotswolds, you know, back in June when we went to that restaurant and then back to our room at the hotel.'

'Sure,' she said. 'I remember that. I was wearing a short burgundy dress, wasn't I?'

'I keep thinking about you bending over the bed, you know, and me pulling your dress up, I wish I could lick you, down there, you know.'

'Yes, I know. I know what you mean. I wish you could too.'

Oh Christ, he thought. He had an erection just by thinking about it. Now he was starting to touch himself up.

'Would you like that? Would you like me licking you down there?'

'Yes, sure. Tell me what you'd like to do.'

'I'd like to kneel down behind you and lick your pussy. Lick your ass, too, all over. What are you wearing now? In bed, I mean. Are you naked?'

'A silk nightdress,' she replied quickly. 'My long silk nightdress, the one with lace panels.' It was oyster-coloured, with coffee-coloured lace. He'd given it her for her birthday. She loved things like that.

'Why don't you put your hand inside your nightdress, Chantal?' he suggested.

'Okay,' she said. 'That feels nice. What are you doing?'

'I'm holding my cock. Jesus it feels big, you know, really hard and stiff.'

'I know. Your cock's really big, Danny. So big sometimes I can hardly get it up me.'

'Think of the way we did it in the hotel. Think that I'm kneeling down behind you with this incredible hard-on and licking you out. God, I can really smell your pussy. It smells good, your pussy. Does my cock smell good to you?'

'A big stiff cock always smells really good.'

'Now I want to pull your nightdress up, all the way. Can you feel the silk sliding over your thighs? Do you dare guess what I'm going to do?'

'You're going to tongue me? Put your finger up my ass?'

'When I've finished licking your cunt I'm going to make you rub your tits all over my cock. And then I want you to suck me, while you're rubbing that creamy silk against me – against my balls, against my backside. And I want my cock right deep down in your throat. You like it deep down in the back of your throat, don't you?'

'Yes, I do,' she said. 'A nice big one. With lots of come for me to suck.'

'How's your pussy feel, Chantal?'

'Wet. Hot and horny. I like the way you talk dirty. I always did. I like talking dirty too, especially over the phone.'

'I'm really glad I called you. Jesus, though, I wish you were here.'

'I wish you were here too, Danny, with your big thick cock right next to me. What do you want me to do now?'

'I want you to bend over like you did over the bed. Then I want to shove it right up you, really hard, you know. Can you feel me moving about inside you?'

'Yes, I can. You really know what you're doing, Danny. Are

you holding your cock right now?'

'Damn right I am. But I'm imagining it's your pussy I'm shafting and we're moving in and out, in and out. That's how it goes, isn't it, in and out, in and out?'

'Yes – in and out, up and down, in and out.'

'You can feel the rhythm, now, can't you? Can you feel my big dick right up you.'

'Oh God, yes. I'm playing with myself, Danny. My legs are wide apart.'

'And I can see your bare ass, 'cause you've got your nightdress pulled right up, haven't you? And I can smell cunt, I can smell you – sexy and sweet, and nice to lick. Go on, lick your fingers for me.'

He knew that her fingers were expertly busy between her legs. She always found it a turn-on to taste her own juices, with or without a lover.

'I'm licking it now, while you talk to me,' she breathed. 'Tasting it, every little drop. Mmm my fingers are all sticky.'

'I bet they are. I wish I was licking them too. And I'm thrusting into you all the time, really hard now, and there's your ass, and I'm going to slap it for you, even while I'm fucking you. You like that, don't you?'

'Yes – slap my bum. Slap me hard. But keep fucking me. Don't stop. Keep your cock up me.'

'God, yes, I feel so big, I just wish I could see you, see my cock going in and out of you from behind, right up there now. Christ, it's so wet, and there's your ass there and—'

'And what?'

'And now I'm up your ass.'

'Oh God, yes. Fuck my ass, Danny. But be gentle with me.'

'Easy now, oh that's tight. That's just so tight. I'm squeezing my cock now, just like it's up your ass. Just a little push now, I don't want to hurt you. Just a push, and a push, and—'

'Oh do it to me. Just fuck my ass, nice and gentle. Oh God, I can really feel you right the way into me now, so big and strong . . .'

His come came boiling out over his hand and in that same

moment he heard sighs and whimpers as she came and then there was nothing, only a brief silence over which he could hear the faint noises of her hotel room, three hundred miles away.

'Was that good?' she said softly after a while.

'Oh yes. You give great phone sex, you know. But it's better still face to face.'

'I can't wait for Friday.'

'Neither can I.'

They spoke for a little while longer, inconsequentially, before ringing off.

He got himself a beer from the fridge and flipped on an early Stan Getz recording – perfect late-night music. He sat down on the big sofa in the living room, the events of the day running through his head. He suddenly remembered Chloe's parting gift and went to fetch his jacket.

He got a bigger surprise than he'd imagined. In his hand was a pair of white silk panties with a phone number written across the crotch in blue felt tip.

Colin Branwell was going through his morning mail when his eyes lit on a glossy brochure that had arrived from an agency called Seeing Double. They were in the lookalikes business and the slickly written text – obviously targeting commercial clients – described the benefits that users of their services could accrue in terms of sales promotions, product launches and other business initiatives. He was struck by the Marilyn lookalike but he guessed it was the Damon and Michael clones he was meant to home into. Branwell Thermoplastics was an up-and-coming player in the racing car components business and by 1999 he hoped to be the preferred supplier to many of the major marques.

They would be having a stand at the Silverstone show the weekend after next and, as he sipped his coffee, he considered the possibilities. It would certainly let him steal a march on Precision Point, his main rivals, but he wondered how the big boys like Ferrari would feel. Branwell Thermoplastics wasn't in quite that league – not yet anyway – and Colin wondered how any of their representatives would react on seeing a Michael Schumacher lookalike selling someone else's products.

It wasn't worth the gamble, he told himself. It would be a laugh but he hadn't got where he was today by throwing caution to the winds. He knew all about strategies for risk management but he didn't want to introduce too many wild cards into his game plan.

He was just about to throw the brochure into the bin when his eye caught the picture of Jeff Stevenson and Carly Morrissey, alias Paul and Carole Chivers. Instantly he felt that familiar stab of desire that he always felt when he saw Carole Chivers on TV. These two looked pretty good, her face was a bit longer than Carole's and his eyes weren't right, but it was a damn good likeness all the same. Inwardly he drooled over the familiar blonde hair – captured to perfection – the generous mouth and the equally generous bosom.

Colin's big fantasy had always been to screw Carole Chivers while his wife Sonja watched, and then to screw Sonja in front of Carole. He'd often talked about it with his wife and she got a kick out of it too – she had, with and without his encouragement, taken several female lovers in the course of their marriage. Inevitably, though, a liaison with Carole seemed doomed to remain forever in the realms of fantasy. Colin may have been MD of a company that made bodyshells for Formula One racing cars but in social terms he and the object of his desires were poles apart.

Colin's business head ruled his heart but his cock dominated everything. In five minutes time he was on the phone to Lesley Carmody discussing fees.

After three or four glasses of Krug Danny felt himself relax, becoming more and more mellow with every sip. And with the mellowness came desire, a feeling so palpable within him that it was if he had turned on a tap. Less than half an hour after he rang her bell, Chloe was lying naked on the big old brass-framed bed upstairs while he was down there between her legs, eating her out.

'No, don't stop,' she hissed when he made a move to do

something different. 'Just keep it like that, okay? Jesus, that feels good.'

She was bucking and writhing around so much, she almost threw Danny off the bed. One thing was for sure – she didn't get this kind of treatment too often.

He broke free for a moment, gulping in great lungfuls of air that were tinged with her heavy perfume and the strong, musky scent of her sex.

'What's happening?' she said, her voice soft and husky. 'Get back down there and eat me out again. I was just about there when you stopped.'

He brought her off quickly and expertly. Danny got the feeling that she hadn't had sex for some while. Heaven only knew what she'd be like when he got his dick into her.

When her palpitations ceased he climbed on top of her, conscious of his cock bobbing there in front of her eyes, of his balls hanging down heavy and full. He would have got her to suck him off there and then but Chloe wasn't ready for that yet. Later on, maybe, after he'd balled her.

He slipped inside her nice and easy. She was loose and wet and just about dying to be fucked. She was laying back on the pillows with her eyes closed and her mouth half-open, naked as the day she was born.

Danny had been surprised how quickly she'd taken her clothes off. They'd sat down, talked for a while about nothing in particular, and then she was in his arms and snogging him like crazy. Then Chloe had stood up and stepped out of her shirt and leggings, and then out of her brassiere, and then out of her panties. Standing beside her in the big, rug-strewn bedroom he'd barely got his shirt cuffs unbuttoned before she was standing there next to him, stark naked and feeling his cock. He knew she'd been waiting for him, building herself up into peak of anticipation. He liked to know a woman had the hots for him.

And Chloe was hotter than most. After all, cool women don't hand over their panties to complete strangers in the middle of restaurants. Especially not with their private phone number on them.

So now he was moving back and forth, back and forth,

building up the rhythm, using the strength in his arms and legs, feeling her spreading her own legs wider and wider to draw him in until she brought her knees up and then wrapped her legs around him, twisting and turning. They rolled over, still locked together, and then it was her turn to be on top of him, her hair wild and loose, the blonde muff almost exactly the same colour. She had generous pear-shaped tits and her nipples stood out big and proud and hard. He rolled them between his teeth, nipping and making her gasp as she flaunted herself above him. She was, he knew, entirely at ease with her own body, sun-tanned without a bikini line.

He grabbed hold of that firm, thirty-something-year-old ass and squeezed the cheeks hard. She moaned and, leaning forward, bit him hard on the neck, so hard it hurt. Hell, he suddenly thought, I hope that didn't leave a mark. Shocked, he pulled her ass down on to him, feeling his cock burying itself right up inside almost to the end of her vagina and then he could feel it coming, that irresistible urge deep inside himself. He carried on thrusting, sharp, vicious stabs now, but he was well on his way. With one last effort he pushed up at her, lifting her whole body clean off the bed and up into the air, and then he was shooting his seed into her.

He must have dozed off. Bad manners, Danny, he told himself when he came round. He could hear the distant hum of traffic along the avenue of large Victorian houses where she lived, even the sound of tyres slick on wet night-time leaves.

She lit a cigarette after, which surprised him, lay back on the bed smoking. He had one hand resting on her thigh, brushing those blonde curls, wet and matted now from his sperm and her juices. Feeling confident with her, the way he usually did when he'd taken a woman for the first time, he slipped a finger inside her, then two. She made no move to stop him, just lay back on the pillows, blowing out smoke. After a while she stubbed out her cigarette and turned her head to face him.

'You really are one hell of a persuasive bastard, you know,' she said to him.

'Oh yeah?' he said. 'What makes you say that?'

'Just the way you do it, that's all. Kind of understanding. A lot of guys these days can be so brutish, sometimes. You're different.'

'Guys have to be aggressive for their work. Kick ass, that kind of thing. I'm not like that.' His magic fingers teased her up to a new peak of lust.

'How much do you make pretending to be what's his name?' she asked, distracted.

'You should know. You hired me.'

'No, I mean in a year?'

'That's not the kind of thing I'd tell a lady.'

'Not even after a little cock-sucking?' she asked, trying to sound really casual. 'You get a lot of offers of blow-jobs?'

'That's private information too, I'm afraid.'

'I bet you do. And I bet you enjoy it.'

'My lips are sealed.'

'Well, let's just see if I'm right, shall we?'

Chloe slid down the bed. Propped up on the pillows, Danny looked on in fascination as her pink tongue flickered for a moment before she began to lick the tip of his cock, probing the little oval hole in the end. She was holding the shaft in her fist, gently pumping it up and down as she did so. Then she sank her mouth down on to him, wide open, and took all of him in, her tongue swirling around him.

He moved as best he could so he could reach down and run his fingers through her hair and along the smooth skin of her shoulders.

'That's good,' he breathed, aware of little other than the sensations of his body. Lying there on her bed, with Chantal hundreds of miles away, he didn't have a care in the world.

Her mouth fitted him like a velvet glove. She really knew how to go down on a guy, treated it with relish. After a while, it got like she was eating him. He was sure her jaws must have been aching by now but she kept on with her lips and her tongue, teasing and tormenting him, licking him up and down his full length before taking all of him back down deep inside her.

She had a rhythm going now, hypnotic and powerful, and Danny surrendered to it. Images of sex began to fill his mind, various women he had known, tits, hair, lips – all the women began to blur into one and the focus of that desire was Chloe Fisher, MD of Fisher Publishing, one-time Businesswoman of the Year and, in Danny's book, quite definitely Fuck of the Week.

When he knew he was coming he kind of grunted and touched her shoulder but she didn't pay any particular attention, just carried on there sucking away at him. Even when he got past the point of no return, when she must have known from the way he writhed and moaned what was going on, she still continued to do him. Now he was fucking her in her mouth the way he'd fucked her earlier in her pussy, strong and sure. And then he couldn't hold back any longer and his seed came boiling up out of his loins.

He was excited by coming in her willing mouth and his orgasm was big and prolonged, the spasms amplified, the desire out of control. All he was aware of was that powerful ejaculation from his body and the feeling of her mouth enclosing him, welcoming him into her, drinking his fluids down, milking him dry, until his body stopped twitching and he fell back on the pillows, utterly drained and blissed out beyond belief.

'Hey,' said Sonja Branwell after a highly successful launch of Branwell Thermoplastic's new air dam matrix. 'Would you like to come back to our hotel afterwards and have a drink with Colin and myself?'

'Sure,' said the woman. 'That would be just great. Let me get rid of my partner and I'll be with you.'

With Colin's encouragement, Sonja had several times been to bed with other women – sometimes with her husband, sometimes without – but this time it seemed they'd gone one step beyond. She didn't really know why she'd asked. She'd just been in that kind of mood, maybe. Everyone at the bar seemed to be acting a little looser than usual, since Colin had clinched a half-million pound deal with a leading Japanese manufacturer.

As soon as she could, she got Colin over to one side.

'I asked her,' she said, real quiet.

'Asked her what?'

'If she'd like to come back to the hotel with us.'

'Jesus fucking Christ, you didn't?' He looked at her in astonishment.

She nodded, gave him a sideways smile.

'What about the bloke?'

'No problem. He's got to be in Leeds by six. The car was waiting for him at the door.'

'When do we meet her?'

'Just as soon as you're ready,' she said, and went to get herself another drink.

He could hardly breathe with excitement. Carly Morrissey looked more like Carole Chivers than he dared imagine. Maybe she seemed a little older than she did on TV and maybe not quite so wickedly slim, but she certainly did the business for him.

Later, back in their suite, Colin was almost trembling as he got undressed. It had all been so easy. Everything was happening just as he had imagined it. There was the bed with the covers drawn back, and there was Sonja in her lemon-coloured French lingerie, kneeling down with her butt towards him.

He climbed up behind her, got his cock into her. She was still wearing her pants and garter belt and everything, best satin and lace, a hundred quid for a pair of knickers, unbelievable really. She felt warm and wet as he slid into her. Watching her strip, he had been aware of the damp patch between her legs.

Sonja gasped. The woman in the chair opposite had a drink in her hand and a smile on her face. She came and sat on the edge of the big, queen-sized bed.

Her eyes took in Sonja, kneeling there with her small, exquisitely-shaped tits almost spilling out of her brassiere, and Colin going into her from behind, naked so she could see his powerful back muscles and his tight butt. Colin had a good figure, worked out every day. He liked to show it off.

For a while Colin worked his dick in and out of his wife's pussy. Then, when he was sure their guest was watching closely, he pulled it almost the whole way out so she could see how long and thick it was. He felt really good doing that, powerful and male, leaning back so he was almost sitting on his ankles, with his cock pulled out almost as far as it would go.

He was still bowled over by the resemblance. He could almost imagine it was Carole herself sitting right beside him. He wanted her to see every last impressive inch of him before she tasted it for herself.

He was surprised he didn't come the moment she sat down, so close he could smell her perfume. He felt so worked up about it all. When he was sure she'd seen enough, he leaned forward again and began working Sonja's pussy once more, his hands on her hips to steady himself, feeling the soft sheen of the fabric of her pants and garter belt.

'Take your clothes off, if you like,' he said to the blonde.

She smiled and stood up. She was wearing a two-piece skirt and jacket, very chic.

Her breasts, as he had envisaged so many times, were magnificent. She was wearing an intricate brassiere of black lace and it held them up to perfection, emphasising the deep cleavage between them. She was also wearing black suspenders and tiny, black lace panties that seemed to be moulded to the wicked fullness of her cunt.

Even as he caught a glimpse of her, he could feel his balls beginning to tighten. He pushed his cock deep inside Sonja's pussy and then withdrew it completely. It stood jutting forward from his abdomen, red and kind of angry-looking, glistening with Sonja's secretions. Colin felt immensely powerful and potent, very sure of himself.

It was as if their guest had read the script. Even as Colin stood up, she pressed herself forward and took hold of his dick, guiding it towards her tits. She frigged it only a couple of times and then Colin's spunk came flying out, all over her black lace brassiere and into the deep channel between her breasts. After the initial rush of elation, Colin felt like a million-ton weight had been lifted from his shoulders.

Sonja Branwell turned round. Her eyes had that just-fucked look, dreamy with lust. Carole didn't need to speak, and neither did they. Their body language spoke volumes. All three of them were at that pitch of sexual desire when anything is possible and everything is desirable.

She crossed the room towards them, her eyes fixed on Colin Branwell. Before his very eyes she pulled down her panties. He held out his hand to her. She took it, parted her stocking-clad legs and placed his palm between her thighs.

'I want you to fuck me,' she breathed, her eyes not leaving his. 'While she watches us.'

The couple separated. She caught the woman's eye and smiled. Sonja smiled back. Of course they didn't know who she really was but Carole knew well enough how grown-ups, like children, liked to pretend. She'd even asked them to call her Carole, though that was pushing things too far. She knew damn well that Carly Morrissey wouldn't do anything like this and besides, her bum was too big. Carole, as she'd often been told, had a peach and perhaps that was why men liked so much to fuck her from behind.

The atmosphere in room sixteen at the Park House Hotel was electric. Carole didn't know what kind of a scene these folks were usually into but it didn't seem to faze them one whit what was happening. Maybe, like herself, they were both too fuck-crazy to think straight.

The next thing was, she was lying flat on the bed with her legs wide apart, still wearing stockings and suspenders and high-heeled shoes, and Colin was guiding his cock up her. Jesus, he had a humdinger on him all right, and he sure knew how to use it. She pressed back against him, trying to impale herself on that huge thing he'd got there between his legs.

'Come on,' she breathed at him. 'Let me see what you've got in you.'

She heard him chuckle and then he really started to fuck her in earnest. She spread her legs to accommodate him more and at the same time to stop herself falling off the bed, so violently did he surge into her. She was aware of the way her tits swung while he screwed her, and of how Sonja seemed utterly mesmerised by them. Women with small tits always seemed to have this things about women with big tits, she'd noticed. It wasn't always that they were envious, or anything

181

like that, just that they were different to what they'd got.

Sonja had taken off her brassiere and the rest of her underwear. Her body was beautiful, long and lean with exquisitely formed pear-shaped boobs and big, big nipples. They looked like strawberries and were no doubt twice as luscious.

'Hey,' Carole breathed to the other woman. 'You want to suck me? I love being sucked, don't you?'

'Love to,' said Sonja. She lay down beside them on the bed, somehow got her head in there and started to lick and suck Carole's nipples. The feeling drove Carole wild. Colin was filling her right up to the root and Sonja was going at her with her lips and her tongue so that she didn't know what week it was.

Seeing his wife making it with Carole seemed to fire Colin up even more. He arched his back, called out something she couldn't quite catch and then pushed himself so hard up against Carole's ass that he pushed her against the padded headboard, Sonja still drooling over her generous cleavage.

At the same time that great cock of his pulsed in a steady stream and he shot his load right up into her. It was the catalyst Carole had needed. Aware only of the shuddering waves of pleasure that rocketed around every last nerve ending in her body, she gave way to her senses and came and came and came, the feeling of desire and release so intense that she bit into the pillow to stop herself calling out aloud.

When she came round, she was lying on her side, Sonja still snuggled right up against her, tonguing her breasts. She looked down. She could see how red and wet and engorged her nipples looked. It excited her. She was sure that only women really knew how to lick and suck another woman.

She reached out a tentative hand and touched Sonja on the shoulder. Sonja smiled and sat up.

Colin was standing at the foot of the bed with a glass of champagne in either hand.

Carole took the proffered glass and sipped. It tasted good.

They showered together, all three of them somehow squeezed into that tiny tiled cubicle. Then, refreshed, she lay down naked on the bed with Colin lying next to her. She'd taken his dick into her mouth and was sucking him nice and slow, tasting her own juices on him. Sonja was there too, lying the other way, and then she opened her legs and Colin went down on her while he continued to work his cock in and out of Carole's eager mouth.

Carole's heart was pounding again and she felt that familiar prickly feeling she always did when she got really aroused, and she closed her eyes to savour it all the more. And then she felt Sonja's hair on her thighs and the next thing she knew, Sonja had nosed in between her legs and was planting little butterfly kisses all over Carole's pussy.

And it was so good, the way she did it to her. Paul could eat pussy like there was no tomorrow and very little of today but the way Sonja did it, licking away around her labia and nuzzling at her clitoris, and then sticking out her tongue and going right into her, it was almost like having a cock inside her.

They lay there in a triangle of torsos and limbs on the tangled bedsheets, each one giving and taking at the same time. Colin brought Sonja off first, and then Sonja licked and lapped at Carole until she went nearly insane before her orgasm hit her and then, still coming the whole time like she couldn't stop the flow, she sucked harder than ever at Colin. By the time his big balls contracted, she was ready for him. She swallowed his come with relish once he'd finished pulsing, he tasted so good.

They must have dozed a while. The next thing Carole knew, it was one in the morning and Sonja was pouring out the last of the champagne. Sonja handed Carole a glass, stood next to her at the bedside sipping her own drink. Then she put the glass between her legs and dipped her pussy in it.

'Here,' she said. 'You going to have a little drink with me?'

It was effortlessly done. Crazed with desire and the power of novelty, Carole did just what was expected of her. She could see the wetness on Sonja's rich dark pussy hair. She stuck out her tongue and licked the champagne off her.

She could taste the grapes and she could taste the cunt taste too, musky and rich. Tentatively, she extended her tongue and drew it along Sonja's vermilion pussy lips, firm and smooth.

'This is South African champagne,' said the other woman. 'But I bet this isn't how they drink it in South Africa.'

Again Sonja dipped her pussy in champagne and offered her sex for Carole to lick. Half-drunk with desire and the sparkling wine, Carole buried her face in that divine muff over and over again, and then she and Sonja were lying together on the bed, their tongues probing each other, and Colin somehow got up behind Carole and got his cock into her again, and he fucked her at the same time as Sonja licked his cock and Carole's pussy, and everyone was coming all over the place and coming out with all these crazy lewd obscene words, and in time Carole didn't know what belonged to who but just sucked and touched and kissed whatever was closest, and the next thing she knew was the early morning light coming in through the windows, the telephone ringing for the Branwell's rise-and-shine call. The morning sun was just coming in through the curtains and her whole body was glowing along with it.

It was a good life being a lookalike, she told herself.

Chapter Eight

Reg Wagstaffe was biding his time, as he usually did. A couple of days after the opening of the new vacuum cleaner factory in Llanwelty, he was sitting in Katryn's mum's living room in Bethesda Drive.

Rex may have been a complete shit but he was a very observant shit. He knew something was going on, something that didn't quite ring true. To his initial muckraker's suspicions was added the lead he'd got from a casual remark at Lesley and Charmayne's party. Other little things had led him to put two and two together – Tina Richardsons' guardedness, for one. Though he was more inclined towards the make-it-up-as-you-go-along school of hack writing, he knew enough abut investigative journalism to know the difference between people who really didn't know what you were talking about and those who did but weren't letting on.

Without letting on to anyone, not even his editor, he'd been on the Paul and Carole trail for weeks. He had kept well in with Lesley Carmody at the agency, booked a couple of her up-and-coming acts for his paper's annual pleasure boat trip up the Thames, and generally made sure that she was kept sweet. If, dropping in casually for a chat and a bit of showbiz gossip, he should chance to look into her bookings diary while she popped out for a moment to photocopy something, well that was just natural curiosity, nothing more and nothing less.

With his press card and the faithful Jimmy in tow with a bagful of Nikons, he had been in the crowd at the factory opening. He'd watched the ceremony, listened to the speeches, but his eyes were on Paul and Carole the whole time. He knew who they were, even if no one else did. A flurry of discreet phone calls had revealed that Carly, the usual Carole Chivers lookalike, was in bed in Bishop Auckland with an unseasonable cold and that her partner had had his contract with Seeing Double terminated a month and more ago.

So he stood and watched and clapped and watched some more, and wasn't in the least surprised to see his quarry slip out with the girl with the stupendous tits in the see-through blouse. It was a shame that Jimmy couldn't get anything usable but the acoustics in the ladies' loo meant that the sound of what they were up to didn't come out too well on his little portable Sony but it was pretty unmistakable all the same. Afterwards, he was able to retrieve Katryn's ripped panties from where she'd kicked them behind the pedestal. He was pleased to note, as he sniffed them deeply and appreciatively, that they were still wet.

They were in his pocket now, to use as a persuader in case Katryn wasn't willing to talk. But, thank the good Lord, she sang like a canary. In twenty minutes he had everything he needed and she had two hundred and fifty quid in cash. He had brought five hundred with him from his float but he'd bid low and she'd taken what he'd offered, without question. Maybe the bottle of wine had helped loosen her tongue. It was deliberately strong fourteen per cent by volume – and he'd gone easy on it himself.

Of course, he hadn't told her the truth – that it really had been Paul Chivers who'd been fucking her. He showed her his card and said he was interested in this dodgy agency and he still wasn't really sure whether she thought he was a hack or a copper. At this stage, it wasn't necessary, and maybe never would be, to let her know any more. Instead, he gave her the usual pitch and a bit of celebrity gossip and within the hour he was heading upstairs with her.

He could see her nice ass ahead of him in tight Levi jeans as he went up the stairs and he licked his lips in anticipation. He reached out and put his hand up there between her legs. It felt damp. Katryn turned round, grinned, and blew him a kiss.

Katryn's bedroom was like Barbie's playroom, a mass of soft toys and clothes and cosmetics and magazines and he almost threw her down on top of the bedclothes, not made since she got up that morning. He quickly got out of his suit and shirt and was pleased the way his dick stood out through his pants. He took them off too and saw Katryn's eyes on him as his dick bounced and wobbled, ready for her, the skin at the end drawn back and the big purple dome ready and willing.

'You want to take my panties off, lover?' she breathed at him, her eyes half-closed.

He tugged down her jeans and then her underwear as she lay back on the bed.

'Lick me now, nice and slow.'

She pushed up her ass and parted her thighs, and Rex knelt on the tangled covers and did what he was told. Her pussy gaped at him, coral pink and inviting – everything seemed to be pink in Katryn's room – and he pushed his face down in that musky-smelling tangle of hair. She was almost overflowing. He rolled his tongue over her lubricious folds a few times and knew she was ripe and ready. Jesus, he thought, this woman just seems to live for it.

He quickly got his rubber on and climbed up on top of her while, outside in the street, he could hear Welsh voices, a milk float going down the hill. Katryn had her legs wide apart and now she hooked them up and over his back, so that he could reach down with his free hand and feel how wet and slippery her pussy was, his cock sliding in and out of it in short, pistoning stabs. He was surprised at how cool his balls felt against the heat of her pudenda. Katryn, it seemed to him, was just one enormous pussy, and he was just one enormous cock.

She pulled up her top so he could see her plump and luscious breasts, the nipples engorged, twin peaks of desire. He leaned forward and licked each of them in turn taking them in his mouth and rolling them around his tongue like a gourmet tasting mangoes. They were as hard and sweet as ripening fruit.

Katryn was sweating up a storm now and thrusting hard at him, her hips powering against his. If that's how you want it you can have it, he half-breathed at her and pushed back just as hard, slamming his groin into her slick wetness. Rex was just one big powerful aggressive ego concentrated in his dick and when he came – not knowing nor caring what she was doing – it was a release.

They lay back in the crumpled bed, Katryn smoking a cigarette. She switched on the bedside radio and for a while they listened to the morning show on Radio 1, saving the need for talking. Rex never could find much to talk about with girls like Katryn. As he'd say to the lads at the bar, he preferred to find 'em, finger 'em, fuck 'em and forget 'em. When it was over, he usually just wanted to get away as soon as possible. This morning, though, he didn't have anywhere special to go, so he lay back with his head on Katryn's mountainous breasts and breathed in her foul tobacco smoke and looked up at the ceiling light fitting and the fly-speckled shade.

Afterwards, Katryn got him to frig her off by hand and then he put his fingers in her and that got her going all over again, and it seemed to get him going too. She tasted Rex experimentally, like she was licking an ice cream cone or something. Then she slid her mouth over the end of his cock and sucked hard at it. It felt good. Rex was all for variety, in whatever form it came. He wondered if she'd done it this way with Paul Chivers, there in the bog in the ladies' room.

She was kind of half-kneeling over him with her big boobs hanging down. Rex liked heavy breasts, low-slung like over-ripe fruit. He had a stack of magazines, with titles like Naughty Forties or D-Cup and Up. He had other magazines, too, and videos, especially of younger girls. Rex was a man of catholic tastes.

He settled down on the disordered bed and looked up at the fly-speckled light fitting again and then down again at Katryn, which was a much better view, seeing she'd turned almost half-way round now and was presenting her gorgeous ass to him. Still she went on sucking him, her fingertips playing with his balls all the while so that it nearly drove him mad. Before he knew it his cock was stiff again while her big tits swung mesmerisingly in front of his eyes. He gazed down at the mysterious folds of her pussy and wondered just what the hell it was that made women like her tick.

Finally she stopped what she was doing and turned round, her hair all tousled, a kind of bleary look in her eye.

'You want to screw me again now, Rex?' she breathed.

She was over on her front with her big bare ass in the air and he came up behind her, his cock feeling heavy and potent once more.

Her lips parted for him and he slid effortlessly inside her, right up to the hilt. She was soaking wet down there and there was a musky smell in his nostrils, a cunt smell that he liked a lot, the same one he'd smelt on her panties. Katryn knelt there, rocking back and forth with her eyes closed and pressing her ass against him, fantasising about God knows what, maybe Paul Chivers or something, and Rex was making these big vicious shoves into her and gasping out loud with the effort of it all, looking at those dimpled cheeks and the big heavy breasts and the cunt smell filling his nostrils, feeling pretty animal.

Neither of them lasted long like this. Katryn started grunting and squealing like he was hurting her or something and he could see she was starting to go red in the face. He could feel the urgency in his own loins urging him forward, stabbing his cock into her pudenda, feeling lewd and potent and powerful all at the same time which was how he liked it, and then he could tell she was coming because her grunts turned to gasps and she was kind of trying to screw herself sideways around his cock, and in that instant he let fly and could feel the big thick jets of semen coming welling out of him and pouring into her.

His legs felt weak and kind of trembling as he got off the bed and fastened his belt. Katryn was lying face down on the bed, breathing heavily. Her eyes were closed and her features seemed somehow coarser now, different to how they'd looked downstairs in the cluttered living room.

He'd got everything he wanted now from her, there was no point in hanging around any longer. He pulled his shirt back on, fastened his tie, checked the tape recorder in his pocket. He wondered where Jimmy had got to. There was a half-way reasonable-looking pub in the town and he fancied a drink.

He found the torn white panties in his jacket pocket.

'Here, these are yours,' he said and tossed them on the bed.

'Armadillos have very special pricks,' said Leonie Swallow.

She was sitting with a group of colleagues in the staff common room. Conversation, as usual, veered between incestuous bitching and lewd innuendo. It was probably worse than what went on in the student bar downstairs.

'How come?' asked Don Willis, who taught twentieth-century poetry.

'How's your physiology?' she asked.

'Works pretty well.'

'Okay. The male penis is an organ that, to function properly, needs strength.'

'That much is true,' said Don.

'I read the other day,' observed Terry Freeman, senior lecturer in applied engineering, 'that you burn off about a dozen calories achieving penetration with an erect penis – and about five thousand if you haven't got a stiffie.'

He was dry like that, Terry Freeman. When the laughter had subsided, Leonie went on with her story.

'The penis needs strength but, unlike an arm or a leg or any other load-bearing structure, it doesn't have a solid skeleton. Instead it works hydraulically, through internal fluid pressure.'

'It pumps itself up, like a bicycle tyre?'

'Sort of. The fluid builds up in fibres that run up and down your willy in a spiral. But not in an armadillo.'

'What happens there, then? Does it have a bone in it or something?'

'No. World experts in penis technology have discovered that, uniquely among the animal kingdom, the armadillo's fibres aren't spirals but are in two sets of rod-line structures, at right angles to one another.'

'So instead of being like a helical spring, it's more like the scaffolding around a chimney or a church tower.' An engineer like Terry would always make a comparison like that, thought Leonie. Specific, highly practical and exactly right.

'Some run along the little chap's chopper,' she went on, 'while others run around it.'

'What is the benefit?' asked Don.

Terry was in like a shot.

'More resistant to buckling, I should imagine. If you've got all this right-angle bracing inside your dick, it won't compress like a spring if it meets resistance. It makes for a much more rigid structure. Basic engineering, really.'

'But how do they know that?' asked Don. 'I mean, do they have a lab full of disembodied armadillo dicks and they blow them up with a bicycle pump to see what happens? No joke, a stress fracture in your willy, I should imagine.'

Leonie's mobile phone trilled. She pulled up the aerial.

'Leonie? Hi, it's Lesley. Can we talk?'

'Sure, yes.' She got up, went on to the balcony outside the common room. Most of her colleagues didn't know about Seeing Double.

'Sorry,' she said. 'Walls have ears. Okay to talk now.'

Lesley sounded worried.

'Look,' she began, 'have you spoken to Rex Wagstaffe recently?'

'Not that I know of, no. I can't say he's my number one person, to be honest.'

'Well, if he does call you, don't say anything more than you have to.'

'May I ask why?'

'This is strictly confidential, but I think he's on to something about Paul and Carole.'

'There have always been rumours about them.'

'Yes, but I think he knows something. And if he knows about them, he knows about us. You were at that party too.'

'Why do you say that? I mean, what do you think he knows?'

'I think he knows that Paul and Carole have been getting their kicks by pretending to be lookalikes, and then picking up anyone they fancy.'

'How's he sussed them?'

'I don't know. He asks a lot of questions.'

'Who's he spoken to?'

'I know he rang Tina the other day.'

'I thought she isn't doing the Scully thing any more.'

'She isn't.'

'What did she tell him?'

'I don't think she told him anything. I think it was what she didn't tell him that he found significant.'

'Like the dog that didn't bark in the night.'

'I'm sorry? You've lost me there.'

'In one of the Sherlock Holmes stories, the murderer is identified because a guard dog didn't bark. It didn't bark because it knew the assailant.'

'Right. I see what you mean. So I think we'd better be cautious, that's all.'

'What about our friends?'

'Paul and Carole? Well, I didn't want to alarm them at this stage so I haven't told them anything. But I've stopped any bookings and they're not doing any more engagements.'

'What about me? I'm supposed to be in Edinburgh at the weekend for the film festival. They're relaunching all of Marilyn's movies on CD-ROM.'

'That's okay. Just be good, that's all. Watch your back. And if you see Rex Wagstaffe, run a mile.'

'Think I got a big one,' said Rex Wagstaffe.

'You got a big one?' replied Brian Levitt, hard-bitten editor of the *Daily Bleat*. 'Come in and have a biscuit.'

Brian Levitt seemed to live on tea and biscuits, reflected Rex as he closed the door behind him. There were two moments of crisis in his daily routine – when the paper went to bed, and when the tea trolley came round. He looked at Rex through horn-rimmed glasses.

'Yeah, I got a big one all right,' repeated Rex. And he told him just enough of the Paul and Carole story for his tea to go cold, untasted.

'Great stuff, Rexy boy,' said Brian Levitt when he'd finished. '"I WAS TV STAR'S LOVE CHILD SURROGATE." "MY NAKED ROMPS WITH MR PERSONALITY." "DREAM LOVER CAROLE LIKES IT *EIGHT* TIMES A NIGHT." I can see the headlines now. We'll do a million. Hope it's as good as the teenage porn stuff you've done.'

A copy of that morning's *Daily Bleat* was open on the desk in front of him. TEEN VICE PROBE SHOCKER ran the banner headline. Rex's by-line was nice and prominent. It was the third and final instalment of the *Daily Bleat*'s crusade against the nation's moral iniquity. It had gone down well. Even the old man had been pleased.

Brian Levitt selected a Jammy Dodger and munched, stabbing a finger at the latest issue.

'Good stuff there, Rex. Pretty we couldn't print half of it. "HEREDITARY PEER MUNCHED MY CLIT". "THREE IN A BED POP STAR STUNNER". "TEENAGE VICAR MOTORCYCLE SEX FIEND HORROR."'

He could – and frequently did – go on like this for hours. Whole pages, whole editions even, of the *Daily Bleat* issued from his becrumbed lips with little evidence of conscious thought. Brian Levitt would rewrite the front page at a moment's notice and, while he tended to pay little regard for the niceties of grammar and sentence construction, there was no doubt he knew what the people liked.

The motto 'NO ONE WENT BROKE UNDERESTIMATING THE TASTE OF THE PUBLIC' was engraved on a stainless steel plaque above his desk.

Still, Brian was a nice guy and knew which side his bread was buttered. He had the smooth, easy manners of a PR consultant and – uniquely among top journalists who'd come up the hard way – a reputation for never losing his temper.

'Look at the tits on this one, Rex,' he said, suddenly lurching off at a tangent and propelling a 10x8 glossy photograph across the desk. Charm and cunning played a great part in Brian Levitt's rise to fame but logical thought rarely did. He was quite capable of writing a leader on one theme that seamlessly veered off on another tack entirely. A tirade against the greed of old-style trade unionists could blend effortlessly into a flag-rallying paean for the national football team. He was reputed never to reread anything he ever wrote.

'About my next story,' Rex ventured. 'Paul and Carole the bonking afternoon duo.'

'Sure,' Brian responded. 'When do we run it? What have you got?'

'Just as soon as I get the one piccy I need. I got Jimmy working on it. I got everything else, all the facts.'

'Don't bother too much with them, old love,' said Brian, reaching for a Hobnob. 'Let the facts take care of themselves, as long as it's not libellous. The story's the thing. What's holding up the picture?'

'I'm after just the right one.'

'I'd like to see Carole with some great cucumber shoved up her twat,' said Brian dreamily. 'And blowing some guy in bondage gear, a great big black guy with a ten-inch dick.'

'We could never print that.'

'I wasn't thinking about printing it. I was thinking about putting it in the bog downstairs. Now fuck off, Rex, I got to see the old man at eleven.'

Despite Lesley's assurances, Tina was worried. She knew she hadn't done anything reprehensible herself but people like Reg Wagstaffe never let truth stand in the way of a good story.

Providence, as it happened, took a hand. The day after her divorce from Ray came through she had a phone call from Anthony, the barrister who'd taken the naughty pictures of her in her Scully kit. She was convinced she'd never hear from him again.

'I was wondering,' he said in that soft and pleasant voice of his, 'whether you might be able to do me a favour?'

'That depends what it is,' she replied. With Christopher's considerable salary to add to the money she had in the bank, she was certainly far from hard up and, besides, she wasn't entirely sure she wanted to do things like that any more.'

'We have the local Law Society dinner coming up and I wonder if we could use your professional services. We'd be happy to pay the market rate.'

'You'd have to go through my agency first but the truth is, I'm not doing the lookalike thing at the moment.'

'I'm sorry to hear that. What led up to this? I thought it was all going rather well for you.'

'It was but various things started to go wrong.' She gave him a quick run-down on the sequence of events that had led to her decision to withdraw.

'The other thing is,' she said when she'd finished, 'we think there's a journalist sniffing around.'

She could sense a momentary stiffening in his tone of voice when he asked who and what.

'It can't be anything to do with what happened between us,' she was quick to reassure him. 'I've not breathed a word to anyone, believe me.'

'I understand. I have every confidence in you. Wagstaffe, you say his name is. What kind of thing is he looking for?'

'Any whiff of hokey pokey, you know the score.'

'What do you know about him? Has he contacted you?'

'Yes, but I didn't tell him anything.'

'Good. Has he called back?'

'No.'

'Let's hope it doesn't come to anything,' he said in a lawyer's reassuring tones. 'I'm sure it won't.'

Two days later Tina had another call from Anthony.

'Your man, Wagstaffe,' he began, 'I've been looking into him, courtesy of a friend of mine. I think you might find what we've discovered rather interesting. Would you like to have dinner with me and I'll tell you what my friend came up with?'

Christopher was away in Tokyo on company business. She carefully took his ring off her finger before she said yes to Anthony.

'I mean, God damn it, if Wagstaffe blows the lid on us we're sunk.'

Lesley had never seen Carole so angry.

'He doesn't know for sure. And no one else seems to have suspected anything.'

'I'm just amazed we got away with it in the first place. That people didn't realise who we were.'

'They saw who they expected to see. They expected to see lookalikes so they saw lookalikes. The lucky few had it off with the lookalikes, or at least they thought they did. How often did you do it?'

'Four or five times, that was all.'

'That was enough,' said Paul. 'I don't want to take the risk any longer.'

'Why do you do it? Or why did you do it?'

'For the adrenaline, I guess. The feeling of doing it and then getting away with it. Most of the time, life isn't dangerous enough. That's the trouble with having money. It makes everything so safe.'

'Maybe you should take up mountain-climbing or Formula One racing then.'

Carole glared at her. 'What's his story going to be, then?' she asked.

'I would have thought it's pretty obvious,' replied Lesley. 'Glam TV couple put it about a bit with the hoi polloi, or words to that effect. Daytime TV Bonkers, you can imagine the headlines.'

'I'd rather not. But how do we stop him?'

'I haven't a clue,' said Lesley. 'I wish I did, but I don't.'

Tina felt his hand on her knee, under the crisp white table cloth that stood out with startling geometry against the black table. *Christ*, she thought, *he wants to touch me up in the middle of the most fashionable Japanese restaurant in the country.*

Anthony turned and leaned towards her. She parted her legs to make it easier for him. His hand slid up her thighs, on to the tops of her bare legs, feeling how soft and cool she felt despite the heat. Tina looked up anxiously, but the waiters were at the other end of the room. Discreetly placed screens blocked them off from the view of the other well-heeled diners, who were far too well-mannered to stare at the stunning red-haired girl with the extraordinary facial resemblance to you-know-who.

For a couple of minutes or more his fingers delicately brushed across her skin as she sipped her wine. He knew it was making it tingle, making her long for him. He knew she wanted his fingers there, his tongue, his penis. For more than an hour he had engaged her in effortless, well-practised conversation. He knew the way to turn a hanging judge around – flatter the bastard – and a beautiful woman like Tina was a pushover. He was kind and warm and understanding and she was just like putty in his well-manicured hands.

His fingertips moved higher. She glanced anxiously around the room. No one could possibly see them, unless they knelt down on the floor and looked up. She felt reassured, and was able to relax. She parted her legs a little more, moved forward in her seat so that his fingers brushed against her sex.

He stroked her delicately, between her legs. He was looking straight into her eyes.

Now his fingers slid underneath, against the moist lips of her pudenda, the palm of his hand cupping her pubic mound. She had to push herself almost off the edge of the chair so he could reach her and so she was leaning right back. She glanced out of the window and saw people coming and going at the other end of the restaurant, paying their bills, ordering extra courses. She poured the last of the wine into their glasses, trying to look nonchalant. She realised her hands were shaking and she nearly dropped the bottle.

Anthony's middle finger roved around her labia, probing between the folds, finding at last the entrance and slipping inside her. She had not been particularly wet before but now her juices were beginning to flow, easing the passage of another finger and then another, until he had three fingers buried in her, there at their table in Divine Wind, with people stuffing noodles and sushi and things only a few yards away.

She felt wild, recklessly guilty over Christopher, in his hotel on the far side of the Earth. How ironic that she should be with a QC in a Japanese restaurant. Maybe he was eating Japanese too, at that very moment, six thousand miles away.

'Come on, Anthony, someone might see us,' she heard herself say for form's sake but he could tell she wanted him to go on, to push on into her, to push her over the edge. With the ball of his thumb he found her clitoris and he massaged it with infinite gentleness, all the while his fingers twisting and sliding and turning inside her. Already she was pushing out to meet him, trying to force herself on to him, ready to be penetrated.

She didn't reach a climax, though she was close to it – she felt too inhibited by the other people in the restaurant and

197

the waiters hovering around the place. She whimpered and moaned and sighed quietly enough for Anthony to think he had brought her off. He withdrew his hand. As he brushed back a lock of his hair she could see him smell her musky pussy smell on his fingers, strong and exciting.

Over coffee, he told her all he had managed to discover about Rex Wagstaffe. She had no idea where he had got this information but he said it was from 'an unimpeachable source', which probably meant someone in the police. Rex the crusading journalist, guardian of public morals, was an extremely high consumer of porn on the Internet. In 1973 and again in 1977 he had received heavy fines for having sex with under-age girls. Anthony had no idea how, the second time, he had avoided a prison sentence. In 1982 and 1983 he had come under police suspicion of involvement in similar goings-on, but nothing had ever been proved and his name, for the moment at least, had remained unblemished.

This was, to say the least, ironic – as Anthony was quick to point out. Last week the *Daily Bleat* had lifted the lid on Britain's teenage porn scandal. Beneath shock horror headlines was the name of Rex Wagstaffe, the intrepid custodian of the nation's well-being. Tina, who didn't read the *Daily Bleat*, had no idea.

'It's all in here,' said Anthony at length, removing a slim envelope from his inside jacket pocket. 'Use it as you will but please do not attribute anything to me. As far as our friend Mr Wagstaffe is concerned, I don't exist.'

He paid their bill and they made their way out into the night. It was almost dark outside, just a faint trace of colour in the sky, not a great deal of traffic about. The air was warm and the stars were incredibly bright, high up there between the buildings.

He fucked her against a column in the underground car park where he had left his black Audi. It was kind of weird down there, with the big concrete columns and the overpowering smell of stale water and fuel, the distant sound of a car moving along the ramps. The security lights bathed their half-naked bodies in an eerie glow, his trousers down around his knees, her dress up around her waist.

She stood up high on her toes and parted her legs and he was pushing inside her, hot and eager. She came almost immediately, kissing him like mad, and then again as he pumped his strong, masculine backside up and down, up and down, his cock seeming to fill her completely until she was oblivious to everything else. When he came into her, it was like a big shuddering spasm for both of them. It seemed to go on and on until finally the feeling subsided and she realised her legs were getting stiff standing like that, and then Anthony withdrew and she wiped herself quickly and discreetly with a tissue from her bag.

She felt guilty but she felt oddly justified. It wasn't like sleeping with the enemy. Rex Wagstaffe was the enemy and now she'd found a way of shafting him.

Riddled with guilt, she called Christopher in Japan when she got home. She didn't say a word about anything that had gone on that evening. He sounded so cheerful and honest, it was like he was giving her absolution.

Lesley got the idea almost as soon as she'd finished talking to Tina. It was so simple, she'd wondered why she'd not thought of it before.

Jailbait was a girlie band that she and Charmayne had been interested in nine months or so ago, while they were still Kirtley Carmody and long before they had any thoughts about getting into the lookalike business. Josh had been keen for them to diversify, to avoid having too many eggs in one basket. Need to try something new, he'd said as they gave him his bi-monthly soaping-down. Don't want to keep ploughing the same old furrow.

They'd seen Jailbait perform live at the Pink Pussycat club and it was obvious why they'd got the name. They couldn't sing for nuts and they used pre-recorded backing tapes but they all looked about fourteen, with the make-up and the tight little asses and rosehip tits. In fact there wasn't one of them who wasn't at least seventeen but, unlike most teenage girls, they actually looked younger than their real age, rather than a couple of years older.

Lesley and Charmayne considered the options, spoke to

Josh about it, followed them around for a couple of weeks to see how the land lay. Their accountant was predictably keen for obvious reasons but his partners went cool on the scheme in the end. Did they really want to get into music? Lesley asked. It was all so sleazy, so full of rip-off artists. A lot of ready cash around, said Josh. Money up front and all that.

They didn't really like the idea of cashing in on this teenage thing either. It seemed, on the whole, like an exercise in bad taste that they could well do without. So she decided to pass up on the opportunity to 'discover' the new Spice Girls and that was when the lookalike thing came along in the shapely form of Tina Richardson and Seeing Double was born.

She'd kept in periodic touch with the Jailbait girls, all the same. For a start one of them, a sexy little strawberry blonde called Cally, just happened to be a dyke and for another, they'd always struck her in some way as representing a solution awaiting a problem.

Now at last she'd found it. Less than half an hour after speaking to Tina, she'd picked up the phone and dialled Cally's number.

It all happened in an anonymous hotel just off the outer orbital ring road, where she'd booked a couple of rooms for the night. Lesley got through half a bottle of vodka before leaving, to give her enough nerve for what was to come, and Charmayne had to drive her.

It seemed that she had to do this one herself. No one else could do it and besides, she was in a sense responsible for Paul and Carole getting in this mess in the first place. She could always have said no when they put the ideas to her but she didn't. The fact that she was half-crazy on cocaine and champagne at the time might have had something to do with it, allied to the fact that Carole was doing it to her with the vibro turned up full while Paul was subjecting Charmayne to the most intensive bout of heterosexual fucking she'd ever witnessed in her life. The scene at the Chivers' house seemed a harbinger of what was to come in this four-star hotel.

They found the equipment remarkably easy to set up. In

the old days, it was a man outside the window with a flashgun camera – not any more. Okay, Josh was going to shin up a convenient tree to try and get some still photographs as a back-up but everything they needed was in this box of tricks set up on the dressing table in a hotel room. It had cost a couple of grand to hire the portable CCTV gear but if it got Paul and Carole off the hook – not to mention the agency – then it would be money well spent.

On the monitor screen they could see a milky image of Cally walking around in a room remarkably similar to the one she, Charmayne and Josh were in. Josh fine-tuned the monitor and the picture was much better; not quite broadcast quality, sure enough, but certainly in the category of admissible evidence. Cally had one mini-camera in her bag, casually lying open on a table and with its wide-angle lens trained on the bed. There was another one on top of a wardrobe. It was like a spy movie from the Cold War days.

Lesley was surprised how readily Rex had waked into the trap they'd laid for him. A website ad on the Internet, a discreetly arranged contact, a grand in cash to Cally and five hundred each to the other girls, half up front and the rest later, and the plum was ripe for the picking. Okay it was a risk but even if the screens went blank or the cameras failed or – and this was the worst-case scenario – the video recording was a washout, they would still have Josh up his tree. Even a couple of usable snaps would be enough.

Lesley drank coffee and waited. It could be a long night. It was certainly hot enough, even with the air conditioning.

Reg Wagstaffe sat on a big, comfortably upholstered sofa while room service came in with a bottle of champagne on ice. Cally declined. The atmosphere in the room was heavy and oppressive, as though a storm were on the way. There was that same humidity, the sense of something rising up, ready to explode, a summer storm in the making.

'You mind if I open a window or something?' Cally asked. 'Even just pull the curtains back a little? We could use some air in here.'

'Better not. What if anyone sees anything?'

'There's nowhere to see anything from. It's all fields out there. Look.'

She drew back the curtain. There were just trees outside.

Before he could answer the girls arrived, Cassandra and Terri, one dark, one blonde, with devilment in their eyes. In any other circumstance, Cally would have greatly enjoyed what was to follow.

She saw Rex start when they came into the room.

'Hi,' he said, motioning them to sit down next to him on the sofa. He gave them the old patter but it was obvious where his interest lay.

Pretty soon, the girls took off their skin-tight clothes. Underneath, they were naked. They lay down together on the bed facing the onlookers. Watching from another floor on the TV monitor, Lesley could see in fuzzy black and white, small, pear-shaped breasts, dark pubic hair. Neither girl wore any make-up and she could see how young and fresh their skins were. She couldn't believe, until Terri showed her a birth certificate, that she really was as old as she said. Cassandra, in fact, was all of nineteen.

To Rex Wagstaffe, however, they were fourteen going on fifteen, just as it said on the Internet, and just the way he liked them. That's what he'd been told and that's what he believed. Hell, he'd seen enough naked teenagers to know one year's crop from the next – and these were vintage 83 or 84.

The girls were kissing now, rolling about the bed together. Despite herself, Lesley felt vaguely shocked by what she saw. It was one thing to see this kind of thing in a blue movie, but quite another to have it acted out right in front of her eyes. All the same, she noticed her heart was beating fast, like it did whenever she and Charmayne or whoever did something a little beyond the pale. There was that little hint of an extra thrill, the buzz to which Paul and Carole seemed so dangerously addicted.

The girls were playing with each other's tits now, nuzzling and nibbling and licking. The watchers in the room could not help but become aroused by the strangeness of the situation, a man they had nothing better than fear and contempt for, the three girls, the anonymously tasteful decorations of the room, the atmosphere of darker secrets that filtered through the overheated air.

Terri had gone down on Cassandra and Cally, compelled for the moment to watch, wasn't entirely unmoved when they slipped one and then two fingers inside each other. She quickly checked her bag, could just see the glint of a lens inside, hoped it was working okay. With its battery pack and transmitter the camera weighed more than she thought.

'I bet their cunts are good and wet,' said the tabloid hack, sniffing his fingers appreciatively and looking right at Cally. 'I guess you're enjoying the show, right.'

She nodded. *That's going to look good*, she thought. The two of them on the bed with their legs apart and him looking right at the camera, smiling. She felt herself to be charged with an electric thrill of sexual potency. Terri and Cassandra swung both ways but she didn't like guys all that much – at least on the sexual side – and she thought she'd want no part in it all. She wasn't looking forward to having to blow him or whatever and yet a deeper, darker side made her want to become involved, despite herself.

Rex Wagstaffe got up and pulled his clothes off, before joining the girls on the bed. They seemed to treat him like a favoured friend, as if they knew all the little tricks he'd like. They were certainly putting on a great act. While he ate one of them out, the other one took his dick in her mouth and sucked him good and hard.

'Like what you see, Cally?' he called out to her, motioning her to join him on the bed. She nodded, beginning to feel aroused. She'd seen plenty more boring things in her twenty years on this earth.

She sat down beside him, still in her T-short and tight jeans, every inch the Lolita fantasy she knew guys like him drooled over. A hand strayed down to her crotch – it was Rex Wagstaffe's. For a moment, she froze – she didn't like guys touching her unless it was on her terms. And yet, despite herself, she felt a sense of mystery. She'd only ever made it with a couple of guys in her life but the idea of doing it for money rather than love had a curious seductive appeal.

The two girls were both tonguing him now, licking him up and down like it was an ice-cream cone. His dick looked big and thick and powerfully distended. He rolled one of the girls over on to her front and got into her from behind. She could see the muscles of his back and thighs working as he powered away. With a few hard shoves, he brought himself off.

'Here,' he grunted at length. 'You want to get your clothes off now? Come and join us on the bed.'

She took almost half a glass of champagne at one pull and stood up. She could almost smell his arousal as he took off her brassiere and pulled down her pants. It was a musky, ammoniac, male smell, compounded with fresh sweat and tobacco, the male scent she had always known. He was rough with her tits as he pawed her, slobbering over them and tweaking her nipples so they stood up hard and fiery red.

They climbed on to the bed together. He made her get on top of him. To her surprise, he put another rubber on. 'When you hang around with girls,' he explained, a cigarette in the corner of his mouth, 'you learn to be extra careful, keep things safe. Nothing about you, honey, it's just a habit I got into, you know what I mean?'

Her head felt hot and heavy, and her heart seemed to be racing faster than usual. It must have been the booze, the bubbly on top of the vodka she'd had earlier with Lesley before setting off.

It was weird, having a real live cock in her. She bobbed up and down, feeling confused and aroused in equal measure. Was this how it was for straight women, the feeling of something missing, this strange absence of arousal? Terri and Cassandra were watching her. She would rather be pleasuring either of them than Rex Wagstaffe, any day of the week, but this was work, this was business. God knows, she needed the money badly enough. She bobbed up and down with renewed vigour.

'Jesus, that's tight,' he murmured. 'I like a slit like that, you know what I mean?'

She was kind of relieved that he came quickly – or was it just time slowing down? – but that wasn't to be the end of the party, it seemed. He pulled off the rubber, dropped it under the bed. Then he rummaged under the pillow and pulled out a mean-looking vibro, black and heavily ribbed, the kind of thing that Cally had seen advertised in the back pages of leather-scene magazines.

It made her feel strangely innocent, all this, even though her head was spinning wildly. She knew she wasn't a prude but everything that was happening seemed to be taking her closer to the edge than she'd ever been in her life before. A little gay-scene fun and games was one thing but this was straight hardcore.

'Look, Rex,' she said at length. 'Do you mind if I sit this one out? You made me feel kind of sore, you know what I mean? It must be the size of that thing you have on you.'

He laughed. The flattery had worked. She was relieved.

After he'd played with it a while around Terri's pussy lips, the vibro slid into her quite easily. She could hear it humming quite loudly, was surprised at how much of its monstrous girth he crammed into her. Terri pushed up to greet it. To Cally's surprise, she came off quickly and cleanly, a couple of times in a row.

'You like that, huh?' The vibro was wet and glistening, angry-looking.

She nodded. Sitting back in the sofa, taking a sip of champagne but almost immediately putting it down again, untasted, she felt unreal. It was like she couldn't move her eyes and her mouth felt very dry; she felt she was going to puke. Rex lit another cigarette. The vibro was still humming away in his hand where he'd pulled it out.

Cally checked the camera in her bag, could see the one on the wardrobe staring down on them.

Now it was Cassandra's turn. She spread her legs invitingly, her rosebud lips in a pout, really playing up to him but her mind, no doubt, on the five hundred quid she was getting for this. Rex Wagstaffe made her spread her legs and then he pushed it into her as far as it would go, moving it up and down like he was fucking her with it. He took hold of her hand, guided it to his cock, made her frig him. Spunk flew everywhere.

Half an hour or so went by, or was it just ten minutes? Cally lost track. Eventually, of course, Rex Wagstaffe got pretty tired and drunk and then he lost interest in her and the two girls and slumped down on the bed and fell asleep. She didn't know what was supposed to happen now. She'd banked on them going down to the bar or something together, and then they could slip away.

Instinct told her to get dressed and make a move. She got up off the crumpled bed, drew the curtains, closed the window. She stepped back into her clothes, fixed her hair in the big mirror in the bathroom, almost ran out of the place on her high heels. The girls came with her while Rex Wagstaffe snored on the bed like a beached whale.

Lesley was relieved when Cally tapped on the door. Of course, they'd seen it all on the monitor. She'd seen Cally reach up for the camera on top of the wardrobe and the crazy dash, the camera still running, along the corridor and up the stairs to their room.

Quickly they got the CCTV equipment back into its case, downstairs to the car. Now that it was over, they all felt this crazy sense of excitement. Charmayne was there, waiting for them. Josh was beside her, a camera on his lap. He'd just spent three hours up a tree in the middle of a field and he was cold and stiff and very hungry.

'How did it go?' he said, teeth chattering.

'Okay,' she replied. 'I think I've got what we want. I could see Rex and the girls clear enough. How about you?'

'I prefer watching blue movies at home,' he said, 'with a big bag of crisps and a bottle or two.'

It was confrontation time. They knew it would be coming, sooner rather than later.

'The way I see it,' said Rex, 'you've got three options. Route one is that you give me Paul and Carole and I run a story on them.'

'A story about what?'

'Oh come on, Lesley. Everyone knows what they're up to. All I need is one big picture for the front page. "SEX-CRAZY TV HOSTS," you know the kind of thing I need. "I BONKED MY TV HERO." "TV CAROLE IN LESBO SHOCKER."'

Lesley nodded. 'Go on,' she said in an even monotone. 'What's option two?'

'Option two is that I drop Paul and Carole and stitch you up instead.'

'You have such a nice way of putting things, Rex.'

'Don't I just?'

'What about us, precisely?' asked Josh, who was sitting in a corner at the back of Lesley's office and, so far, had contributed very little to the conversation.

'That Seeing Double is nothing more than a souped-up knocking shop. I know what goes on here.'

'What goes on?'

'You don't need me to tell you.'

'Yes we do. Tell us what you know.'

'Or think you know,' added Josh softly.

'In a nutshell, you hire out these lookalike people so they can do the business with anyone who's daft enough to want to.'

'Crap. We'd never sanction anything like that.'

'I'm not saying you sanction it. I'm saying that's what happens. Some woman has the hots for a certain American film actor we could name, and for two grand a day or whatever it is you charge they can rent them Danny boy to have their evil way with. They can imagine they're doing it with the real guy, whatever they want.'

'That's just not true. You've got no proof.'

'I know he shagged some woman that time we were down in Norfolk. Don't tell me she didn't imagine he was someone else. I was there, remember. He was dressed up like him, the whole works.'

'Yes but you were paying, Rex. That makes a difference. If anything happened between Danny and some woman – I'm not saying it didn't happen but I'm not saying it did happen either – then that's his private business. He did just what he was paid to do, didn't he?'

'Okay, that's maybe a bad example. But believe me, I've got stuff I know I could make stick. A little girl down in Wales, for a start. Sings like a canary, you know what I mean?'

'Let our lawyers handle that, Lesley,' Josh broke in. 'He's just trying to call our bluff.'

'Think what you like, sonny.'

'What's the third option, then? You said there were three.'

'Option three is the easiest one.'

'We pay you off.'

'You said it, not me.'

'You're so obvious, Rex,' muttered Josh. 'You can't prove anything and we've got nothing to hide. So fuck you.'

'You'd better be careful what you say, sonny. I could have your name in lights.'

Lesley could stand it no longer.

'So could we,' she snapped. 'On a teen-porn movie called *Lolita Meets Moby Dick*. We've got the exclusive rights on that one. Want to see it?'

Josh flipped a remote and the video screen in the office flickered into life. There, in crisp, image-enhanced black and white, was the unmistakably whale-like form of Rex Wagstaffe being fellated by one very young-looking Japanese girl while two others lay beside him, quite naked, on a dishevelled bed.

Josh let it run on for a minute or so. Then he stopped the tape and ejected the cartridge. He handed it to Rex. His face was impassive.

'Here, keep it. I've got a spare copy.'

'And I've got something else for you,' added Lesley, opening her desk drawer. She pulled out a brown A4 envelope, addressed to the editor of the *Daily Bleat*.

'These are some pictures you might like to have for your articles. They're a bit raunchy but I'm sure your readers won't mind. The girls don't look a day over fourteen but the guy looks oddly like you, isn't that interesting? It's amazing what you can pull off the Internet these days. That's where we got it, on a Website in Denmark.'

Rex Wagstaffe never did write the piece he was threatening to write. In fact, he didn't really do very much journalism of any kind, either for the *Daily Bleat* or any other paper. The last anyone heard of him, he was scripting low-budget porno movies in Portugal.

Seeing Double began to change as well. Tina, of course, had been the first to call it quits, and now she was Mrs Francombe instead of Mrs Richardson and very happy indeed being a wife and mother instead of Agent Scully. Danny decided that it was time to give all his attention to his day-job, and then Leonie was offered a full professorship, teaching English at a Mid-Western University, and without them it just wasn't the same any more.

Paul and Carole negotiated a new contract with greatly enhanced rewards for both of them, and decided it was time to concentrate on their careers. They didn't see half as much of Lesley and Charmayne as they used to.

Still, Lesley reflected, it had been good while it lasted. Now she and Charmayne were diversifying into general leisure interests. With Josh's advice and the bank's willing money, they'd sunk most of their energies into a health farm in Somerset. What did it matter if their newly appointed managing director had, back in her youth, been a famous glamour model? Everyone they knew, in one way or another, seemed to have had a touch of colour in their past.

One evening they were relaxing at home. Autumn was coming on and the room was bathed in the warm glow of a log fire, the first of the season.

'Did you fancy Danny?' asked Charmayne, quite casually.

'Didn't everyone?' There – it had slipped out. And yet Lesley had kept her desires to herself for so long. 'How about you? Did you fancy him?'

'He's such a nice guy – and so good-looking.'

'I know. The thing is, I fancy him much more as himself than when we got him dolled up as you-know-who. I could go for a guy like that.'

'I thought you were strictly one for the girls. Most of the time, anyway.'

'Not always. You know that.'

'Do you ever think of him?'

'How do you mean?'

'Well, about you and him, you know, doing it? Being together?'

Lesley smiled. Even in the firelight Charmayne could sense the glow that lit up her features.

'You won't tell anyone?'

'Who could I tell?'

Lesley drew closer, until she was almost whispering in Charmayne's ear. The TV flickered unseen in the corner of the room.

'Well, sometimes I think about him coming round here, unexpectedly.'

'Where am I?'

'Oh, off on business or something. I'm just here on my own.'

'How very convenient, you getting him all to yourself. And then—'

'And then what?'

'What happens next?'

'Oh, you know. We start talking. Maybe we have a glass of wine. And then another.'

'Does he come on to you?'

'Oh yes. I can tell he's really excited by me. I can see how stiff he is, through his trousers.'

'I bet he has a nice prick.'

'I do too.'

'Nice and thick.'

'I bet it is. I like a nice thick one.'

'I wonder if he likes having his prick sucked?'

'I'm sure he does. Don't all men?'

'Do you imagine what it would be like to suck him?'

'Of course I do.'

'So what do you do, when he's with you?'

'He starts to kiss me, really soft and slow. He's so gentle with me but I know that underneath he's really bursting to screw me.'

'Go on, go on.'

'Then he starts playing with my tits.'

'I envy you your tits. Nice to suck and lick and such a lovely shape. I bet Danny would like them. I bet he wants to rub his cock against them. I bet he'd want to come off all over you.'

'Mmmmm, I'm sure he would. I'd really like that. And I imagine him licking me while I'm stroking his cock.'

'Has he taken his trousers off yet?'

'No, that comes later. When we go into the bedroom.'

'So what happens next?'

'We lie down here, on the hearthrug by the fire. I take his lovely long cock out and lick it.'

'What's it like?'

'Lovely. I love the taste of his cock in my mouth.'

Charmayne reached out and began to caress Lesley's breasts. The two women had just showered together and were in their towelling robes. She tugged at the belt and it fell apart, revealing softly perfumed flesh.

'Then we go through into the bedroom. He undresses me very slowly. He keeps murmuring all these lovely compliments, like he really means them. It makes me feel good.'

'Sure it does. What does he say?'

'Oh, about how much he likes me and how he loves my body. And all the time he's stroking me and playing with my tits and sucking my nipples—'

'Let me suck them for you.' Charmayne's tongue flickered over her lover's luscious, strawberry-tipped breasts.

'That feels good,' breathed Lesley as Charmayne took her nipple into her mouth. 'I hope Danny can suck me as nicely as you do, my love.'

'Of course he can. And he's got such a lovely big prick too.'

'Mmmmm – his prick. I sometimes dream about his prick, you know.'

'I can feel you getting wet just talking about it.'

'Am I wet?'

'Oh yes, you're just soaking.'

'Put another finger right up me, my love. Oh, that's nice. Do it harder.'

'Is that like Danny would do it?'

'Oh yes, that's just like his prick. Frig me up and down like he's fucking me. Tell me what he's doing.'

Charmayne drew a deep breath. Her own pussy was on fire and she wanted to be satisfied herself. For the moment, though, she was enjoying pleasuring her friend and lover. Her own time would come later, in bed.

'He's got his cock in you and he's playing with your clitty with his thumb. Can you feel that? Isn't that just like a man?'

'Oh yes. Don't stop.'

'And with his other hand he's squeezing your nipples, really gently, so gentle you want to come just because of the way he's doing it to you. And his tongue, he's licking you all over, like this.'

They ended up sprawled on the rug in front of the fire in an attitude of utter abandon, their words ceased now, everything silent now but for the silken sound of hands on flesh, of lips gently touching and parting, of kisses given and exchanged. Their breathing was becoming harder and more insistent, half-formed sighs and endearments, the fire blazing and popping away beside them and bathing their half-naked bodies in its warm glow.

And then, suddenly, Lesley began to pant and gasp, and to call out first Charmayne's name and then that of Danny Kirkpatrick, and then she ground her hips, with Charmayne's fingers still buried deep inside her, and she came tumultuously and triumphantly, her own wicked tongue seeking Charmayne's, her robe spilling wide open to reveal her wanton charms to her imaginary lover.

Later, in bed, it was Charmayne's turn. They had a familiar routine for times such as this. Imagining that Lesley was Danny gave it added spice, a thrill of the unusual.

Charmayne was sitting up in bed, impatient and at the same time savouring the urgency of the moment. She watched as Lesley took off her soft white robe, revealing the full beauty of her body. She was tall and lithe, almost like a man in some ways, but her sex was proclaimed with her long, colt-like legs and small breasts.

Charmayne stirred impatiently. Lesley was teasing her. It was all a part of their game.

From a drawer Lesley took out their favourite ebony dildo. She held it up, admiring its perfect contours, the beautiful shape. Lesley ran her finger over the exquisitely formed contours, which had found her innermost recesses again and again. She held it up to her mouth and kissed it gently. Be patient, she mouthed to Charmayne.

Then, from a drawer, she took out something that was half garment and half harness, fashioned of soft black leather.

It fastened around her hips with tight buckles and belts that pressed into her smooth white flesh, leaving her sex exposed. Through Lesley's soft downy bush, Charmayne could see pink lips glistening moistly with her secretions.

Lesley tightened more straps. Now the black dildo was fastened to her body, jutting arrogantly forward like a man's penis. She stood there, her eyes fixed on Charmayne, one hand holding the root of her strange ebony manhood, the other caressing her own nipples.

The two women looked at each other in silence, eyes longing. Lesley spoke first.

'I want to fuck you now,' she said, her voice deep and dark, almost like a man's.

Charmayne squirmed with excitement.

'I'm dying for you, Danny,' she breathed. 'It's been too long. I can hardly wait.'

She pushed back the sheets, revealing her nakedness. Though Lesley had seen her friend unclothed many times, the beauty of her body never ceased to inflame her.

'Come and fuck me now,' Charmayne breathed, her eyes closed. Lesley came and stood by the bed, the black dildo heavy and potent.

'Suck me first,' she said, still in that deep voice. 'And I'll lick you at the same time.'

They lay down together, reversed. Charmayne caressed the ebony dildo, tasted it with her tongue. She could smell Lesley's pussy and she could see it too at the same time, the lips puffy and aroused. Down below, her lover began to lick and lap at her own labia, teasing them expertly, the tip of her tongue darting and probing.

Charmayne took the whole of the dildo into her mouth and, at the same time, inserted just the tip of her index finger into Lesley's bumhole. Her friend was very fond of that particular insertion, and she began to moan and whimper as her wanton tongue explored Charmayne's inner folds.

Her tongue seemed to push Charmayne to higher and higher levels of pleasure and yet, somehow, she was still not satisfied. She wanted the dildo in her, wanted Lesley to fuck her hard with it, as hard as a man with a real cock, but it

213

wasn't Lesley she wanted inside her, it was Danny.

Yet when she parted her legs and Lesley climbed on top of her, she found it remarkably easy to maintain the pretence. Lesley knew exactly what to do, her body now so muscular and strong. She fucked her as any man would have done, gentle at first, but then with increasing vigour, until at length she was pounding into her with all the force she could muster, her breasts quivering, the dildo crammed right up inside her one moment and then, at the next, withdrawn almost to its fullest extremity.

They kissed, burning kisses fiercely exchanged, and their tongues danced around each others', and their breasts were crushed together as Charmayne parted her legs and brought them up and around behind Lesley's back, clutching her around the waist, trying to draw her body inside herself.

She could feel the black leather of the harness against her own flesh now, the warmth of the material and the cold silver buckles. When she came, it was with Lesley's dildo inside her and Danny's face imprinted on her imagination.

Imagination, that was the key to it all, she realised as she drifted off to sleep in Lesley's arms. It was all in the mind. You could make yourself believe in anything if you tried hard enough.

Dangerous Desires

J. J. DUKE

*In response to his command, Nadine began
to undress. She was wearing her working
clothes, a black skirt and a white silk blouse.
As she unzipped the skirt she tried to keep
her mind in neutral. She didn't do this kind
of thing. As far as she could remember, she
had never gone to bed with a man only
hours after she'd met him . . .*

There's something about painter John
Sewell that Nadine Davies can't resist.
Though she's bowled over by his looks
and his talent, she knows he's arrogant
and unfaithful. It can't be love and it's
nothing like friendship. He makes her
feel emotions she's never felt before.

And there's another man, too. A man
like Sewell who makes her do things
she'd never dreamed of – and she
adores it. She's under their spell, in
thrall to their dangerous desires . . .

0 7472 5093 6

More Erotic Fiction from Headline Liaison

Vermilion Gates

Lucinda Chester

Rob trailed a finger over Rowena's knee, letting it drift upwards. She slapped his hand. 'Get off me,' she hissed, 'or I'll have you for sexual harassment.' Nevertheless, part of her wanted him to carry on and stroke the soft white skin above her lacy stocking-tops . . .

Rowena Fletcher's not having much fun these days. She's a stressed-out female executive with a workload more jealous than any lover and no time, in any case, to track one down.

Then she is referred to Vermilion Gates, a discreet clinic in the Sussex countryside which specialises in relaxation therapy. There, in the expert hands of trained professionals, Rowena discovers there's more than one way to relieve her personal stress . . .

0 7472 5210 6